Kat Rawlings was the kind of woman who could make him howl at the moon.

And if she could do that, Lucas knew, she could wrap him around her little finger any time the mood struck her.

He'd known that from the moment he laid eyes on her. He would have gotten the hell out of there right then, but his stupid pride had refused to let him run from any woman.

But Kat wasn't just *any* woman. She was the kind of woman who got into a man's bloodstream and refused to get out.

And there was no way in hell he was letting her do that to him. She might be used to getting everything that struck her fancy, but she wasn't getting *him*. He'd had two long years in prison to think about his future. And nowhere in his future was there a place for Kat.

Dear Reader,

Once again, we're proud to bring you a lineup of irresistible books, something we seem to specialize in here at Intimate Moments. Start off your month with award-winning author Kathleen Eagle's newest American Hero title, *Defender*. In Gideon Defender you'll find a hero you'll never forget. This is one of those books that is bound to end up on "keeper" shelves all across the country.

Linda Turner completes her miniseries "The Wild West" with sister Kat's story, a sensuous treat for readers everywhere. Award-winner Dee Holmes once again demonstrates her skill at weaving together suspense and romance in *Watched,* while Amanda Stevens puts a clever twist on the ever-popular amnesia plotline in *Fade to Black.* We have another Spellbound title for you this month, a time-travel romance from Merline Lovelace called *Somewhere in Time.* Finally, welcome new writer Lydia Burke, who debuts with *The Devil and Jessie Webster.*

Coming soon—more great reading from some of the best authors in the business, including Linda Howard, whose long-awaited *Loving Evangeline* will be coming your way in December.

As always—enjoy!

Leslie J. Wainger
Senior Editor and Editorial Coordinator

Please address questions and book requests to:
Silhouette Reader Service
U.S.: 3010 Walden Ave., P.O. Box 1325, Buffalo, NY 14269
Canadian: P.O. Box 609, Fort Erie, Ont. L2A 5X3

KAT

Linda Turner

Silhouette®

INTIMATE™ MOMENTS®

Published by Silhouette Books

America's Publisher of Contemporary Romance

SILHOUETTE BOOKS

ISBN 0-373-07590-1

KAT

Printed in U.S.A.

LINDA TURNER

began reading romances in high school and began writing them one night when she had nothing else to read. She's been writing ever since. Single and living in Texas, she travels every chance she gets, scouting locales for her books.

Prologue

Braced for the fight she knew was sure to come, Katharine Hepburn Rawlings took a position at the opposite end of the study and faced her three older brothers defiantly. Her jaw set stubbornly and her slender shoulders stiff with resolve, she looked nothing like her famous namesake, but she had her backbone, thank God! Her brothers weren't going to like what she'd done, but there wasn't a heck of a lot they could do about it now. The deed was done and she had no regrets.

The only thing left to do was tell the family, which was why she'd called this meeting with her brothers. She hoped her sisters-in-law weren't hurt because she'd excluded them, but these three were the only ones she had to convince that she knew what she was doing.

Dragging in a calming breath, she resisted the urge to twist her hands together nervously and instead adopted the serene expression worn by her mother in the portrait over the fireplace. "I quit my job," she announced baldly. "I won't be going back to Santa Fe."

Silence fell like a stone . . . and lasted all of ten seconds. "What happened? Was somebody giving you a hard time?"

"I knew this would happen. It's one of the teachers you work with, isn't it? An overeducated bookworm who doesn't know how to keep his hands to himself. He probably took one look at you and fell like a ton of bricks."

"Just give us his name and we'll take care of it, sis," Cooper assured her. "Gable, you know the superintendent of the Santa Fe schools, don't you? Give him a call—"

"No!" Struggling to hold on to her patience, Kat glared at them in exasperation, affectionate amusement tugging up one corner of her mouth. She loved them to death, but, Lord, they were something! As overprotective as a bunch of old hens with a new chick, they would lock her away in the henhouse until she was forty if she let them. "This has nothing to do with a man," she said dryly, "so you can save the call to the superintendent. I just don't want to teach anymore."

The unexpected announcement, coming out of left field, stunned them into silence. Gable was the first to recover. Frowning, he said, "But this is what you've worked for, what you wanted. I thought you loved it."

Touched by his confusion, Kat felt her eyes burn with the sheen of tears. How could she make him understand? She had only been a child when her parents had died, and the loss could have been far more traumatic than it had turned out to be. Thanks to Gable. As the oldest and the only one of age at the time, he had shouldered the responsibility for the rest of them, as well as the ranch, and she'd never once doubted that her world was secure or that she was loved.

He had done so much for her that she could never repay him. So when he had started talking college and Flynn and Cooper had added their two cents, she'd never thought to protest. They'd always wanted more for her than they had for themselves, so she had gone away to school and tried to convince herself that she loved it. But after being away from the ranch for eight years—first with school, then because of her job—she had realized that what she wanted and what her brothers wanted for her were two different things.

"I thought I could learn to love it," she said huskily, "but it isn't what I want to do with the rest of my life."

Flynn, who knew all about chasing dreams after hitting the rodeo circuit to find his, winked at her, his smile understanding. "I don't blame you, brat. Some of those kids are little monsters. So what *do* you want to do? Stay in Santa Fe and get a job as a secretary, or what? You know we're behind you, no matter what you want to do."

Her heart thudding, she let out the breath she was holding and grinned. "Good. Because I've decided to come home and start my own cattle company with registered Texas longhorns."

"What!"

"The hell you are!"

"Have you lost your mind? Working in the hot sun with stinking, bad-tempered cattle is no job for a woman!"

It was Cooper who made the unfortunately sexist remark, but the words could have come out of any of their mouths. Her spine snapping straight and her blue eyes flashing, Kat retorted, "There seems to be a misapprehension here. I'm not asking for your permission. I'm *telling* you what I'm going to do."

"Dammit, Kat, you can't be serious!"

Ignoring Gable's objection, she continued coolly, "I've been saving my money, and with the small trust fund left me by Mom and Dad, I have enough to start my own herd. Granted, I have only enough for a cow and a bull at this point, but it's a start."

Cooper, slower to lose his temper than his two brothers, couldn't quite hold back a grin. "I don't know why we didn't see this coming. You've been riding hell-bent for leather since you were three and helping with roundup since you were old enough to wrap Red and the rest of the hands around your little finger. Why longhorns?"

"Because they're what the West is all about. They're beautiful and hardy, and a longhorn cow can put a calf on the ground for ten years after most cows stop breeding. They can gain weight on the open range, and their meat has very little fat and it's more tender than most beef. In today's market, that's important."

She had done her homework; she fairly oozed confidence. Still not liking the thought of her soft skin weathering in the summer heat and drying out in the winter cold, Gable could think of a hundred reasons why this was a bad idea. But it only took one look at the willful set of her rounded chin to warn him that she was in no mood to listen to anything negative. "This isn't what we wanted for you," he grumbled.

"But it's what *I* want for me," she replied, some of the tension easing out of her at his disgruntled tone. "And you always said you wanted me to be happy, didn't you?" she wheedled. "So relax and let me be happy."

"Yeah," Flynn drawled, his blue eyes, so like Kat's, dancing devilishly. "And thank your lucky stars she didn't decide to raise ostriches or turn this place into a chicken farm or something. We could have been knee-deep in feathers.''

He did, Gable had to admit, have a point. "All right, brat," he said with a chuckle, "start your own longhorn cattle company if that's what you want to do. You're going to, anyway."

Her dimples flashing, Kat didn't bother to deny it. "It's so nice having a supportive family. I don't know what I'd do without you guys."

Chapter 1

"Trust me, Kat, honey, I'm just the man you need for the job. What I don't know about cattle ain't worth knowing. So whaddaya say? Have we got a deal or what? You hire me and before you know it, you'll be making money hand over fist."

Standing on the porch of the cabin at the springs, Kat kept her distance from Brody Hucklebee and just barely managed to hide her distaste. The Double R ranch hands had called her sweetheart and honey for as long as she could remember, but Brody wasn't one of the men she'd grown up with and she didn't appreciate his familiarity. He had a reputation for being a lazy good-for-nothing, and if her brothers knew he was on the Double R to apply for the ranch hand position she'd advertised in the paper, they would have a fit.

"The ad only came out today," she hedged. "I'm sure I'll get other calls on it, so it'll take me at least a week to interview everyone. I'll get back with you."

It was a clear dismissal, one that not even someone as thickheaded as Brody could miss. His mouth twisted into a grimace of a smile. "Just don't wait too long, darlin'. This ain't the only job in the county, and I just might find myself something else if you don't make up your mind quick like."

Unimpressed, Kat almost told him she knew for a fact that the world wasn't beating a path to his door to hire him. But he had a nasty temper, and she had no intention of tangling with him in any way, shape or form. If he wanted to think he was in hot demand, it was no skin off her back. "You do whatever you have to do, and I'll do the same. Now, if you'll excuse me, I have things to do."

She escaped inside and shut the door firmly behind her, wishing, just for a second, that she'd had a dead bolt installed before she'd moved in. But Brody wasn't dangerous, just so full of himself he was obnoxious. Outside, she heard his pickup roar to life and gravel jump out from beneath his tires as he hit the gas. Within seconds he'd rounded the curve that took him out of the rocky canyon that formed the western boundary of the ranch, and the only sign that he'd ever been there was the dust that slowly settled back to the ground.

The silence that followed was immediate, soothing, complete, broken only by the musical gurgle of the springs as the clear water tumbled over its rocky bed a stone's throw away from the cabin's front porch. When she'd moved into the cabin last week over the objections of her brothers, the constant, unceasing murmur of the water had reminded her of just how alone she was in the canyon that was miles from the ranch headquarters and the Victorian home she had grown up in. A half-dozen times she'd been tempted to pack her things and go back to the house. But if she had, she would have stepped back into the role of little sister. Her brothers, unfamiliar with treating her as an equal in the business, would have given her unsolicited advice, then been hurt if she didn't take it. And that was something she was determined to avoid.

So she'd stuck it out and gradually grown accustomed to the playful rhythm of the springs...much to the disgust of her brothers, who had placed bets on how long it would take her to admit she'd made a mistake.

Her mouth twitched, her eyes glinting at the memory of their indignation when they'd learned the full extent of her plans. Not only did she intend to set up her longhorn cattle operation separate from the rest of the family holdings, she was going to hire her own cowboys, buy her own cattle and eventually buy or lease more land when she needed it—all without anyone's assistance. Talk about outrage! she thought, chuckling. The fat had really hit the fan then. They'd tried reasoning with her, pleading with her, and—when that hadn't worked—arguing with her. If they could have gotten away with it, they would have sent her to her room until she came to her senses.

But she was twenty-six, not sixteen. Her days of needing their permission to do anything were long gone, and they would...eventually...come to accept that. Hopefully before she was forty. But for now she had to prove herself to them, and they weren't going to make it easy for her.

Living by herself at the cabin helped. It was a simple structure of rough wood and paned windows, with a rock fireplace that climbed one wall and a deep porch that stretched across the front. Cooper had had electricity installed after he and Susannah had been married, and it had all the comforts of home. But what Kat loved the most about it was its seclusion. Located at the entrance to the canyon where the springs ran in and out, it was one of the remotest areas on the Double R. Miles from everything, it wasn't all that easy for her brothers to drop in on her whenever the whim struck them. Not that that stopped them, she reminded herself, grinning. She still saw at least one of them every day.

As if her thoughts had the power to conjure, she heard the sudden sound of a vehicle coming up the gravel road to the cabin and almost laughed aloud. Which one would it be this time? she wondered in amusement. Yesterday, Cooper had shown up with a pound cake Susannah had made. The day before that, Gable put in an appearance with the excuse that he was going to town and thought he would see if she needed anything. He could have called, of course, but he'd conveniently forgotten that the cabin now had a phone. And then two days ago there was Flynn, who had baldly admitted that he'd just stopped by to nose around and make sure she didn't screw up since she obviously didn't have any idea what she was doing. If she hadn't wanted to laugh so badly, she would have punched him one. Lord, what was she going to do with them?

Moving to open the front door, she stepped out on the front porch, the teasing smile she couldn't contain stretched across her face. But the rusty green pickup that pulled a horse trailer into her yard and braked to a stop didn't belong to one of her brothers, and the man who stepped down from the truck wasn't anyone that she had ever seen before. Kat took one look at him and could only stare.

The first thing anyone with eyes would notice about him was his height. Six foot four if he was an inch, he was tall and rangy and stood as straight as a fence post. Another ten pounds added to his slim frame wouldn't have hurt, but Kat knew better than to mistake his leanness for weakness of any kind. The rolled-up sleeves of his shirt revealed forearms that were sinewy and rock-hard.

At five foot ten, Kat was no shrimp herself and wasn't often impressed with a man's stature. She wasn't altogether sure she liked the feeling. But while it was his height that drew her first glance, it was his face that held her motionless on the porch.

He wasn't even close to what she would normally have called good-looking. His cheeks and angular jaw seemingly carved in granite, his mouth was unsmiling, and his jet black eyes were hardly friendly. If there was any softness in him, Kat decided, openly studying him, it was buried deep.

In spite of that—maybe because of it—he had sex appeal written all over him. Just by walking down the street, he could have drawn the eye of every woman within a six-block radius. Herself included.

"I'm here to apply for the ranch hand advertised for in the paper," he said stiffly. "Is your husband around?"

If Kat had needed any verification that he was a stranger, she just had it. Everyone in the county knew she was single. "No, he's not," she replied with a smile that didn't come as easily as she would have liked. "I'm not married." Crossing the porch, she took the steps down to where he stood and held out her hand. "I'm Kat Rawlings. I placed the ad. And you're—"

He stared at her offered hand as if it was a rattler that was going to reach out and bite him at any minute, and for a long moment, Kat didn't think he was going to answer her or shake her hand. Then his fingers, hard and callused, closed over hers.

Heat. It was as instantaneous as the sudden flare of a match, jumping from his hand to hers, lightning quick. Startled, her eyes flew to his, but his expression was shuttered, revealing nothing. Without a word, he released her. Her heart inexplicably skipping a beat, she frowned down at her hand as if she'd never seen it before.

"Lucas Valentine," he said finally in answer to her query, his deep growl of a voice shattering the sudden, tense silence. "Your ad said you were looking for someone experienced in working with longhorns. How big a herd do you have?"

Her pulse still throbbing in a disturbing rhythm, she had to physically force herself to focus on business. "Actually I don't have one at all now," she admitted wryly. Quickly and succinctly, she told him of her plans to start her own cattle company. "I'm virtually starting from the ground up, so there's a lot of work to be done. This is my baby, so it'll be kept separate from the rest of the family holdings. A barn and corral have to be built before I can start to buy the first of the herd, and fences strung, of course." Turning toward the door, she said over her shoulder, "Why don't you come in and I'll make some iced tea and you can tell me about yourself. I know you're not from around here. I was born and raised here and—"

But instead of following her inside, he leaned back against the front fender of his truck, crossed his arms over his chest and stayed right where he was. Surprised, Kat stopped short and turned to face him, a frown gathering on her brow. "Is something wrong? If you don't want tea, I've got coffee—"

His jaw rigid, Lucas shook his head. Acid dripped in his stomach just at the thought of stepping into that cabin with her. "I'd rather talk out here. What do you want to know?"

He could see the questions in her eyes, the curiosity that cats were so famous for churning in the blue depths. A lifetime ago, he might have been captivated, but now he only ran his gaze over her in a way that was deliberately insulting. She was pretty, he'd give her that, and she no doubt knew it. A woman like her, with her pampered skin, delicate features and dimpled smile, always did. But he'd tangled with her kind before and he saw her exactly for what she was. Spoiled, headstrong, a poor little rich girl who was used to getting her way. Just the type of woman, he reminded himself, he'd run up against before and walked away from with scars that he would carry with him for the rest of his life.

"Well, if you're more comfortable out here, then I guess we'll do the interview here," she said, letting her breath out in a huff of impatience as she stepped back out onto the porch and sat down on the old willow porch swing. Her blue eyes, as sharp as cut glass, snared his. "So where are you from?"

"Texas."

Kat waited expectantly for him to elaborate, but he only stared back at her, offering nothing more. Torn between frustration and amusement, her eyes began to dance. "Well, that certainly narrows things down, but how about being a little more specific? It's not that I'm nosy or anything, but are we talking East Texas or West? Big city or one horse town? Or does the place even have a name?"

He *almost* smiled. Kat saw his mouth barely twitch and found herself holding her breath, waiting expectantly, but like a dream that never materialized, the moment was gone before she could so much as blink. "The Cedar Break Ranch, outside Austin," he replied curtly. "Then the Angel spread of Gonzalez, and the K-Bar near Dallas."

Impressed in spite of herself, Kat lifted a delicately arched brow. Getting information out of him might be like pulling hen's teeth, but his work history was impressive. "Those are three of the most famous longhorn ranches in the country. Most cowboys would give their right arm to work for even one of those operations. How'd you end up out here?''

"I wanted a change of scenery."

Just as before, he didn't elaborate, irritating Kat no end. What was it with this guy? She started to ask him just that, but there was something in the black depths of his eyes, a No Trespassing sign that warned her to back off, that had the words turning to dust on her tongue. Her heart thumping for no reason that she could think of, she swallowed.

"If your references check out," she said huskily, "then I suggest we try a two-week trial period to see if we can work together. If either one of us decides we don't like the arrangement, there'll be no hard feelings. Okay?"

The last thing Lucas wanted to do was work for a woman...especially one like Kat Rawlings. She was young and bold and too damn pretty for her own good. The minute she'd told him she wasn't married, he should have gotten the hell out of there. But his prospects weren't all that encouraging that he couldn't afford to be picky. He had exactly ten dollars in his pocket and less than a quarter of a tank of gas in his truck. And nobody else in the area was hiring—he knew because he'd tried them all. If he didn't take this, he'd very well likely have to sell his truck, horse and stock trailer just to get by until he could find something else further down the road.

"You do have references, don't you?" she asked with a frown when he hesitated. "Because I can't hire anyone without checking out their previous work history first. It's nothing personal. I just don't like surprises."

"Then you'd better know right up front that I just got out of prison," he said flatly, without missing a beat. "That's why I left Texas."

He hadn't meant to tell her, at least not so bluntly, but something about her casual assumption that they had a done deal after only a few minutes of conversation rubbed him the wrong way. Little fool! Didn't she know that it was a big, bad world, and there were any number of bastards out there just waiting to take advantage of a sweet young thing like her? He saw her pale, heard her gasp, and hoped he'd scared the hell out of her. She deserved it. Damn her blue eyes, she didn't know him from Adam, yet here she was, ready to invite him into her life without a thought to the risk she was placing herself in. For all she knew, he could be an ax murderer and cut her to pieces during the middle of the night!

"Prison," she echoed, shocked. "You were in prison? For what?"

"Rape."

Wanting to shock her, he fairly spit the single, damning word at her, then stood back and waited for her reaction. He didn't have long to wait. What little color there was in her face drained away. Sucking in a sharp, silent breath, she took a quick, involuntary, condemning step away from him.

Lucas's mouth twisted mockingly, the bitterness that knotted his gut an old, familiar friend. He should have been accustomed to such reactions by now. Over the past month, prospective bosses, sheriffs in little one-horse towns, barflies looking for fresh meat who refused to believe he wasn't tempted by their come-hither smiles and swaying hips had all reacted the same way. As soon as he mentioned rape and prison in the same breath, the world judged, then condemned him, without once asking for the rest of the facts.

He told himself he didn't give a damn. About anything or anyone. If Miss High and Mighty Rawlings wanted to believe he was a scum bag, he wasn't going to waste his breath trying to change her mind. There were other jobs down the road, other ranches where the bosses might not be quite so judgmental.

But he only had ten bucks in his pocket.

The thought stopped him cold, infuriating him. He needed a job, and like it or not, Kat Rawlings was the only one hiring within forty miles. After what he'd just told her, there was no way in hell she would consider him for the position without a damn good explanation. Even then, with the stench of prison still clinging to him, he could hardly blame her if she wanted nothing to do with him.

"I spent two years in Huntsville for a rape I didn't commit," he said stiffly. "I was working for John Kent at the K-Bar, outside of Dallas, when his daughter, Melaney, decided she wanted me for her sixteenth birthday present." Not so much as a flicker of emotion showed in his black eyes. "She was just a kid, but she was hot to trot and spoiled rotten. When I tried to make her understand I wasn't interested in little girls, she went crying to her daddy that I raped her."

"But if you were innocent, how were you convicted? There had to be evidence—"

"All circumstantial and concocted by Melaney, then twisted by the DA, who owed John Kent everything he owned for backing his reelection campaign."

Listening to himself and the wild story he repeated by rote, Lucas wouldn't have blamed her if she'd laughed in his face and ordered him off her property. Even to his own ears, he had to admit he sounded like a loser crying sour grapes, but, dammit, he was telling the truth! If she didn't believe him, that was her problem.

"He claimed I raped Melaney to get back at her father for not giving me a raise, and the jury bought it, hook, line and sinker," he continued coldly. "Nobody gave a damn that I was the one who really got screwed. I spent two years in prison before Melaney finally admitted she lied about the whole thing."

Studying him shrewdly, Kat's first instinct was to believe him. Growing up at the Double R, the family ranch that was located in the remote desert country of Southwest New Mexico, miles from the crime of the city, didn't guarantee anyone a Pollyanna existence. All of her brothers, at one time or another, had been victims of greed, jealousy and vindictiveness, and something in Lucas Valentine's black, stony eyes told her he was telling the truth.

But Kat knew her own weaknesses, and jumping to the defense of the underdog was one of them. She wasn't looking for a cause to take on, she reminded herself, just the best ranch hand she could find for the money. With her brothers watching her every move, just waiting to jump in and take over, she didn't want to make a mistake before she'd even bought her first cow. Which meant she had to consider the facts objectively.

By his own admission, the man was an ex-con, and he hadn't volunteered that information until he had to. So he claimed he was framed. What else could you expect an ex-con to say? *Yeah, I did it, so what are you going to do about it?*

Silently snorting at the thought, she said firmly, "I'll still need references to verify your story. If everything checks out the way you claim, you've got a job."

If she'd hoped to surprise him, she could have saved herself the trouble. Lucas Valentine didn't so much as blink at her willingness to accept him for what he was. "Sheriff Whitaker can verify my prison record. Brad Hawkins at the Cedar Break and Preston Thomas at the Angel should be able to tell you all you need to know about my work." Leaning back against the front fender of his truck, he crossed his arms across his broad chest, obviously prepared to sit there as long as it took. "I'll wait here while you call."

Kat only nodded and turned to pull open the screen door. "Make yourself comfortable," she advised. "This could take a while."

She called the sheriff first, knowing the other two calls hinged on what he had to say. Settling into a corner of the red plaid overstuffed couch that faced the old rock fireplace, she reached for the phone. All business, she greeted Riley Whitaker as soon as he came on the line and said, "Lucas Valentine is out here applying for the job I advertised in the paper. What can you tell me about him?"

"Probably the same thing he's told you," he replied bluntly. "He came in the first day he was in town. He wasn't exactly broadcasting the news, but he didn't want to keep any secrets from the law, either. Claimed he didn't want any trouble."

"So he told you about his prison record?"

"Yeah. I have to admit I had my doubts about him at first," he confided. "He's a tough-looking customer— hard as stone. But I called the Texas State Board of Corrections, and his story checked out. He served two years in Huntsville. Then the victim came forward and admitted she'd lied. This time, she must have been telling the truth— she passed a lie detector test. Valentine was released last month, and it seems he couldn't get out of Texas fast enough. Can't say I blame him."

Shaken, Kat stared out the front window to where Lucas still patiently leaned against his truck. Two years, she thought, trying and failing to imagine what it must have been like for him to be locked up for something he didn't do. A spoiled little rich girl had taken two years of his life, two years that he could never get back. No wonder he was cold and bitter. Who wouldn't be? If some tight-jeaned little tart had done to one of her brothers what Melaney Kent had done to Lucas, she'd have snatched her ball-headed!

"What about the rest of his record?" she asked quietly. "Does he have any prior arrests?"

"Nope. He's clean as a whistle. Not even a speeding ticket. You gonna hire him?"

Kat smiled, sudden amusement tugging at one corner of her mouth. Leave it to Riley to cut straight to the chase. "If his work history checks out," she replied. "Unless you can think of a reason why I shouldn't."

"Oh, I can think of three six-footers," he said with a chuckle, "and their last names are the same as yours. They're going to have a stroke. But I'm sure you won't let that stop you."

Kat laughed. He knew her too well. "I haven't for twenty-six years. Why would I start now?"

Grinning, she thanked him for his help, then called information for the numbers of the two Texas ranchers Lucas had given as references. When she finally made her last call and hung up fifteen minutes later, she had all the answers she needed. Whatever Lucas Valentine was, he wasn't a liar.

Stepping out onto the porch, she found him right where she had left him—slouched against the front fender of his truck. From the indifferent expression on his chiseled face, he didn't look as if he gave a damn whether she hired him or not. Irked, she said bluntly, "Hawkins and Thomas did nothing but sing your praises. The job is yours if you want it."

Not surprised that his former bosses had come through for him, Lucas simply stared at her. What the hell was he going to do now? In the month since his release, he'd roamed the West, picking up work where he could, hoping to earn enough so that one day he could buy himself an acre or two in a remote area where no one would ever bother him again. But the jobs never lasted too long before the fences seemed to close in on him, strangling him until he couldn't breathe, and all he could think of was breaking out, getting away. So he moved on, the restlessness that had first crept under his skin while in prison clawing at him, always eating at him, driving him on.

He didn't know anything about the woman standing in front of him except that she was rich, attractive and no doubt used to having her own way, come hell or high water. Trouble in tight jeans, he thought grimly. And he'd had enough trouble to last him a lifetime. He would just tell her to stuff her job, then take a hike and not stop until he'd put at least a hundred miles between himself and the lady.

But the ten dollars in his pocket wouldn't take him nearly that far. And as much as he knew Kat Rawlings was a problem he wanted no part of, she was the only rancher in the area who was hiring. Which meant his choices were simple. He could either sell his truck, Thunder and his horse trailer and hit the road with his thumb out...or take the job she offered him. Neither, he admitted, eyeing her warily, held much appeal. But beggars couldn't be choosers. "What's the salary?"

Kat named a salary that she knew didn't compare to what he must have been making in Texas, but her budget was limited to the small trust fund she'd inherited from her parents, and the majority of her money would be needed to start her herd. Registered longhorns didn't come cheap.

"It's not much," she added defensively, taking his silence as criticism, "but that includes room and board, of course. As the operation grows, there'll be raises and bonuses, but I can't promise when or what they'll be since I'm just getting started. Everything depends on the market, though with your experience, I'm sure you know that."

Realizing she was chattering, she clamped her teeth together, half expecting him to tell her she was crazy if she thought she could get him or any other experienced cowboy for the insulting amount she was offering. But the silence grew heavy and uncomfortable between them, and still he continued to study her. Almost as if she were some strange new breed of animal that might jump out and sink her teeth into him the very second he was stupid enough to drop his guard, she thought in growing annoyance.

"Look, if it's not enough," she began defensively, "then maybe you'd better look somewhere else—"

"I'll take it," he retorted, cutting her off. "For now."

Hardly hearing the rider he added to his acceptance, Kat was stunned by the relief that flooded through her. He was just another footloose cowboy who spent more time on the road than he did in the saddle as he moved from ranch to ranch, avoiding ties and commitments and getting nowhere fast. He might be good at what he did—after talking to his former employers, she couldn't doubt it—but it wasn't as if he was the *only* cowboy available who could help her, she thought irritably. She needed a hired hand. Anyone with moderate skills would do.

Telling herself she didn't care if he stayed two weeks or two years, she nodded, ignoring the pounding of her heart. "Fine. You can start immediately."

An hour later she was showing Lucas where she wanted the barn built when her three brothers drove up. It took only one look at their set faces to know that they'd been talking to the sheriff. Cursing Riley Whitaker, Kat didn't know why she was so surprised he'd called them. Riley had a reputation for discretion—when someone told him something in confidence, it never went any further—but he and her brothers were friends and Riley could be as protective of her as her family. He had probably called the Double R the minute she hung up.

Watching her brothers study Lucas suspiciously, she had to stifle the urge to give all three of them a quick, hard shake. When were they going to realize that she was all grown-up and able to take care of herself? "I thought you guys were going to the El Paso auction this afternoon," she said by way of greeting as they piled out of Gable's truck. "You're going to be late if you don't get a move on."

"We're going," Cooper said. "We just stopped by to see how you were doing."

"Yeah," Flynn added. "We saw your ad in this morning's paper and we were wondering if you'd gotten any response." Baldly turning his eyes to the man who stood silently at his sister's side, he lifted an inquiring brow.

Kat bit back a grin. Trust Flynn to be about as subtle as a sledgehammer. "As a matter of fact, I did." With a wave of her hand toward her brothers, she glanced at Lucas. "I'm sure you've already figured it out, but these mother hens are my brothers—Gable, Cooper and Flynn." Her chin lifting to a challenging angle, she turned back to her siblings. "This is Lucas Valentine..." she said smoothly, then dropped the bomb "...my new hired hand."

She didn't have long to wait for the explosion. The words were hardly out of her mouth when Flynn nearly strangled on a curse. "Your what? You can't be serious!"

Cooper, seeing Lucas Valentine's jaw tighten to granite, explained, "We haven't got anything against you personally, Valentine—"

"You just don't want your sister working with a convicted rapist," Lucas finished for him coldly. "Don't worry about it. I've heard it before."

"We won't apologize for being protective of Kat," Gable retorted. "Regardless of what you have or haven't done in the past, you're still a stranger, and we don't know a damn thing about you. We've got a right to ask a few questions."

Kat bristled at that, her blue eyes dark with irritation. "Not when I'm doing the hiring and paying his salary, you don't."

The reminder struck home. All three stiffened. Any other time, Kat would have been amused by their protectiveness, but their jaws were still set stubbornly, their stances just short of belligerent. And there was nothing amusing about the look on Lucas's face.

"I wish you could see yourselves," she told her brothers in disgust. "Talk about rude! You're all ready to string him up from the nearest tree, and you don't even know the facts."

"We talked to Riley," Cooper said sternly. "We know all about his prison record."

"Then you know he didn't get out of prison on a technicality or because the courts suddenly decided there wasn't enough evidence to convict him," she replied. "*He's innocent!* He spent two years in prison because a woman lied. He didn't do anything."

Standing there listening to her plead his case, Lucas refused to let himself be taken in by the passion of her defense. It didn't mean a damn thing. The boss lady was trying to keep her hired help, nothing more.

He started to tell her to save the speech—he didn't stay where he wasn't wanted—but he never got the chance. Gable, her oldest brother and obviously the one the others turned to for advice, searched his face with sharp, shrewd eyes and seemed to find what he was looking for. "Like Cooper said, this isn't personal. Kat's living out here all by herself, so I'm sure you can understand why we're concerned. But if she's already hired you, she must be satisfied with your references, and we'll have to trust her judgment." Giving him a cool smile, he held out his hand. "Welcome to the Double R."

Lucas eyed him suspiciously, not sure he trusted the hand held out so straightforwardly to him or the man who was willing to give him a break. But there was no guile in the dark brown eyes that squarely met his, no ulterior motives. Still half expecting him to jerk back his hand at any minute, Lucas cautiously returned the shake. "Thanks."

"Yeah," Flynn grumbled as he and Cooper both offered their hands. "Welcome aboard. We're not usually so suspicious—"

"Since when?" Kat teased.

"But she's the only little sister we've got," Cooper finished for Flynn as he scowled at their *little* sister. "You'll be on her payroll, but we're going to be running two cattle companies on one ranch until her herd gets so big she has to lease more land. So you can stow your gear in the bunkhouse with the rest of our ranch hands, then drive out here every morning to work."

Lucas almost laughed at Cooper's very obvious maneuvering. He had accepted Lucas's explanation for his time in prison and welcomed him to the Double R, but Cooper was going to make damn sure Lucas didn't sleep anywhere near his sister.

Lucas almost told him he didn't have a thing to worry about. Kat Rawlings might be beautiful and desirable—the hottest catch in seven counties for all he knew—but she left him cold and scared the hell out of him at one and the same time. He wouldn't touch her with a pool cue, let alone sleep within a thousand yards of her. If there hadn't been a bunkhouse around, he would have driven to the middle of the desert and bedded down in a sleeping bag in the back of his pickup rather than stay anywhere near that cabin of hers.

"That'll be fine," he assured her brothers. He was there to work, nothing else, and their sister couldn't have been safer with him if she'd been a cloistered nun. Just as soon as he saved some money for gas and put a little aside for the land he wanted to buy, he was out of there. It was just a matter of time.

Chapter 2

If he'd let himself, Lucas could have been right at home at the Double R bunkhouse. It was spacious and comfortable, and the cowboys who lived there were more than welcoming. Quick with a joke and a handshake, they were open and friendly and more than willing to accept him into their ranks without knowing a damn thing about his past.

Another lifetime ago, he would have been just as open, just as accepting, and made himself at home within a couple of hours. But he wasn't the man he had once been, and he'd learned the hard way that the world might forgive and forget a lot of things, but serving time in prison wasn't one of them. And while cowboys were generally accepting of just about anyone who carried his share of the load, even they wouldn't have been able to overlook a rape charge and time served behind bars. That tainted a man forever.

So he kept his past to himself and stiffly returned their handshakes and words of greeting, then passed on the nightly poker game. It wasn't the best beginning—more

than a few of the hands took his refusal to join the game
as criticism of their gambling—but Lucas offered no explanation as he retired to his bunk. If they wanted to think
he was a stiff-necked jerk, let them. That was better than
what he was, and anyway, he didn't give a damn what any
of them thought of him. He wasn't there to make friends—
he didn't want them or need them. Because if they ever
found out about his past, they would turn their backs on
him quicker than he could spit.

Intending to be long gone before that happened, he
found himself an empty bunk off in a corner by itself and
stretched out on his back. The card game was loud and
boisterous, but he closed out the noise by just shutting his
eyes and escaping to a dark, quiet place in his mind where
no one could bother him. It was a trick he'd learned in
prison, one he'd had to perfect to break free of the nightmare of his inhuman surroundings. The need for that escape hadn't faded just because he was free now. There were
some memories a man was never free of.

Within minutes he was asleep and never knew when the
game broke up and the rest of the cowboys found their
own beds. But the peace Lucas sought in sleep didn't last.
It never did. Sometime after midnight, he woke abruptly
to the sounds of men snoring and mumbling in their sleep.
In the blackness of the night, it wasn't the walls of the
bunkhouse closing in on him but the iron bars of his cell
in Huntsville. His insides twisted into knots, his fingers
curled into the sheets. He felt the familiar cold sweat break
out on his skin, the nausea roll in his stomach, and he
swallowed a strangled curse as he fought for control.

It had been a month, he told himself fiercely. A whole
month since he'd heard the prison door clang behind him
for the last time, shutting him out instead of in. The sweats
and terror that had brought him abruptly awake night af-

ter night in his cell, dragging him back to his trapped existence, should have ended weeks ago. He was free. *Free,* dammit! He could go where he wanted, do what he wanted, without answering to anyone. The horror of the past two years was finally over. He was never going to be locked up again.

But even as he tried to reason with the panic backing up in his throat, he knew he was wasting his time. His heart was thundering in his chest, his lungs straining, and the demon clawing at him wasn't going to let go until he got outside where the air was damp and clean and there wasn't a wall in sight for as far as he could see. His teeth clamped tight on an oath, he rolled out of bed and silently reached for his boots and the sleeping bag he'd stowed under his bunk with the rest of his gear.

The early October night was clear and cloudless, the breeze that whispered over his bare shoulders comfortably cool. But even if it had been the dead of winter and colder than hell, there was no way he would have stepped back into the bunkhouse right then. The sleeping bag clutched in one hand and his boots in the other, he made his way to his truck in his stocking feet. With a flick of his wrist, he sent the down bag rolling out before him in the bed of the pickup. It wasn't, he acknowledged grimly as he climbed onto the tailgate, the first or last time he would sleep in his truck.

He was up again before dawn, ready to get started on earning the money that would take him away from the Double R. If the other cowboys, who were only just stirring to life, noticed that he'd left the comfort of his bunk for the unforgiving hardness of a bed in his truck, no one said anything. And that was just fine with him. Before any of them could work up the nerve to ask the questions he saw in their eyes, he was gone, headed for the cabin and Kat Rawlings.

Working for her, he figured, wasn't going to be all that difficult. She'd claimed this longhorn venture was her baby, one she planned to be directly involved in, but that was big talk for the only daughter of one of the richest families in New Mexico. She might have good intentions, but you only had to look at her to see that she'd never done a day of hard, physical labor in her life. She probably slept till noon every chance she got and wouldn't like getting her hands dirty. She might think she wanted to help him, but the second she broke a sweat, she would head for the coolness of the cabin, and he'd be left to do his job in peace.

For once in his life, he just might have landed butter-side up, he thought as he braked to a stop in front of the cabin—*if* he could convince Miss High and Mighty Rawlings to stay out of his hair.

The cabin windows were dark, just as he'd expected. Relieved, he pushed out of his truck, but he'd only taken two steps when he stopped dead in his tracks.

She wasn't sleeping in, as he'd imagined. She wasn't even lingering over breakfast in the cabin. Instead, she was already working at the spot she'd selected to build the barn on, staking it out in spite of the fact that the sun had just started to peek over the horizon.

The bubbling murmur of the springs had drowned out the sound of his arrival, so she hadn't heard him drive up and was totally engrossed in what she was doing. Transfixed, Lucas couldn't take his eyes from her. Tall and slim as a willow, she was dressed for work in well-worn jeans that hugged her hips like a lover, an oversize, long-sleeved shirt tied at the waist, and scuffed boots that had seen better days. With her dark hair scraped back in a ponytail that hung halfway down her back, she could have passed for a sixteen-year-old with no trouble at all.

She shouldn't have looked the least bit appealing. In the early morning light, her face was free of makeup, her sensuous mouth bare of lipstick. But she wasn't a woman who needed makeup to enhance ordinary looks. Oh, no, he thought, his gaze locked on her soft mouth. She had the classic features of a model—high cheekbones, elegant nose, flawless skin. And a smile that could knock a man clean out of his boots. Without even glancing at him, she somehow managed to steal his breath.

Just as quickly as the thought slammed into him, Lucas stiffened, furious with himself and her. Did the woman need to knock him on the head with that hammer of hers before he remembered that she was nothing to him but someone to be avoided? What the hell was wrong with him?

More than half tempted to climb back in his truck and keep right on driving until he'd left the Double R far behind, he had no choice but to stand his ground when she suddenly looked up and spied him. Her smile as quick and sudden as a flash of sunshine on a cloudy day, she waved enthusiastically, greeting him as if he were a long-lost friend. "Good morning!" she yelled. "I was so excited about getting started this morning that I couldn't sleep. Come on over and tell me what you think."

If she was hoping for a smile, even a polite good morning, Kat was doomed to disappointment. His long legs easily eliminating the distance between them, he slowly took in the area she had meticulously staked out for the new barn. Hands on her hips, she could hardly stand still. "Well?"

"You've been busy," he retorted. "Nothing left to do now but clear the land, then buy the lumber and start building."

His coldness wiped the smile from her face like a backhanded slap. Hurt, she tried to remind herself that what was a dream come true for her was just a job to him and she couldn't expect him to share her enthusiasm. But it didn't help. He could have at least said good morning.

But Lucas Valentine obviously didn't like to waste time on pleasantries. She'd hoped that since they were going to be working so closely together they could find a way to be friends. After all, she had grown up surrounded by cowboys and was as comfortable around them as she was with her brothers. But something warned her Lucas wasn't the type of man a woman could ever feel easy with.

Studying him unobtrusively through her lashes, she was struck anew by the intensity that seemed to roll off him in waves. He cloaked himself in coldness and appeared to keep his emotions on a short leash, but his black eyes opened onto his soul and he couldn't hide what he was—a man of fierce passions. He would hate with fervor. And love with a keenness that would transcend time. If he ever allowed himself to want a woman again, he wouldn't play by the rules. He would boldly let her know that he wanted her in his arms, in his bed, then set about convincing her that was what she wanted, too.

Suddenly realizing where her thoughts had wandered, Kat's heart jerked in her chest. What was she doing? she wondered wildly, her cheeks burning with mortification. Trying to scare off her first employee before the first workday had even begun? The man had every right to be a woman-hater, and he didn't have to spell it out for her to know that he didn't trust her—or any other female—as far as he could throw her. If he found out she had only to look at him to start fantasizing about the kind of lover he would be, he'd be gone faster than she could say "adios." And who could blame him?

Shaken, she swallowed to force moisture into her suddenly dry throat and managed to say easily, "So, I guess you're ready to get started." Pulling a folded piece of paper from the back pocket of her jeans, she handed it to him. "I drew up some rough plans last night. As soon as we get the building site cleared, we can make a trip into Silver City for the materials we'll need."

Lucas merely looked at her. He had no intention of riding a half a mile down the road with her, let alone the sixty to Silver City. "I'll clear it," he finally said flatly. "You go on into town and get what you need. It'll save time."

"But I don't have any idea what to buy!"

"I'll make you a list," he said. All business, he snatched up the tape measure she had used earlier to pace off the stakes for the perimeter of the barn. With her help, he took the necessary measurements, then used the back of the plans to figure out all the supplies that would be needed. "You won't be able to carry everything in one trip," he said as he handed her the list, "so right now just buy the first five items. That's all we need to get started on the framework."

Kat wanted to protest, but he was right. It was stupid for her to insist on helping him when he could do the job by himself and she could be back with the supplies by the time he finished.

So an hour and a half later, she walked into the hardware store in Silver City only minutes after it opened, excitement dancing in the depths of her blue eyes. After pondering her decision for months and worrying about how her brothers were going to react to her plans, she was finally getting started on her dream.

Grinning from ear to ear, she greeted Rick Hellerman, whose family had sold building supplies in Silver City for longer than anyone could remember. "Hi, Rick. How's it going?"

"Well, if it isn't the terror of the Double R," he teased as he tugged on her ponytail just as he had when she was a kid. "Last time you were in here, you were looking to buy a rope to hang Flynn with."

Kat laughed, the memory he dredged up making her eyes dance. "Lord, I'd forgotten about that. I should have strung him up when I had the chance. He's been dealing me nothing but misery ever since." Telling him what she needed, she almost laughed as his eyes widened in surprise. "This time I need a heck of a lot more than a rope. I'm building a barn."

He whistled softly. "You aren't kidding. Let me get someone to help me, and we'll get you all taken care of. Your pickup out front?" At her nod, he said, "Good. Give me a couple of minutes, and I'll have you all loaded and ready to go."

He left her looking at nails, and Kat sent up a silent prayer of thanks that Lucas had been specific about everything, right down to the nails. Otherwise, she could have been there all day just deciding what to get.

"What you doin', darlin'?" a smug male voice drawled behind her. "Waiting for me?"

At the first sound of Vince Waters' provocative greeting, Kat stiffened. Not today, she thought, just barely managing to stifle a groan. She was in too good a mood to deal with Vince today. Or any other day, for that matter. But he was just like a bad penny and she knew from past experience that he wasn't going to go away until she acknowledged him.

Forcing a smile that was little more than a grimace, she reluctantly turned to face him. "How are you doing, Vince?"

"Better, now that I've seen you," he replied, leering as his blue eyes swept her up and down. "You look good enough to eat this morning, honey."

Inwardly wincing, Kat tried not to gag. What had she ever seen in this man? When she'd first moved back home, he'd asked her out and she'd made the mistake of going. She'd been regretting it ever since.

The son of a wealthy local rancher, he was tall and dark-haired, with a square jaw and rugged features that were undeniably attractive. But as far as Kat was concerned, that was all he had going for him. After only one date, he'd started making demands on her, demands that two weeks later still had the power to make her steam. Possessive to a fault, he'd actually insisted that she have nothing to do with the cowboys she'd known all her life. Talk about nerve! She had refused any more dates with him, but she'd quickly learned that he had an ego the size of Texas. Accusing her of playing hard to get, he'd flatly refused to take no for an answer and had been pestering her ever since.

"So how about going out to dinner with me Friday night? I can pick you up at seven."

He was, Kat decided, frowning at him, the densest man she'd ever had the misfortune to meet. One word to her brothers was all it would take to get him out of her life forever, but she didn't want to do that. She'd lived on her own for years in Santa Fe without once running to her brothers for help, and she could handle Vince. Even if he was stubborn as a motherless mule.

"Sorry," she said without an ounce of regret, "but I'm going to be too busy to go anywhere. Rick is filling my order for the barn I'm going to build, and that's going to take all my time for quite a while to come. Why don't you ask Pat Bobkins? She's back in town, and the two of you would probably get along great."

He didn't so much as blink at the suggestion. "You hired him, didn't you?"

Confused by the sudden change in subject, Kat frowned. "Hired who?"

"That drifter who hit up every ranch in the county for work," he snarled. "You hired him to help you with that crazy longhorn scheme of yours, didn't you?"

"It's not crazy!" she began, her eyes snapping like blue fire.

Swearing, he hit a display of antifreeze with a force that almost sent it crashing to the floor. "Damn! I can't believe your brothers let you do something so stupid! What were they thinking of? You don't know a damn thing about this jerk."

"Excuse me?" she gasped. "Did you say 'let' me? My brothers don't *let* me do anything, Vince Waters! In case you hadn't noticed, I'm an adult, and I don't answer to them or any other man. Especially you! I know all I need to know about Lucas Valentine, and if you don't like it, that's tough! Now, if you'll excuse me, I think Rick has my truck loaded."

"Kat, honey—"

"And don't call me honey!" she threw over her shoulder as she stormed out. "In fact, don't call me anything. Just stay away from me!"

Her thoughts churning angrily and her foot heavy on the accelerator, Kat traveled the sixty miles back to the Double R in record time. The gravel ranch road that led to the springs was washboard-rough, but she bounced over its uneven surface without once checking her speed. Damn

Vince Waters! she fumed as the cabin, nestled among the trees in the rocky canyon, came into view. He actually believed he had the right to tell her who she could and couldn't hire. Who the hell did he think he was?

Steam practically spilling from her ears, she could have raged for a good thirty minutes more, but when she headed toward where the barn was going to be and spied Lucas working in the hot sun, the sight of him drove every other thought from her head. He was stripped to the waist, his golden tanned skin glistening with sweat as he struggled to move a heavy boulder. Muscles straining across his impossibly broad shoulders, his granite jaw set determinedly, he threw his weight against the crowbar he had wedged under the rock and seemed to will the stubborn chunk of stone to move. Slowly, reluctantly, it did.

Feeling as if she'd just been hit in the gut, Kat braked to a stop. There was a roaring in her ears, but it was a long, timeless moment before she realized it was the wild thundering of her heart. Taken aback, she swore softly under her breath and sternly ordered herself to get a grip. If her pulse was jumping crazily, it was just because she was still grinding her teeth over Vince Waters. It had nothing to do with Lucas.

But it wasn't Vince she couldn't take her eyes from. It was the man standing in front of her, and, Lord, he was something to see. Lean and bronzed and as hard as the rock he pitted his strength against, there wasn't a spare ounce of fat on him anywhere. A fine matting of black hair dusted the center of his chest before narrowing to a thin trail that wandered down his torso. With a will of their own, Kat's eyes followed that seductive path to a spot just below his navel, where it disappeared beneath the worn jeans that rode his hipbones.

If he hadn't frozen then, Kat didn't know how long she would have stared at him. But his sudden stillness caught her attention, jerking her back to awareness. Startled, her gaze flew up his body to his face, only to find him scowling at her with black, angry eyes.

Mortified, she felt color surge into her cheeks like a bloodred tide, and it was all she could do not to look around for a hole to climb into. She'd been out in the sun too long, she thought in growing desperation. What other reason could she have for staring at Lucas as if he was the flavor of the month? She wasn't looking for a man. Any man! The male of the species—especially in her part of the country—had a hard time standing back and letting a woman run things without trying to take over, and she wasn't letting anyone take over her or her dream. Especially a man like Lucas Valentine.

After what he'd been through, he was hard, bitter and as wary as an abused bull. Right now, all he wanted was to be left alone, which wasn't surprising. But once his anger wore off, once he dropped his guard enough to let a woman get close to him, watch out! She'd thought Vince Waters was possessive, but he was tame compared to what instinct warned her Lucas would be once he decided to make a woman his. He would take control in a relationship, and that was something she was determined to avoid at all cost. She was crazy about her brothers, but she'd been struggling against their natural need to protect her for years. Now that she'd finally declared her independence, she answered to no man, and that was just the way she liked it.

"So quit your staring, Kat," she said under her breath as she pushed open the cab door to her pickup and climbed out. "He's just another cowboy."

But her pulse didn't react to him as if he was just another tall drink of water in boots and a Stetson. When she moved to the back of the truck to start unloading the supplies and he started toward her with a disapproving frown darkening his brow, her pulse skipped like a schoolgirl's, irritating her no end.

"What do you think you're doing?" he growled when she reached for one of the heavy beams that would be used for the barn's framework. "This stuff weighs a ton. Let me have that." Taking the lumber from her before she could stop him, he jerked his head toward the front porch of the cabin. "Go sit down in the shade. I'll do this."

It was the wrong thing to say, especially when the sight of the sweat trickling through his damp chest hair turned her throat as dry as the dust under his feet. Deciding it was time they got a few things straight, Kat planted her clenched fists on her hips and faced him squarely, her chin set at a belligerent angle. "Look," she huffed, "I don't know what kind of women you're used to, but if you think I'm some kind of weak city girl afraid of breaking a nail, you can think again. I'm not going to sit on the porch and watch you work. Okay?"

She was right about that, he thought grimly. She wasn't watching him at all! He'd seen the sudden awareness in her eyes when she'd driven up and it had turned his blood to ice. Melaney Kent had had that same hot look when she'd decided she wanted him, come hell or high water, and that was exactly what her interest had turned his life into—hell. He'd be damned if he'd go through that again with another spoiled little rich girl.

He opened his mouth to tell her not only was he not going to work shoulder to shoulder with her, he wasn't going to work with her period, when he noticed that the sweat was already beading on her brow, and she hadn't even started to work yet. Shutting his mouth with a snap, he figured she wouldn't last ten minutes in the heat. He could wait her out.

"Have it your way," he said indifferently. "You're the boss."

Without another word, he dropped the beam in the spot he intended to stack the lumber. When Kat followed him and dropped another beam beside the first one, he ignored her and returned to the building materials piled in the back of the pickup, counting the minutes in his head. Even though it was October, the sun was unrelenting in its fierceness, and fall still seemed weeks away. Any second now, Kat was going to cry uncle and retreat to the shade.

But she didn't. She hung tough, matching him step for step, carrying her share of the load in spite of the fact that her shirt was soon damp with sweat and her hair slipping from its ponytail to cling hotly to the back of her neck. Not once did she offer a word of protest or complain in any way. And when the truck was empty, all the lumber neatly stacked to one side, the bags of ready-mix concrete she'd bought for the support posts piled to the other, she still didn't retreat to the porch to cool off. Instead, she grabbed a pick from the tools she'd assembled earlier to clear the building site. Within seconds, she was attacking a scrub mesquite.

For Lucas, it was too much. He'd been patient, but to his disgust, she showed no signs of tiring. In fact, she had more energy than a buzz saw and seemed to get stronger with every passing minute. But enough was enough, dammit! He had to put a stop to this nonsense right here and now before things got out of hand.

Snatching up the crowbar he'd been using earlier, he thunked one end of it in the dry ground and clutched it like a staff, glaring at her in annoyance. "Don't you have something better to do?"

Surprised, Kat glanced up from the mesquite she was trying to uproot and frowned at him in confusion. "Like what?"

"I don't know," he retorted with an impatient gesture. "But there's got to be something in the cabin that needs your attention. Why don't you go do it and leave me to take care of this?"

So it had come—the showdown she'd been expecting all day. Setting her pick down, she straightened to her full height and met his irritated gaze head on. "If I wanted to spend my days doing housework, I'd find a job as a housekeeper. Now, you want to tell me what's wrong or do I have to guess?"

"I don't need your help," he said bluntly, then immediately corrected himself. "No, I not only don't need your help, I don't *want* it. Okay? You hired me to do a job, so I'd appreciate it if you'd back off and let me do it."

Not surprised by the request that sounded more like an order, Kat struggled to hold on to her patience. "I told you when I hired you that I planned to work *with* you. If you had a problem with that, then why didn't you say something then?"

"Because I didn't believe you." Exasperated, he scowled at her as if she were the cause of all his problems. "How was I supposed to know you were serious? It's hot as hell working in the sun all day and I thought you'd wilt like a pansy after about five minutes."

She lifted her chin at that, her eyes narrowing dangerously. "That was your first mistake, cowboy. I'm no hothouse flower."

"No, you're a woman. And I don't work with anything that wears skirts, boss lady. Ever."

For the first time in what seemed like hours, Kat's mouth twitched in amusement. "In case you hadn't noticed, I'm not wearing a skirt."

Oh, he'd noticed all right. Too much. His eyes black with determination, he met her gaze unflinchingly, his jaw as unyielding as a stone mountain. "I don't work with women," he repeated coldly.

Kat could understand why he'd be leery of women, but he had nothing to fear from her. "Look, I'm not interested in you as a man," she said bluntly. "I just want to get my barn built, then start on the fences I'll need before I can buy my cattle. Obviously, there's a lot to do, and two pairs of hands are better than one."

His mouth a flat line, Lucas had to give her credit. The lady gave a good argument. There was only one thing wrong with it—he hadn't imagined the interest he'd seen in her eyes when she'd gotten back from Silver City. Regardless of what she said, she was as aware of him as he was of her. And that scared the hell out of him.

"I can handle it by myself," he growled. "I know what I'm doing and you don't. You'll only slow me down."

"Then we'll just have to go slow," she said impishly. "Because I'm not going to go away and let you build *my* barn without putting a few nails in it myself."

So that was that. She was the boss and she was pulling rank. Releasing his hold on the crowbar he still held, he watched it fall over into the dust, then lifted mocking eyes to hers. "Then *I'll* take the porch and you can do all the work. Let me know when you want to switch places."

Kat couldn't believe he was serious, but he didn't spare her a second glance and headed for the cabin. As she watched in stunned disbelief, he dropped down into one of the old willow chairs on the porch and propped his feet up on the railing as if he intended to make himself comfortable there the rest of the day.

Frustrated, she just barely resisted the urge to throw something at him. Who the hell did he think he was? *She* was in charge here, not him, and she'd work if she wanted to. And if he didn't like it, he could take a hike. She was looking for a ranch hand when he first showed up on her doorstep, and she could look again if she had to.

But even as she considered firing him on the spot, she knew she couldn't do it. After all he'd been through, his hostility toward women was perfectly understandable. And he was, according to his former employers, a hell of a cowboy who could do just about anything that needed doing on a ranch. All she had to do was find a way to convince him to do his work with her at his side. Because she *wasn't* giving in to him, no matter what.

Stiffening her spine, she shrugged as if she couldn't care less what he did. "Fine. If that's the way you want it, that's okay by me," she told him, and determinedly turned back to the mesquite that had so far stubbornly resisted her efforts to dig it up.

She could feel Lucas's eyes boring into her back and knew he was just waiting for her to cry defeat. He was, she decided with a small smile, going to have a long wait. Her brothers could have told him a mule didn't have anything on her when it came to stubbornness.

Her dimples deepening at the thought, she took a firmer grip on the pick and swung it down into the hard, sun-baked earth. Her hands stung as the impact rippled up her arms, but she hadn't been kidding when she told him she was no hothouse flower. Working the dry earth free from the pointed end of the pick, she swung it again and again until she was finally able to tug the mesquite free. Tossing

it aside, she moved onto the next one without missing a
beat.

From his relatively cool spot on the porch, Lucas
watched her clear the building site of all plants and bushes.
In the cloudless sky, the heat of the sun had only intensi-
fied, and the temperature was rising steadily. Kat's shirt
was clinging to her back and breasts, her hair curling in
damp ringlets around her brow. She was hot, there was no
doubt about it. But would she stop? Would she even admit she needed a break? Hell, no!

Studying her through narrowed eyes, Lucas wanted to
curse her, to storm off the porch and grab her and give her
the good, swift shake she deserved for driving him crazy.
Did she think it was easy for him to sit here and watch her
sweat and strain while he relaxed in the shade? Just because he'd spent time in prison and wanted nothing to do
with women didn't mean he was a complete monster. A
half-dozen times, he'd almost come to her aid, unable to
sit there another second when she obviously needed his
help. But he'd stopped himself every time, sure the heat
would get to her any minute.

It hadn't.

She had no business being out in the sun working like a
fieldhand, damn her. But she'd proved her point. She was
stronger than he'd thought and more than capable of doing some of the less difficult tasks. That did not, however,
mean she could build a barn by herself. She probably
wouldn't even know where to start. All he had to do was
bide his time and wait for her to admit it.

Savoring the moment in anticipation, he sat back, his
mouth curling slightly as she tossed the pick aside and
turned toward the cabin. Don't be smug, he told himself,
his eyes locking with hers. The boss lady had a lot of pride

and he had no intention of stomping that into the dirt. Now that things were finally going his way, he could afford to be gracious.

But instead of crossing to the porch and the shade as he'd expected, she stood her ground, her gaze never flinching from his. If he hadn't known better, Lucas would have sworn she knew exactly what he was thinking. Shaking her head as if to say, "Oh, no, I'm not giving up yet," she headed for the tools assembled next to the building supplies. Without sparing him a glance, she reached for the posthole digger.

Swearing, Lucas jumped to his feet. Enough was enough.

Chapter 3

"Hellfire and damnation! You have got to be the most hardheaded woman I've ever met in my life!" Grumbling, he stepped off the porch, his long legs quickly eating up the space between them as he stalked toward her. "What does it take for you to admit you're in over your head?"

Hot and sweaty, her arms aching from the unaccustomed exercise, Kat was more than ready for a fight. She gave him a smile that was guaranteed to set his teeth on edge. "Obviously more than a few hours in the sun," she said with sugary sweetness, and had the satisfaction of watching his eyes narrow. "Now, are you going to help me or what?"

Help her? He wanted to turn her over his knee! But he didn't dare. Grinding an oath between his teeth, he stopped five feet away from her, wisely keeping his distance. "You don't know the first thing about building a barn."

Heat flushed her cheeks. Leave it to a man to worry about technicalities. "I've been to barn raisings before. I have a general idea of what's involved."

"Then where do you start, Miss Know It All? Huh? Tell me that."

"With the foundation, of course. Anyone knows that."

It was a good guess, but Lucas wasn't impressed. Arching a mocking brow at her, his gaze dropped to the tool in her hand, then lifted back to her face. "Then I suppose you know the first thing that goes up are the support posts. How deep do we set them? How far apart? Do you even know which ones are the support posts? Go ahead, pick one out. I dare you."

He had her and they both knew it. But would she admit it? No way. Waving her hand airily in the direction of the building supplies, she said, "They're over there somewhere. I'm sure I could find them if I had to. *And* put them up."

Stubborn. The woman gave a whole new meaning to the word. More than half tempted to walk out then and there, Lucas scowled at her in growing frustration. A bullheaded, willful woman was something he wanted nothing to do with. So why the hell was he still there? The ten dollars in his pocket wouldn't take him far, but it would take him miles away from her; and right now that sounded damn appealing.

His decision made, he had actually started for his truck when, from the corner of his eye, he saw her set the posthole digger aside and reach for one of the support posts that weighed nearly as much as she did. "Dammit to hell, woman, are you *trying* to hurt yourself?" he thundered, rushing to her side. "Give me that before you strain your back!"

Snatching it out of her arms, he was too incensed to notice that she gave it to him thankfully, without a word of protest. It wasn't until he tossed it to the ground and turned back to scowl at her that he saw her dancing eyes. "What are you looking at?"

"You," she said, grinning. "Does this mean you've changed your mind?"

Too late, he realized he'd been set up, but there wasn't a dang thing he could do about it now. The lady might have pushed his buttons, but he didn't doubt for a minute that she would try to build the barn by herself if he walked out and she couldn't find anyone else to help her. Just the thought of a ramshackle barn collapsing on her had his stomach twisting sickeningly.

Frowning down at her, he swore in defeat. "Do you always get your way?"

Dimples flashing, she didn't bother to deny it. "Whenever I can finagle it. My brothers say I'm a spoiled brat, too stubborn for my own good."

"They're right," he agreed, refusing to let her see the sudden grin that tugged at his mouth. Little witch. She was already cocky enough as it was. If he made the mistake of letting her know she could amuse him, he'd have more trouble on his hands than he could handle. Sobered by the thought, he deliberately turned his back on her. "Enough of this jawing. We're wasting daylight and we only have a few hours of it left. We need to mark off where the support posts go, then start digging. Where's the tape measure?"

The next few hours passed in a red-hot haze. The ground was as hard as stone and digging any type of hole in it was no easy task. Exhausted but unwilling to admit it and give Lucas one more reason not to work with her, Kat tried to dig her share of the holes, but her quivering muscles just wouldn't cooperate. Without a word of protest, she turned the posthole digger over to Lucas and stood back to watch, knowing he appreciated the room.

Fascinated in spite of herself, she had to admit that he really was something to see. Unmindful of the sun that beat down on his bare back, he ignored the sweat beading his skin, pulled on work gloves, then drove the posthole digger into the ground with a strength that seemed to steal the air from her lungs. The rock-hard muscles of his arms flexing with his every movement, he tightened his grip on the long-handled tool and repeated the process time and time again, until he was satisfied the hole was deep enough.

Her heart thundering against her ribs, Kat tore her eyes from him, knowing that if he caught her gawking like a kid in a candy store, he could very well walk out on her—this time for good. Sternly ordering herself to straighten up, she stayed well out of his way, waiting until he started digging the next hole before she moved forward to rake the dirt out of the one he had just finished.

But when all the holes were dug, he couldn't continue to the next step without her help. Support posts had to be set in each of the holes, then temporary braces attached to them so they would stand straight until the cement could be mixed and poured around the base of each post.

It was a simple enough procedure, one that shouldn't have set Kat's pulse jumping in her veins. After all, they'd worked quite well together over the course of the afternoon, and once Lucas had accepted the fact that she wasn't going to go away, there hadn't been another cross word between them. There was no reason to be so skittish of the man, she chided herself. He wasn't going to bite her, for heaven's sake!

But as she stepped forward to hold the first post steady so he could hammer the brace into place, her arm accidentally brushed his. Skin barely grazed skin, but he felt it. Sucking in a sharp breath, he drew back so swiftly, the pole almost fell over and conked them both on the head.

Startled, Kat grabbed it just in time, her blood suddenly throbbing in her veins. Tension, hot and fiery, crackled between them. "Lucas—"

"Hold the pole steady," he growled, snatching up a hammer and nail to attach the braces.

"But—"

"I don't want to hear it," he said coldly. His eyes, dark and wary, locked with hers for a brief, hostile moment before he turned his attention back to the task at hand. When she opened her mouth in protest, he only pounded the brace into place, drowning her out before she could say a single word.

Her brows knit in a single dark line of temper, she gave serious consideration to telling him what she thought of his arrogant tactics the minute he stopped hammering. Did he think she didn't know what he was doing? She'd felt the heat, the fire that seemed to leap from his skin to hers the second he'd touched her; and she wasn't any crazier about the attraction than he was. She'd have told him that if he'd given her half a chance. They needed to talk about it, acknowledge it, then find a way to dismiss it.

But the sun was blazing down on them, they were both hot and sweaty and tired, and neither of them was in any shape for anything that even resembled a civilized conversation. Biting her tongue, she mutely held the next board that needed to be nailed, determined to get along at all cost.

The bee came out of nowhere. Holding the post steady as Lucas started to hammer the brace in place, Kat didn't see it until it suddenly buzzed angrily in front of her face. Alarmed, she stumbled back, forgetting the boards lying right behind her on the ground.

"Watch out!"

The furious hum of the insect filling her ears, Kat hardly heard Lucas's warning. She took another step back, only to land half off a board. Her ankle turned, and pain shot up her leg. Gasping, she started to fall.

It happened so fast, she didn't have time to think, to protest. Then, in the next instant, she found herself snatched close to a hard, masculine chest. Her eyes wide, she looked up to find herself caught in the heat of Lucas's gaze, her hands flat against his bare chest, her mouth only inches away from his. Stunned, her heart started to knock out a frantic beat in her chest.

Let her go.

Somewhere in the back of his mind, the order ground out by his protective inner self registered, but instead of pushing her away, his wayward fingers tightened, drawing her impossibly closer. It had been years since he'd touched a woman, years since he'd allowed himself to *want* to touch one. How could he have forgotten, even for a second, what it was like?

She was soft, huggable, squeezable-soft, the kind of soft that blew a man's good intentions straight to hell. And even though she'd been working for hours and they were both damp with sweat, her scent was as clean as sunshine and so damn tempting she made his head swim. If she'd been a drug, she'd have carried a warning label. And like a junkie who couldn't remember the last time he'd been high, all he could think of was tasting her, drawing her in, losing himself in her.

Lost to everything but the feel of her under his hands, he didn't hear the truck barreling up the rocky drive until it was almost upon them. And by then it was too late. He'd been caught gazing down at Kat with calf eyes, no doubt by one of her brothers. Great, he thought furiously, snatching his hands back and stepping away from her. *That was just great.* After one day on the job, he was going to be thrown off the Double R for daring to touch baby sister.

But the man who stepped out of the custom-painted, aquamarine one-ton truck wasn't a Rawlings. Lucas didn't know him, but he took one look at him and sized him up for what he was—a rich rancher with soft hands. Dressed in fancy western clothes that probably cost more than Lucas made in a month, he looked like he didn't know one end of a cow from another and didn't have to. His kind always had somebody to do the dirty work for him.

Whoever he was, he was mad as hell.

"Looks like you've got company," Lucas told Kat without taking his eyes from the man who was stalking toward them with long, angry strides. "And don't look now, but he's about to blow a gasket. You know this jerk?"

Oh, yes, she knew him, Kat thought with a groan at the sight of Vince storming toward her like an overprotective father. Too well. "His father owns the Broken Arrow Ranch on the other side of Lordsburg," she said in a quick undertone, then forced a smile as the other man approached. "Hey, Vince, I wasn't expecting to see you today. Say hello to Lucas Valentine, my new hired hand. Lucas, this is Vince Waters."

Lucas started to offer his hand, but something in the other man's eyes warned him he'd be setting himself up for a scathing cut. So he only nodded and wasn't surprised when Vince didn't so much as acknowledge him.

"I want to talk to you," he told Kat coldly, ignoring Lucas. "Now."

Outraged by his rudeness, Kat said through her teeth, "This isn't a good time, Vince. In case you hadn't noticed, we're busy."

"Too bad," he retorted, "because I'm not going anywhere until I've had my say." Taking her arm abruptly in a vice-like grip, he started to tug her over to the shade of the porch.

"What the hell—"

At Lucas's angry snarl, Kat's heart jumped into her throat. "It's all right," she told him quickly, motioning for him to back off. "I can handle Vince. Just give us a few minutes, okay?"

Fury burning in his gut at the sight of her slender arm wrapped in that grip, Lucas wanted nothing more than to take Waters apart piece by piece. But the silent plea in her blue eyes begged him not to interfere, and to his disgust, he found he couldn't deny her. "All right," he muttered roughly. "But I'm not going anywhere."

Relieved, Kat allowed Vince to haul her only a few steps away before she reached over and pried his ruthless fingers from her arm. The tilt of her stubborn chin just dared him to touch her again. "You try that again," she hissed, "and I swear to God I'll break your fingers. What do you want?"

Not the least disturbed by her hostility, he said harshly, "For you to get rid of *him*." He nodded toward Lucas, his pale blue eyes nearly silver with antagonism. "I told you this morning how I felt about you hiring him. You should have fired him by now."

He didn't bother to lower his voice, didn't care that Lucas overheard every word. Gasping indignantly, Kat couldn't believe his nerve. Who the hell did he think he was to come to *her* ranch and throw his weight around as if he owned the place? Seething, she struggled to hang on to her temper, but she'd never been able to stomach a bully, and that was all Vince Waters would ever be.

"I don't care how you feel," she said icily. "You're not in charge."

"Well, someone besides you damn well needs to be," he snapped. "He's a bum, for God's sake! A two-bit drifter who probably doesn't have two nickels to rub together. I don't want him anywhere near you."

"Then I guess it's a good thing for both me and Lucas that you don't have any say around here," she tossed back. "He's staying, Vince. For as long as he wants the job."

"The hell he is—"

"And if you don't like it," she continued without missing a beat, "that's too damn bad. Just because I was foolish enough to go out with you once doesn't give you the right to come out here and order me around. You don't own me, and I don't have to do what you say—now or ever. Have I made myself clear?"

Hot color flushing his face and his beefy hands balling into fists, he spit out a curse that most men wouldn't repeat in a woman's company. "You're making a mistake," he warned. "I only came because I was concerned about you."

Kat didn't believe that for a second. Vince Waters liked to control people and everyone in the county knew it. "Don't be," she retorted. "What I do has nothing to do with you. Now, if you'll excuse me, I'm going to have to ask you to leave. Lucas and I have work to do."

Making no attempt to pretend he hadn't heard the entire conversation, Lucas tensed at Kat's curt dismissal of the big rancher, half expecting the angry man to grab her any minute and shake her. If he did, Lucas vowed, it would be the last time the bastard ever lifted a hand to her. Waters could rage all he liked at her—the boss lady could obviously hold her own with him—but he wasn't touching her. Lucas dared him even to try.

A hundred feet away, the springs tumbled merrily, but no one noticed. Silence stretched uncomfortably, tension gathering in the air like an approaching storm. Seeing the fury building in the other man's glittering eyes as they locked with his, Lucas didn't doubt for a minute that Winters would like nothing better than to stomp him into the dirt. Just let him try, he thought grimly, not the least concerned that he was outweighed by a good forty pounds or more. If the moron made the mistake of thinking he could take him on, Lucas was going to bring him down...*hard.* As far as he was concerned, Waters was just another thug with more brawn than brains. Any man who would use his size to intimidate a woman was nothing but scum and deserved everything he got.

Not that he was having much luck bringing Kat into line, Lucas noticed in appreciation, mockery hardening his eyes as he watched the boss lady stand up to the overgrown giant like a bantam hen. He had to give her credit—she had guts. But he didn't like to think what would have happened if he hadn't been around.

Braced for a sudden attack, he waited patiently, prepared to use the dirty tricks he'd learned in prison to teach Winters that he was a force to be reckoned with, but the rancher had obviously already decided that himself. Just when Lucas thought he was going to charge him like a mad bull, Winters muttered an expletive and swung back to face Kat.

"If I can't talk any sense into you, then maybe it's time I talked to your brothers. Then we'll see how stubborn you are." Tossing the threat down as he might a gauntlet, he stormed over to his pickup and slammed into it, sending gravel flying as he raced off, too furious to care that his custom paint job was taking a beating.

"Well," Kat said, releasing the breath she hadn't realized she'd been holding. "I guess he told me. I'm shaking in my shoes."

The quip should have lightened the tension, but it didn't even touch it. In the abrupt silence left behind by Vince's departure, their eyes met and suddenly they were both reminded of what the other man's unexpected arrival had interrupted. Between one heartbeat and the next, the air started to hum.

Her heart racing in a way it hadn't the entire time she'd had to deal with Vince, Kat tried to put the incident into perspective. Lucas had only grabbed her close because she'd almost tripped trying to get away from that stupid bee. It had been an instinctive action, nothing more, and it hadn't meant a thing. Given a choice, Lucas wouldn't have touched her or any other woman with a ten-foot pole.

If she could still feel his hands on her, it was only because he'd surprised her. If her throat tightened and her heart jerked at the thought of being that close to him again, she was overreacting to something that had happened for the first and last time. He'd caught her off guard, and for a second, she'd just forgotten who and what Lucas Valentine really was—a hard, bitter man with a chip on his shoulder that he'd never let any woman get close enough to knock off.

"He's a jerk," Lucas growled. "Forget him."

She could have told him that she'd forgotten Vince the second he drove away. *He* was the one she was having a problem with. But after working with him only one day, it didn't take a genius to figure out that he didn't want to hear that anymore than she wanted to say it. Unable to look at him for fear he'd read her thoughts in her too-expressive eyes, she cast a quick look at the sun, which had already started to set. "We might as well call it a day. It'll be dark soon."

She escaped inside, thankful for the chance to put some distance between them. Determined to put him out of her head, she cooked herself supper, took a bath, then crawled into bed with a murder mystery she'd been trying to start for the last week. But it couldn't hold her attention, and without quite knowing how it happened, she found her thoughts wandering back to Lucas.

Groaning, she tossed her book aside and slammed her eyes shut, but it didn't help. All she could think about was the moment when she'd looked up and found herself only inches away from Lucas's very impressive chest. Suddenly hot, she threw off the sheet that covered her and told herself this had to stop. Yes, there'd been a spark of tension between them, but that was to be expected. They were virtual strangers who had to work closely together. But the awkwardness would ease with time; they just had to be patient. Tomorrow would be better.

But it wasn't.

The minute Lucas arrived for work soon after dawn and his black eyes met hers, Kat felt awareness crawl back under her skin. From there on out, the day went downhill.

She knew that she was mostly to blame. For some crazy reason, she was nervous, and whenever she was jumpy, she chattered. She just couldn't seem to help herself—even when Lucas's response was usually limited to a grunt and a scowl. If she hadn't been so disgusted with herself, she would have laughed. He was clearly bored to death and not the least bit interested in her rantings, but still, she couldn't stop talking.

Tension took on a whole new meaning after that. They took a break for lunch, then another one during the hottest part of the day, but it didn't help. The hours seemed to drag by. Ignoring the sun that beat down on her unprotected head, Kat wished that she could ignore Lucas as easily as the heat. But he was too close, her awareness of him so strong she felt she'd suddenly developed radar where this one infuriating man was concerned. He couldn't move without her heart flip-flopping in reaction.

Horrified that he would notice, she quickly glided out of his reach when the work brought them close. He didn't say anything, but she saw his jaw tighten and his eyes narrow. As giddy as a young girl who had suddenly discovered that the boy next door was fascinating, she yammered on about childhood skirmishes with her brothers.

Later, Kat told herself that the argument that erupted right before quitting time was inevitable. They were both tired, their nerves strung tight. It only took a request, spoken in the wrong tone of voice, to set sparks flying.

"Tilt the wheelbarrow more," he said curtly, raking wet concrete around a support post with a hoe. "You're pouring too slow."

"I'm not Hulk Hogan," she snapped. "Hurry up! This is heavy!"

Muttering a curse, he grabbed the wheelbarrow, his hand inadvertently sliding over hers before he caught the handle and sent the wet cement sliding into the hole. "Watch it, boss lady," he warned in a low voice that seemed to come from the depths of his being. "You're pushing your luck."

"And you're pushing yours," she tossed back angrily as he dropped the wheelbarrow. Too agitated to notice how close she was to him, she punched him in the chest with her index finger. "Get this straight, Valentine. I don't take orders from you. So if you want me to do something, you ask. You don't *tell*. You got that?''

His frown fierce, he caught her finger in a tight grip. "Yeah, I got it. I got it loud and clear. Now, you get this—"

Hardly hearing him, Kat stared at his large, callused hand holding hers captive. Heat, like an unexpected rose in the desert, bloomed in her stomach. Startled, she jerked away, her only thought to put some space between them.

One minute he had a death hold on her hand, and the next she was a dozen feet away and backing up as if she couldn't get away from him fast enough. "Dammit to hell," he roared, "don't *do* that!"

Automatically freezing, Kat blinked at him in confusion. "What?"

His mouth twisted bitterly. "Save it, okay? I'm not blind. You've been as jumpy as a kitten on a hot rock all day. Every time I get too close, every time I accidentally touch you, you can't move fast enough to get away from me. What's the matter? You think the prison stench will rub off on you? Or are you afraid that it's been so long since I've had a woman that I'll jump your bones the first chance I get?"

"Of course not!"

Lifting a brow in patent disbelief, he drawled, "Yeah, right. Like I said, *save it*. Actions speak louder than words, and I read you loud and clear, sweetheart."

Kat couldn't have been more stunned if he'd slapped her. He thought she was *afraid* of him? Good Lord, was he blind or what? Sure, she jumped out of her skin every time he came near her—because her heart dropped like a yo-yo just at the thought of him touching her.

Tell him, a voice whispered in her ear. *You have to tell him.*

But she couldn't. Caught in the trap of his resentful gaze, she searched the rigid lines of his face for any sign of softness, but his expression was as stony as the canyon that surrounded them. Prison had left him a bitter man, and the last thing he would want to hear from her was that she was attracted to him in any way, shape or form. He wouldn't care that her reaction to him had caught her off guard, that she was fighting it and didn't want it any more than he did. The admission alone would be enough to damn her in his eyes and he wouldn't be able to get away from her fast enough.

"There's a logical explanation," she began, only to stop with no idea of where to go from there. What could she possibly say to him to make him understand?

"What I can't figure out is why you hired me in the first place when you obviously can't trust me as far as you can throw me," he said accusingly, too incensed to notice her floundering excuses. Struck by a sudden thought, his gaze sharpened suspiciously. "Or are you another one of those bleeding heart liberals looking to give an ex-con a second chance?"

"You're not an ex-con."

"The hell I'm not! Then what the devil was I doing in a cage for two years, surrounded by filth you can't even imagine? I was there, lady, and it was no picnic. There was one toilet in the middle of a cell for twelve men. *Twelve* men," he repeated furiously. "I couldn't even go to church without suffering through a strip search first."

Kat paled, the image his words painted sickening her, infuriating her. "It was a mistake," she said fiercely. "Nothing but a horrible mistake."

She was fighting mad, her blue eyes glistening with tears...for him. Fury clawing at him, Lucas wanted to rage at her that he didn't want her to defend him, to cry for him, to tell him what he was. But his throat closed at the sight of the pain in her eyes. He was a fool of the worst kind, he told himself angrily. What else could he be? He'd spent two years locked up like an animal, vowing every day of his incarceration that no woman ever again would be able to get to him. Yet this one not only could, she had. Every time she smiled or scowled, every time she stood nose to nose with him and told him exactly what she thought of him, she twisted him in knots.

Dammit, why did she have to be so drop-dead gorgeous? Any other woman would have been wrung out after a day of hard labor in the heat, but not this little cat. Oh, no. Even in dirty jeans and a shirt that was definitely the worse for wear, she somehow managed to look like she'd just stepped out of an ad for designer fashion. Color flared high in her cheeks, her hair was tumbling wildly around her shoulders and was sexy as hell, and all he could think of was reaching for her.

He had to get out of there. The thought hit him like a fist in the gut, driving the air from his lungs. Now. Because if he didn't, he was going to do something incredibly stupid.

"Tell that to the ranchers in Texas who refused to hire an *innocent* man because they had to protect their wives and daughters from me," he said bitingly. "Maybe they'll believe you. I know better."

He brushed past her, heading for his truck. "Where are you going?" she asked in alarm. "Damn you, Valentine, we made a deal! You can't walk out on me—"

"Oh, no?" he taunted, jerking open the cab door. "Watch me."

Before she could so much as blink, he climbed into the truck, fired it up and started out of the canyon with an ease that annoyed her no end. Fuming, her mouth hanging open in disbelief, she stared after his departing truck, tempted to throw a rock at it. If it broke the rear glass and conked him on the head, it was no more than he deserved.

Insufferable man! What had ever possessed her to hire him? She should have known the minute she met him that he'd be as immovable as a stone mountain—it stuck out all over him. But she'd been so sure she could handle him. Talk about smug! What had she been thinking of? He was nothing like the cowboys she'd grown up with, cowboys who were as much a part of the family as her brothers and just as likely to give in to her. Lucas Valentine wouldn't give in to her if she got down on her knees and begged.

Which is why you're so fascinated by him, her conscience dryly pointed out to her. *For the first time in your life. you've come up against a man you can't wrap around your little finger, and you don't like it.*

She wasn't a woman who lied to herself, and she knew the truth when it hit her in the face. Her heart thumping madly, the memory of the way his lean, tough torso had glistened in the sun playing in her head, she couldn't deny the obvious. He made her go weak at the knees.

Not that anything would come of it, of course, she assured herself quickly. She had no intention of giving in to the strange new feelings he stirred in her. She had too much work to do to be distracted by a man, especially one like Lucas Valentine. He had enough emotional baggage to fill a freight train. And even if she would allow herself to give in to her attraction to him, he had made it clear he wanted no part of her.

She should have been relieved, but an unfamiliar restlessness curled through her, disturbing her in a way she couldn't put a finger on. Suddenly realizing she was staring after him like an infatuated teenager, she whirled abruptly, muttering a curse. She was just hot and sweaty and had been standing in the sun too long, she thought in disgust as she headed for the springs. Things would look a lot different after she cooled off.

Chapter 4

Forced to drive at a snail's pace because of the rutted condition of a road that was little more than a rock-strewn cow path, Lucas tried to get a handle on the anger churning in his gut. But all he could think of was Miss High and Mighty Rawlings practically jumping out of her skin every time he got too close. Bitterness bubbled like hot oil in his stomach. Did she think he couldn't read her like a book? Couldn't see that she couldn't stand to be within four feet of him? He wasn't blind, dammit! He didn't have to be hit over the head to know when a woman didn't want him anywhere near her.

Lies, he raged, a muscle ticking in his jaw. She'd said all the right things, even cried for him, and the lies had been so clever, he'd almost been taken in. Just like a raw kid with peach fuzz on his face, he thought in disgust. He should have known better. From the moment he'd gotten out of prison, he'd run into the same prejudices time after time. People were quick to express regret over what had happened to him but couldn't quite forget that he'd spent the last couple of years with the dregs of society. Surely some of that wickedness must have rubbed off on him.

Hypocrites. They were all hypocrites—Kat Rawlings included, he thought resentfully. Just then, he lifted his gaze to the rearview mirror in time to see her head for the springs and plunge in, clothes and all. Caught off guard, he watched her surface, her sodden hair streaming down her back like a black river as she lifted her face to the sun. And just that quickly, heat coiled in his gut.

Snarling a curse, he dragged his eyes back to the pitted road and ruthlessly forced himself to concentrate on finding the smoothest route back to the bunkhouse. But it was Kat he saw in his mind's eye, Kat who tempted him without even trying. All too easily, he could picture her standing in the water, a slow smile sliding across her face, her eyes welcoming as her fingers slowly moved over the buttons of her blouse, releasing them one by one, until the garment parted to reveal breasts that were pale as ivory and pouting, just aching for his touch—

The image was so clear, so vivid, he was reaching for it before he realized what he was doing. Growling yet another savage curse, he jerked his attention back to his driving...just in time to see a mountain lion streak across the road right in front of him.

"What the hell—"

He didn't remember slamming on the brakes, but in the next instant, the wheels had locked up in spite of the fact that he hadn't been driving that fast. Unable to find purchase on the gravel-covered trail, the tires started to skid. In what seemed like slow motion, the truck began to slide toward a boulder that was as big as a house on the right side of the road.

His mouth pressed flat in a thin white line, Lucas fought the wheel, but there was nothing he could do. With a bone-jarring crash, the pickup plowed sideways into the rock and shuddered to a stop.

For a long moment, Lucas just sat there, his hands biting into the steering wheel, his heart pounding like thunder in his ears. Releasing a string of curses that should have turned the air blue, he surveyed the damage. The force of the impact had mashed in the passenger door, which thankfully wouldn't affect the running of the truck. But he only had liability insurance and no money for any unnecessary repairs, so now he was going to have to run around in a junk heap. Great. That was just great!

Wishing he had a piece of dynamite to blow up the damn boulder for getting in his way, he climbed out of the pickup to make sure the situation wasn't any worse than it appeared. But as he came around the front of the truck, he caught sight of a flash of goldish brown in the trees that lined the springs and realized the mountain lion hadn't kept going as he'd thought. It stood unmoving among the cottonwoods and stared right at him as if it could see into his soul.

Stopping in his tracks, Lucas went completely still. He'd never been so close to a big cat before, and this one was sleek and golden and utterly magnificent in the late afternoon shadows. Last night at the bunkhouse, he'd heard some of the men talking about the cat. Apparently, it had come down out of the mountains because of the long dry summer and had been spotted several times out on the range by some of the hands. Someone had said the lion must be close to starving if it came so close to the ranch, but from what he could see, it seemed to be in superb shape. Its coat appeared to be supple, and even from a distance he could see that its big amber eyes were bright and clear.

And wary as hell, he realized, stiffening. If it decided he was a threat and sprang at him, he didn't have a thing to protect himself with. Unconsciously holding his breath, he waited, tensed for an attack. Long seconds later, however, the cat grew tired of the staring game and turned away. In the blink of an eye, it silently disappeared into the trees.

Shaken, Lucas just stood there, staring at the spot where the lion had been, awed by the experience. Then he remembered Kat. She was probably still at the springs, relaxing in the water, unaware that there was any danger within twenty miles.

Immediately concerned, he cursed himself for being a fool. Kat Rawlings had grown up on the Double R. She knew every inch of it. And if ever there was a woman who could take care of herself, it was the boss lady. She didn't need him rushing to her side, and he sure as hell didn't want to. He'd never had the least inclination to be a knight and had no intention of changing at this late date.

And there was nothing to say the mountain lion would turn north, toward Kat, anyway, he reasoned. The springs ran for miles along the base of the rocky ridge of mountains that formed the western boundary of the ranch, and for all he knew, the big cat could have headed up into the mountains or followed the springs south.

The matter settled, he turned his attention back to his truck. The passenger door would never be the same again, but the front right wheel had managed to avoid the rock, so there was no axle damage. Evidently there was a God out there somewhere, he thought cynically. Circling back around to the driver's side, he climbed behind the wheel and carefully edged the pickup away from the boulder.

He'd intended to head straight for the bunkhouse, but like a magnet pulling at iron filings, his thoughts were drawn back to the springs...and Kat. The water was cold; she probably wouldn't stay in it long. But that didn't mean she would immediately go inside to change. The sun wouldn't slip behind the canyon wall for nearly an hour, and there weren't that many really hot days left. She could have stretched out on the bank to catch some rays. With the murmur of the springs echoing in her ears, she would never hear the mountain lion silently stalking her as it moved through the trees like a shadow...until it was too late.

The decision seemingly made without any input on his part, he found himself turning toward the cabin—and Kat. A curse ripped the air like a scalpel. He was going to take five minutes to warn her about the cat. That was it. He hadn't sunk so low that he could drive off and leave a woman—or anyone else, for that matter—to face a mountain lion alone. He would do the decent thing and warn her. Then he was getting the hell out of there.

Goose bumps skating over her skin, Kat rose from the water, chilled to the bone but invigorated. Ruefully, she looked down at herself, her mouth twitching into a grin. Her shirt was plastered to every curve, her sodden, heavy jeans molded to her hips and thighs. One glance at her boots told her they were no doubt ruined, but she couldn't regret the loss. They were her oldest pair, and the plunge had been worth it.

A teasing wind whistled down through the canyon, playfully tugging at the leaves of the cottonwoods. Lifting her face, Kat let the sun warm her, but for the first time that year, she caught the fresh scent of autumn in the air. Smiling, she closed her eyes and hugged it to her, delighted. When she opened them again, it was to see Lucas driving toward her, the passenger door to his truck dented in in a way it hadn't been when he'd left ten minutes ago.

Alarmed, she stepped toward him as he got out of his truck, forgetting that she was still standing up to midcalf in the springs. She started to trip, then caught herself and began wading awkwardly toward the rocky bank. "What happened to your truck?"

If he heard her, he gave no sign of it. Standing as if turned to stone, he took in her drenched state in a single, all-encompassing glance. Not so much as a flicker of reaction registered on his rugged face. Then, as if he couldn't help himself, his gaze sharpened. With infinite slowness, his eyes dropped to her breasts.

Gasping, Kat felt the stroke of his hot look as surely as if he'd reached out and tenderly stroked her. Beneath the wet, clinging material that barely concealed her from his knowing eyes, her dusky nipples puckered. Heat flowed through her like warm honey.

Her heart thumping and her knees quickly losing their starch, she knew she should cover herself. But her hands hung heavily at her sides, and her mouth was so dry, her tongue had to lick her lips for moisture. Then his eyes moved deliberately downward.

With a thoroughness that left her light-headed, he took inventory of every curve, every shallow, ragged breath she dragged in, every sweet inch of skin revealed by the sodden blouse that clung to her like a lover. And when his gaze finally, reluctantly, swept back to hers, she felt as if he touched her with flames of fire. Hot and hungry, his black eyes consumed her.

Kat never knew how long she stood there, dazed. It seemed like an eternity before it finally hit her that her wet clothes left nothing to the imagination and she was all but naked in front of him. Shock at her own boldness rippling through her, she stiffened, her cheeks burning.

"Oh, God!"

She would have bolted for the cabin, her only thought to escape the heat blazing in his eyes and the strange feverishness he lit deep in the heart of her. But her pride wouldn't let her run from him, wouldn't let him see what he did to her. Her feet refused to budge and she faced him defiantly, as regal as a queen, silently daring him to so much as mention her ragtag state. But on the inside, she was shaking. She'd never felt so vulnerable in all her life.

"I thought you'd left," she said flatly. "What do you want?"

His body hard with an ache he didn't want, his hands balled into fists to keep from reaching for her, Lucas almost groaned at her choice of phrasing. *Want?* he thought harshly. What the hell did she think he wanted when she stood in front of him like a half-drowned waif, every sensuous curve of her just begging for his touch. He wanted *her,* damn her blue eyes! He wanted to drag her down into the dirt and strip her bare so he could see the enticing swell of her hips and the crests of her breasts that so coyly peeked out at him from behind her wet blouse. But just seeing wouldn't be enough. Oh, no. He'd have to touch her, taste her . . . every hot, delectable, maddening inch of her.

And that was just for starters, he thought grimly. What he could do to her in bed, what they could do to each other, would set the sheets on fire.

And possibly land your butt back in jail, a caustic voice whispered in his ear. *Remember, that's how spoiled little rich girls play. They tease and taunt and try to drive you out of your mind. But God help you if you don't play the*

*game their way. They don't just turn and walk away. They
find a way to get rid of you for good.*

Deep in the depths of his soul, he heard the clang of a
cell door sliding shut behind him, cutting off escape.
Memories, black and cloying, clawed at him with razor-
sharp talons, tearing at him until his blood ran cold. If he
lived to be an old, old man, he would never forget the moment when he'd realized that he was well and truly caught
in a living nightmare. By day, the despair had been so deep
there was no climbing out of the abyss. And the nights...
God, he still wouldn't let himself think about the dead of
night, when rage seemed to cry from the very walls, turning the close air thick and heavy and cold.

His set face carved in harsh lines, he deliberately dredged
up the hated images when he looked at the woman in front
of him. To his disgust, it didn't make him want her any
less.

Furious with himself, he stood his ground, keeping a
good twenty feet between them. "Last night in the bunkhouse, some of the boys were talking about a mountain
lion they'd seen around the ranch," he told her tightly.
"Apparently there wasn't much rain this summer and the
creeks are going dry in the mountains. The cat has come
down for water and is sticking around to eat. So watch
yourself. He's probably dangerous and you could end up
getting hurt if you're not careful."

The warning delivered, he climbed back into his truck
and once again turned onto the rough trail that led to the
bunkhouse. This time when he drove away from her, he
didn't look in the rearview mirror. He didn't have to. He
could see her with his mind's eye as clearly as if she stood
before him.

Shivering in the warm wind that swirled teasingly
around her, Kat hugged herself and stared after Lucas's

truck long after it had disappeared from view. Silence drifted into place around her, but she couldn't hear it for the echo of his last words in her ears.

Watch yourself. He's probably dangerous and you could end up getting hurt if you're not careful.

Had he been warning her about the cat? Or himself?

Her heart stumbled over itself, and Kat tried to dismiss the idea as ridiculous. Lucas Valentine couldn't hurt her. She wouldn't let him. But as she hurried into the cabin to change, she could still feel the melting warmth that had seeped through her when his eyes had lingered on her breasts.

And suddenly, she knew she couldn't spend another evening at the cabin by herself, alone with her thoughts. For the first time since she'd moved to the springs, she needed the noise of other people, companionship, to fill the emptiness and block out the reflections that were too disturbing and persistent. She'd had a hard day, she told herself as she quickly pulled on jeans and a flowered cotton shirt, then slipped into a pair of flats. That was all it was. If she was discontent, it had nothing to do with the tall, antagonistic cowboy she'd spent most of the day with.

Taking a last glance in the mirror, she decided to join the rest of the family for dinner. It was Thursday night, the one night of the week when everyone tried to get together for supper and catch up on one another's lives.

Considering the fact that they all lived within ten miles of one another, that should have been easy. But ranch business often required one or more of her brothers to be gone overnight. And her three sisters-in-law were hardly homebodies themselves. Now that Tate had finished medical school, she'd joined Josey's practice at the clinic they ran out of her grandparents' old place down the road from the Double R homestead. As the only doctors for forty miles, the two of them were kept hopping. And on the rare nights when they were both able to attend the family dinner, Susannah wasn't always available. As the author of the popular Ace MacKenzie books, she was often tied to her computer by a tight deadline or off on a research trip with Cooper, scouting out new locales for her stories.

Ten minutes after she'd closed the cabin door behind her and driven out of the canyon, the Victorian mansion she'd grown up in came into sight, its lighted windows visible for miles. An anachronism set in the middle of an unforgiving land, it had stood thus for well over a hundred years. Flynn and Tate had built a more contemporary house down the road; even the old Patterson place, where Susannah and Cooper lived, was more modern than the ranch headquarters. But the mansion, complete with wide verandas both upstairs and down, whimsical gingerbread trim and high-ceilinged rooms that were a pain to heat, was and always would be home.

As a child, she'd thought it was as big as a castle. She'd raced through its long halls, slid down the banister like a little hoyden, and played dress-up in the attic. She found it comforting that generations of Rawlingses after her, starting with Gable's tribe, would do the same. Smiling at the thought of her nieces and nephews, she parked behind Cooper's pickup and hurried inside.

"Aunt Kat!"

The cry came from Haily, Tate's thirteen-year-old daughter, and it started a stampede down the stairs from the playroom. Gable's Mandy, now five, and his two-year-old twins, Brian and Joey, charged after Haily, and right on their heels was Cooper's pride and joy, the curly-haired moppet, Lainey. Laughing, Kat went down on her knees to hug them all and within seconds found herself flat on her back with kids hanging all over her.

Alice, more adopted mother than housekeeper, came out of the kitchen to see what all the ruckus was about, her lined face breaking into a smile at the sight of the young bodies wrestling in the entrance hall. "Well, we've finally got the whole clan together. I guess I didn't cook all afternoon for nothing."

Extracting herself from the pile of kids, Kat grinned. "You mean everybody was able to make it? Has anyone called the wire services yet? This is news!"

"We were just waiting for you to get here," Josey said, chuckling as she urged the kids upstairs to wash their hands. "The guys were just talking about sending a posse out to look for you."

Kat arched a brow in surprise. "Oh? Why?"

"Because we thought you might be in trouble," Flynn replied with his usual bluntness as she followed Josey into the den. "You're late."

Cooper, seeing the warning sparks flash in Kat's blue eyes, quickly moved to defuse the sudden tension. Amusement curling the corners of his mouth, he draped a long arm around his sister's shoulders. "Don't pay any attention to him, brat. In two months, when Tate has the baby, he's not going to know if he's coming or going. You can do whatever you want and he'll never notice."

"Yeah, but what about the rest of you?" she tossed back, her frown belied by the sassiness dancing in her eyes. "How old do I have to be before you finally realize I can take care of myself?"

"Fifty-three sounds good to me," Gable said dryly. "How 'bout you, Flynn? You got any problem with that?"

"That's just the figure I was looking for," he said with a chuckle. "What do you think, Coop?"

"I think I value my skin too much to say," he retorted, casting his sister a wary glance as she carefully removed his arm from around her shoulders. "Easy, little sister," he warned. "Don't lose your cool. We're just funning."

When she merely looked at them, all three men started to squirm, bringing a chuckle from their wives. "Give 'em what for, Kat," Tate encouraged her. Seven months pregnant, she was always ready to give a good ribbing, especially where her husband and brothers-in-law were concerned. "If they had to answer to you the way they expect you to answer to them, the rest of us would never hear the end of it."

"They wouldn't do it," Susannah retorted, her teasing smile bright with love as it locked with Cooper's. "Would you?"

"Of course not. But we're—"

Suddenly realizing what he was about to say, he shut his mouth with an audible snap, but it was too late. The Rawlings women jumped on him like ducks on the first june bug of the summer.

"Men?" Josey asked archly.

"Of course," Tate said. "Men don't need to answer to anyone. They're big and tough and strong and can take care of themselves."

"Which is something us helpless females could never do," Kat added. "We haven't got the sense to find our way home without directions." Batting her eyelashes, she gave Cooper a sweet smile. "Is that what you were going to say, big brother?"

Heat climbing into his cheeks, Cooper hedged, "Well, not exactly—"

"It's okay, honey," Susannah assured him, giving his hot face a loving pat. "Everyone knows the Rawlings men are dyed-in-the-wool chauvinists. You can admit it."

"Now just a dang minute," Flynn began. "Lumping us all together isn't exactly fair—"

"Oh, no?" Tate replied, grinning. "If I remember correctly, you were the one who was pacing the floor like a worried father just because Kat didn't get here when you thought she should."

It was a good point, and from the rueful twinkle in his eyes, it was obvious he knew it. Shrugging as if to say *I tried,* he didn't say another word.

Josey, her arms folded over her chest, gave her husband an arch look. "What about you, honey? Have you got anything to add to this little discussion?"

Gable, wiser than his brothers, only smiled and slipped an arm around his wife's waist. "How about, let's eat? I don't know about the rest of you, but I'm starving!"

Laughing, they called the kids from upstairs and all retired to the dining room.

After that they wisely steered the conversation away from Kat and her affairs. The summer had been a busy one, both for the ranch and for the family and there was a lot to discuss. The peppers they had started planting soon after Susannah came into the family were doing well, and this year they would have a record crop. A buyer for one of the country's leading salsa makers had made an offer for the entire harvest, and they had to decide whether to accept it since the price he was willing to pay was somewhat less than the current market price. They could either take the "sure" thing, which paid a little less money, or gamble that the price would still be up when it came time to harvest and they could find a buyer for the whole crop. After much discussion back and forth, they all voted for the sure thing.

And then there was Flynn. The whittling he'd started while riding the pro rodeo circuit had brought him more success than he'd ever dreamed of. His carvings were in top galleries from L.A. to Chicago and selling like hotcakes.

If he'd wanted to, he could have spent most of his time traveling to and from the shows, his work was that much in demand. But after he'd married Tate and adopted her daughter, Haily, he'd surprised everyone by becoming a homebody, refusing to go anywhere—even if it was for his own good—if he couldn't take his family along.

"Talk to him," Tate told the rest of the family in exasperation. "There are artists who literally wait years for the Stevenson Gallery in New York even to notice them, and they're practically begging him to do a show next month."

"Flynn, that's wonderful!"

"You've got to do it—"

"We can make a vacation of it, take the whole family."

They all spoke at once, but Flynn only shook his head. "Tate can't travel then, and I'm not leaving her. The answer is no."

His tone was adamant and brooked no interference. Cooper and Gable exchanged a look—they would have done the same thing. "If they want your stuff bad enough, they'll wait until after the baby comes and Tate and the kids can travel with you," Gable said quietly. "Talk to them. They'll probably cooperate."

"And if they don't," Kat added, "you don't want to do business with them, anyway."

The rest of the family agreed, and from there, the conversation turned to baby names, the going price for cattle, the pros and cons of buying a fancy, high-ticket tractor or getting along with what they had, and Susannah's newest bestseller. Letting the sounds of her brothers' low voices and the children's chatter wash over her, Kat relaxed in a way she couldn't anywhere else. When she'd been away at school, then teaching in Santa Fe, she hadn't realized just how much she missed ordinary, quiet evenings with her family. Not once did she even think of Lucas Valentine.

But then the meal was over, the table cleared, and all the women helped Alice with the dishes. Exhausted from being on her feet all day at the clinic, Tate had Flynn take her and Haily home soon after that and the party started to break up. Saying her own goodbyes, Kat was hunting for her purse when Gable caught up with her and asked to talk to her in his study.

Distracted, she should have realized then that he'd just been biding his time, waiting all evening to bring up the one subject she didn't want to talk about. But his expression was so solemn that she thought there was something seriously wrong. Her heart jerking in her breast, she followed him into the study.

Shutting the door behind her, she leaned against it, a frown worrying her brow as she watched him take a seat behind the old desk that had been their father's and his father's before that. "What is it? What's wrong? Is it Josey? The kids?"

His lips twitched at her flair for the dramatic. "Relax, honey, this has nothing to do with the family. Everyone's fine as far as I know. I just wanted to talk to you about a visitor I had yesterday afternoon."

Surprised, she racked her brain for the name of anyone who could have dropped by the Double R yesterday and put that look on his face. She couldn't think of a soul. "Who?"

Giving her a look from her childhood, one that missed little, he said, "Vince Waters."

The name hit her like an accusation. In her effort to push Lucas from her mind, she'd completely forgotten Vince and his childish threat. "Don't you think I'm a little old for you to call me on the carpet?" she asked curtly.

"I'm not calling you on the carpet—"

"No? Then what would you call it?"

Frustrated, Gable frowned at the stubborn jut of her chin. "Look," he said, letting his breath out in exasperation, "can't we sit down and discuss this like two civilized adults? I'm not lecturing you, honey. I'm just concerned."

Her favorite brother, Gable had locked horns with her more times than she cared to remember. But he only had to speak to her in that quiet, patient voice of his, and she found it impossible to hang on to her anger. Biting back a smile, she scowled at him. "You're not going to talk me into letting Lucas go, so don't even try. If that's what you called me in here to discuss—"

"Vince said—"

"Vince Waters is the biggest jerk who ever walked on two legs," she retorted heatedly, pushing away from the door to prowl restlessly around the study. "He's got this twisted idea in his head that he has the right to run my life just because I was stupid enough to go out with him once. Every time I turn around, there he is. He's driving me crazy!"

In the process of leaning back on two legs of his chair, Gable straightened abruptly, bringing all four chair legs down to the floor with a snap. "Has he been bothering you?"

Kat hesitated, knowing she only had to say yes to have Gable and the rest of the family come down on Vince like a ton of bricks. After they got through with him, he'd never darken her doorstep again. It was, she admitted, a tempting thought. But once she allowed them to handle one problem for her, it would be difficult to draw the line on others. The independence she'd started to establish by moving to the springs would go up in a puff of smoke, and she would have no one to blame but herself.

"Not the way you mean," she replied, sinking into the chair in front of his desk. "You know Vince. He thinks he's God's gift to the women of New Mexico, and he's having a hard time believing I don't find him irresistible. Don't worry. I can handle him."

Gable nodded, satisfied. If any woman could put Waters in his place, it was Kat. But he was still disturbed about the wild tale the other man had rushed over to tell him yesterday. As much as he disliked Waters, he had to admit he hadn't sounded like he was lying.

Picking up a pencil to beat out a staccato rhythm on the desk top, he studied Kat through shuttered eyes, wondering how to ask her about the incident without having her go all prickly on him. But she was so damn touchy about being a "grown woman" now, she would probably blow up no matter what he said.

Deciding to just spit it out, he said, "All right, then, I'll let you take care of him. Valentine, however, is another matter."

Her spine snapping straight as a poker, she shot him a warning look. "I already told you I'm not letting him go. There's nothing left to discuss."

"Now don't get your jeans in a wad, brat," he said with a grin. "I'm not asking—or telling—you to fire Valentine."

"Then why bring him up?"

"Because there's the little matter of the big clinch Waters saw you in with your new hired hand," he retorted. "Or was he lying just so he could stir up more trouble?"

Caught in his unwavering gaze, Kat felt just like she had when she was caught kissing one of the neighbor's sons when she was sixteen. Lying then hadn't helped any more than it would now.

Her face hot with revealing color, she clenched her teeth on an oath and silently damned Vince Waters for tattling on her as if she was a first-grader who had stolen his pencil. Her blue eyes hot with indignation, she met her brother's gaze unflinchingly. "If you're asking if I'm getting romantically involved with Lucas, the answer is no."

"I wasn't asking," he pointed out quietly. "I was just telling you what Waters said. I was concerned."

"Because you think Lucas really is a rapist? Is that what you're saying?"

Gable struggled not to snap back at her sharp question. Lifting his hands into the air as if she held him at gunpoint, he forced a crooked smile. "Hey, I'm not the bad guy here. I love you, remember? And I've got a right to be concerned when I hear that my baby sister has been seen in the arms of a man with a shady past. That doesn't mean I think he's capable of rape," he added quickly before she could protest. "He could be as pure as the driven snow for all I know. He's a stranger, honey. You've only known him a few days, so can you cut me some slack here? I'm worried, okay?"

Put that way, she couldn't stop the flush in her cheeks from deepening. *Watch it, girl,* her conscience taunted her. *You're acting damn defensive for a woman who supposedly isn't interested in a man.*

"It wasn't a clinch," she said, managing to answer evenly in spite of the wild skipping of her pulse. "I was trying to get away from a bee and Lucas caught me when I accidentally tripped."

It was a logical explanation . . . and far too simple for a lie. Gable's eyes started to twinkle. "I see. And I suppose that it was just dumb luck Waters drove up just in time to get an eyeful and jump to the wrong conclusion."

"That's right." Too furious to sit still, she jumped up to pace around the study. "I wish you could have heard him. He was horrible, stomping around like he owned the place...like he owned *me!*" Whirling, she faced her brother in growing indignation. "He actually demanded that I fire Lucas right in front of him! I couldn't believe it."

Leaning back in his chair again to watch her pace, he said, "Waters always has had the sensitivity of a jackass. Forget it."

"Easy for you to say," she quipped. "You're not the one he thinks he's in love with."

"No, I'm not," he said, laughing. "There is a God."

She sent him a reproving glance that would have been fierce if she could have stopped her lips from twitching. "This isn't funny."

He only grinned, unrepentant. "Oh, I don't know. There's a certain twisted humor here if you look at it the right way. What are you going to do about Waters?"

"Pull out my shotgun the next time he so much as shows his face," she said promptly. "I've got no use for varmints, and if that doesn't convince him I'm serious, nothing will."

Anyone else who heard her might have thought she was kidding, but Gable knew her too well. "If you've got to pull the trigger to get your point across, just make sure you shoot into the air. What about Valentine?"

Wariness crept into her eyes. "What about him?"

"Since he seems to be working out so far, I assume you're going to keep him on as long as he'll stay?"

"He's a hard worker. I'd be a fool to let him go."

Satisfied, Gable reminded her that if she needed any help, all she had to do was ask. But as he watched her leave, he couldn't quell the niggling thought that despite all her claims to the contrary, she was more than a little interested in Lucas Valentine. And for no other reason than that, Gable planned to keep an eye on him.

Chapter 5

Half expecting Lucas to be a no-show the following morning, Kat sighed in relief when his pickup rolled into the yard just as the sun peaked over the horizon. He greeted her cautious good-morning with a grunt that could only be called surly, then hardly said two words for the next eight hours, but he was there and that was all that mattered. Resolving to get along with him no matter what, she steeled herself not to make the same mistakes she had yesterday by shying away from him every time the work brought them close. But it wasn't easy. His brooding looks tugged at her heartstrings and sent a thousand butterflies swooping into her stomach. She wanted to chatter, but held her tongue, his set, closed expression not encouraging conversation.

In spite of that, they managed to work amazingly well together. Over the next four days, the barn came along nicely, better than Kat had dared to hope. Even her brothers, who dropped by occasionally to check on their progress, were impressed at the way the building was slowly coming together.

But the progress didn't come without a price. The near silence was driving her up the partially built walls. And she didn't even want to think about what the growing sexual tension was doing to her. Every move, every softly muttered curse, every dark, resentful look Lucas sent her set her heart thundering in her breast.

Disgusted with herself, she fought the attraction with all her stubborn pride, but it only got worse. At night she found herself embroiled in hot, vivid dreams in which Lucas played a major role—dreams so real she could practically smell the spicy scent of his after-shave. The dreams destroyed her inhibitions, and she woke up reaching for him, disappointment catching her off guard when her fingers found nothing but the cool sheets.

By Monday, she knew something had to change. She couldn't continue to endure the long silences without going quietly out of her mind. So when they took their first break at midmorning, a break that usually stretched interminably, Kat perched on a rock near the building site and openly studied Lucas as he got a drink of water from the large cooler she kept nearby.

When he turned to find her eyes on him, he went perfectly still, his brows knit in an intimidating scowl, the glass he held frozen halfway to his mouth. "What?"

Not surprised by the sudden wariness she saw in his eyes, she gazed at him curiously. "I was just wondering how you became a cowboy. Were your parents ranchers?"

Something flickered in his eyes, something that was there and gone before she could read it. "Why do you want to know?"

She shrugged. "Just curious. We've been working together for almost a week, and it just struck me that I don't know anything about you."

"You know about the two years in Huntsville," he retorted coldly. "Nothing else matters. Now, if you're through with the chitchat, let's get back to work." With a long swallow, he drained his cup and slapped it back down on the water cooler, then turned toward the barn.

A smart woman would have taken the hint and let it go. But she was antsy, her nerves shot. If she could just get him to talk, to open up about himself, she might be able to forget this silly infatuation she had for him and go about the difficult task of becoming friends with him.

Following him, she helped him hoist a board into position, her eyes shifting to where he stood at the other end of the piece of siding. It had taken them all day yesterday to put the roof on, and they'd started on the outside walls first thing this morning. With every board needing to be measured and cut before it could be hammered into place, they hadn't gotten very far. "Did you have a tree house when you were a kid?"

His jaw rigid, he never took his eyes from the nail he was about to pound. "No."

His answer was short and terse and hardly encouraging, but Kat didn't so much as blink. "My brothers didn't want me to have one, either. In fact, they flat out refused to build me one. So I did it myself."

She laughed at the memory, her voice unconsciously husky. "It was a pitiful excuse for a tree house, but it was mine, and I loved it. I built it way up in the top of a cottonwood by the creek and used to think I could see all the way to China. Actually, it just overlooked the old Patterson place, but that was good enough for me. Then, when

I was eight, my brothers found out about it when I fell out of it and broke my arm, and that was the end of that.''

Her words flowed over him like the quiet murmur of the springs, and Lucas steeled himself against the seductive pull of her voice. He didn't want to hear about her childhood any more than he wanted to tell her about his. The less he knew about her, the better and the easier it would be to walk away.

Tightening his grip on the hammer he held, he hit the nail squarely on its head, rudely drowning out her reflections. But the fierce pounding didn't block out the image of a dark-haired little girl that took shape in his mind.

Even at eight, Kat Rawlings would have had her fair share of feminine wiles. Adventuresome and into mischief every chance she got, she must have given her brothers fits. The word *no* would have been nothing more than a challenge. His mouth twitching at the thought, he found it all too easy to picture her with her long curls scraped back into pigtails and grass stains on her jeans. Small and sassy, her bright blue eyes defiant, her quick grin full of trouble, she must have been a handful.

And she hadn't changed. *No* was still something to challenge, something she refused to accept gracefully.

And he found that too damn appealing. Muttering a curse, he hammered the nail completely into the board, then stopped to grab another nail from the pouch tied around his waist. In the ensuing silence, Kat immediately began chattering again.

"Your parents must have been as protective as my brothers were. And boys are so rough. I bet you were always coming home with scrapes and bruises and torn jeans. Your poor mother must have worried herself to death over you."

When she waited expectantly for a response, Lucas vowed to let her wait until the cows came home. If she wanted to spill her guts without any encouragement from him, that was her choice. But he'd told her all he was going to. Moving around to her other side, he placed the second nail into position and drove it into the board with a single powerful stroke.

The silence grew thicker with every beat of her heart, and Kat just barely resisted the urge to throw something at him. Stubborn old goat! Let him try and give her the silent treatment. She would show him how much it bothered her!

"I know you probably hated it, but you were lucky to have your mom fuss over you. I don't remember much about mine. Not that my brothers weren't great," she added quickly in case he jumped to the wrong conclusion. "They were. I knew they loved me, but they were guys and they just didn't have that special touch that a mother does. You know what I'm talking about. Your mother must have—"

"She couldn't have cared less if I was alive or dead," he growled harshly, furious with her for unknowingly finding just the right button to push to get a response out of him. "She never wanted kids, hated being tied down. Up until I was twelve, she never let a day pass without letting me know what a burden I was. So save your fantasies for someone who deserves them. Mothers aren't what they're cracked up to be."

Stricken, Kat could only stare at him. "What happened when you were twelve?"

His teeth locked tight, Lucas swore he wasn't going to say another word. He didn't need or want her pity; he just wanted her to leave him the hell alone. But the words and the black anger that had been with him longer than he could remember just came spilling out. "My dad got drunk and was killed by a bull on a ranch in South Texas. He was a tough old bastard, and if it hadn't been for him, Maggie would have run off the first chance she got. But she knew he'd come after her, so she stayed. Once he died, though, there was nothing standing in her way. Certainly not me."

"She left you? She just ran off and left you? You were only a boy!"

At her horrified tone, a smile that had nothing to do with amusement curled up one corner of his mouth. So it was finally hitting her that not everyone grew up in a fairy tale. "Welcome to the real world, boss lady. It's not a pretty place, is it? Anything else you want to know? Such as how I tracked old Maggie down when I was thrown in jail for rape? Maybe you'd like to hear how she turned me down flat when I asked her for bail money and told me I could rot for all she cared. Yeah, my mom is something else, a real fine example of motherhood."

He practically threw the words at her, hoping he had shocked her. Then maybe she would realize that her world was one nonstop picnic compared to the one he grew up in. He was hard and jaded and as tough as an old piece of beef jerky, and instead of trying to befriend him, she should be thinking about running for cover.

But instead of recoiling from the ugly picture he painted with his harsh words, she stood her ground, her blue eyes dark with sympathy and an interest that couldn't be denied. Sudden, unexpected heat slamming into him, he cursed and turned away. But he could still feel the warmth of her gaze and it totally unnerved him. Didn't the little witch know better than to look at a man like that?

"If you've heard enough, then I suggest we both get back to what we were doing." Handing her her hammer, he went back to work.

By the end of the week, the situation was so explosive that it would have taken only one wrong word from either of them for the tension to blow up in their faces. The strain getting to her, Kat couldn't forget what Lucas had told her about his parents and childhood. Her heart breaking for him, she wanted to believe that he'd made the whole thing up just to shock her, but the pain of his lonely existence was there in the depths of his cold, shuttered eyes for anyone to read.

Haunted by his memories, she regaled him with funny stories about the ranch and her brothers in order to lighten the mood, but she couldn't draw so much as a glimmer of a smile from him. Tight-lipped, he only stared at her unblinkingly, silently warning her to back off. Frustrated, she wanted to shake him good, but her heart jumped in her breast just at the thought of getting close enough to touch him.

She needed a break...from the cabin, from the long hours she'd been putting in, from Lucas. So when some of her old friends from high school called Thursday and invited her to go out with them the following night, she leapt at the chance. The change of scenery would do her good. And if she was lucky, she just might meet a man who could take her mind off Lucas for a while.

Deciding to knock off early Friday afternoon, she started to put her tools away at four. When Lucas glanced over at her in surprise, she fought the need to shuffle her feet like a kid caught playing hooky from school. "I'm going out with some friends tonight, so I'm going to quit early and clean up," she said, then wanted to kick herself for feeling she had to justify her time off to him. She was the boss, not the other way around. "Why don't you go ahead and stop for the day, too? It's been a long week and you could probably use a break. I know I could."

They'd just finished the last wall, but Lucas hadn't stopped to celebrate. Picking up the scraps of sawed lumber that cluttered the site, he said, "I'll finish here first."

He had that hard jut to his jaw, the one that told Kat it wouldn't do any good to argue with him. Opening her mouth to object, she shut it with a snap, refusing to even acknowledge the guilt that tugged at her. If he wanted to work longer than he had to, she certainly wasn't going to beat herself up over it just because she was going out to have some fun.

She hurried into the cabin to clean up, and just as she was tucking a rose-colored peasant top into her black jeans she heard the wild honking of a horn outside. Grinning, she took only a second to run some lipstick over her lips and brush her hair back from her face before rushing outside.

Angela Trent and Jenny Blake had been her best friends since grade school. They'd laughed and played together as kids, then shared their deepest, darkest secrets with one another when the only topic of conversation became boys. And when she'd left for college and then started teaching in Santa Fe, they'd kept AT&T in business burning up the phone lines.

She loved them like sisters, but when she stepped out on the porch just in time to see them making a beeline for Lucas, who had come around from the back of the barn to see what all the honking was about, she wanted to kill them. They had that look in their eyes that she was all-too familiar with. *Good-looking man in sight.*

Groaning, she took off like a shot, trying to cut them off. But it was too late. Angela, petite and blond and as angelic-looking as her name, gave him a smile that would have knocked a lesser man out of his shoes. "Well, hi, stranger. You must be Kat's new cowboy. I'm Angela Trent."

"And I'm Jenny Blake," the tall redhead at her side purred as she boldly ran her green eyes up and down Lucas's whipcord-lean frame. "Kat didn't tell us you were so—"

"I'm ready," Kat said merrily, cutting off Jenny before she could say just what Lucas was. Knowing the other girl's boldness, Kat didn't want to even speculate what adjective she'd almost used. "I see you've met Lucas, so I guess we can go. I'm starving! How does steak sound?"

"Oh, but we can't go yet!"

"We haven't had a chance to talk to Lucas," Angela protested, shooting Kat a disapproving frown before turning back to him with a sweet smile. "The three of us haven't been out to dinner with a man in ages, and I—for one—would just love it if you'd come with us," she confided breathlessly. Daring to touch him, she reached out to slowly trail a finger down the hard muscles of his arm. "My pickup's not very big, but I'm sure we could all squeeze into it. It'll be fun. Please say you'll come."

Flabbergasted, Kat could only stare at her friend as if she'd never seen her before. Who was this brazen woman who was coming on to Lucas like a starving woman eyeing the only crumb of bread in sight? The shy one in the group—at least on the surface—Angela never openly flirted until she had at least three beers down her and knew she had a sure thing.

Lucas, far from being a sure thing, was the last man on earth she and Jenny should have hit on. Chancing a glance at him, Kat saw the cold glint in his eyes, the unyielding flatness of his tightly pressed mouth and the barely suppressed hostility in the stiff way he held himself. Alarmed, she quickly grabbed her friends by the arm and started to tug them away. "Sorry, guys, but Lucas isn't interested—"

"How do you know? You didn't give him a chance to say anything."

"Trust me," she assured them, pulling them toward Angela's candy-apple red truck. "I know what I'm talking about."

"I think you should let him answer for himself," Jenny retorted, stopping in her tracks. Whirling, a slow, seductive smile started to slide across her mouth. "Lucas," she began, only to frown in surprise at the sight of the empty spot where he'd stood only seconds before. "Why, he's gone! Where'd he go?"

Her hands on her hips, Kat gave her a reproving look. "Back to work. I told you he didn't want to go. Lucas is kind of...shy."

Angela snorted at that. "Him? Good Lord, why? He's the best-looking thing I've seen in ages. One smile and he could probably have women dropping at his feet like flies."

"Believe me," Kat muttered under her breath, "that's the last thing he wants." Forcing a smile, she linked arms with them. "Forget Lucas. We've got a lot of catching up to do. Let's get started."

They had dinner at a new steak house in Lordsburg, then decided to go to the Crossroads afterward for a couple of games of pool and dancing on the postage-size dance floor. A local cowboy hangout that had, on more than one occasion, been busted up in a fight, it was not exactly Kat's idea of after-dinner entertainment. Especially when she

hadn't been able to get Lucas out of her head all evening.
There would be cowboys coming out of the woodwork,
every one of them reminding her of the one she'd left at
home. But Angela and Jenny were in the mood to honky-
tonk, and she didn't want to be the only killjoy in the
group. Reluctantly, she tagged along.

The minute they stepped inside, Kat knew they'd made
a mistake. It was Friday night and payday. Every cowboy
in the joint had that swagger that only came with money
in the pocket. Beer flowed like rainwater through a gutter,
while cigarette smoke spiraled toward the low ceiling,
where it collected in a gray cloud. Laughter and cursing
floated on the dank air, and on the jukebox, a gravelly-
voiced Waylon Jennings was stuck in a groove so that one
line of the song repeated itself over and over again without end. Nobody seemed to give a damn.

"I don't think this is a very good idea," Kat said quietly, shivering as the volatile mood of the bar seemed to
reach out toward them threateningly. "Why don't we drive
into Silver City instead and maybe catch a movie? There's
a new romance—"

"We can find romance right here," Jenny cut in, wink-
ing at a boyish cowboy at the bar who didn't look old
enough to drive, let alone drink. "Lighten up, Kat, it'll be
fine."

Seconding the idea, Angela quickly found a seat at the
only empty table in the place. "Yeah, I can't remember the
last time I've seen so many men in one place. Look, there's
Tommy Martinez! Boy, he's sure changed since high
school, hasn't he?" Pushing her way through the crowd
toward him, she abandoned Kat and Jenny without a
backward look.

Amused, Jenny arched a delicate brow. "Looks like it's every woman for herself tonight. Hang on to the table while I get us a drink."

She was back seconds later, her green eyes twinkling as she slipped into the chair across the table from Kat. Kat, expecting a beer, blinked in surprise at the mixed drink Jenny set in front of her. "What's that?"

"A hurricane."

"A *hurricane!*" Kat echoed, horrified. Pushing the glass across the table, she frowned. "Are you out of your mind? You know I never drink anything stronger than a beer."

Jenny only laughed and pushed it back at her. "You're not going to get drunk on one drink. Anyway, I told the bartender to go easy on the liquor, so it hasn't got enough punch in it to knock over a fly."

"Easy for you to say," she tossed back, tentatively reaching for the drink. "You're not the one who gets loop-legged over antihistamines. How'd you talk the bartender into making these, anyway? I didn't think they served anything but beer and straight liquor here."

Mischief sparkling in her eyes, Jenny grinned without apology. "They don't, usually. But Fred—the bartender—asked me out and I told him if he'd make me a couple of hurricanes, I'd think about it."

Laughing, Kat had to admit the drink was good. And the liquor was so mild, she hardly tasted it. She took another sip, and glanced across the room to find Angela stepping into Tommy's arms on the small dance floor as a love song slid under the needle on the old-fashioned jukebox. "It looks like Angela's not wasting any time," she told Jenny.

"She always was crazy about the man, she just never had the nerve to tell him. Now that he's divorced, I guess she's decided she'd better grab him while she can. A man like Tommy won't walk around free for long.''

Her elbow on the table, her chin resting in her palm, Kat watched the chemistry spark between Angela and Tommy and did her best to squelch the tiny bit of envy that entered her heart. She didn't have time for a man, she reminded herself as she took another swallow of her drink. But she couldn't deny that right then, just for a moment, she ached to be held. And the man who came to mind looked an awful lot like Lucas Valentine. Without even closing her eyes, she could see him reaching for her, feel her heart jerk in her breast....

Across from her, Jenny suddenly stiffened. ''Uh-oh, here comes trouble,'' she warned Kat. ''Don't look now, but Vince Waters just walked in and he's scouting the joint like a hound looking for a fox.''

Swearing, Kat didn't have to ask who the fox was—since Vince had been hunting her for over a month now, the answer was obvious. She hadn't seen him since the day he'd caught her and Lucas in a clinch, though, and she'd foolishly started to hope that he'd finally gotten the message that she wanted nothing to do with him. She should have known better.

''God, I knew we shouldn't have come here,'' she said under her breath. ''Maybe he won't see me.'' Thankful that she and Jenny were sitting in the shadows and half turned from the door, she sat perfectly still, not moving so much as an eyelash.

''It wouldn't have mattered where we went,'' Jenny replied. ''You know how Vince is. He's like a dog with a bone. Once he went looking for you, he wouldn't have stopped till he found you.'' Her eyes trained on Vince's intimidating form, she swore softly. ''Well, hell, he's seen you. Here he comes.''

Kat groaned, but it was too late to escape. Before she could do anything but take a bracing swallow of her drink, he was pulling out the third chair at their table and straddling it backward.

"Why don't you pull up a chair and join us, Vince," Jenny drawled sarcastically, her green eyes dark with dislike. "Oh, I forgot, you don't need an invitation. You just push your way in without waiting to be asked."

"That's right," he said smugly. "It saves a lot of time." Dismissing her as if she was a pesky child, he turned to Kat. "I've been looking all over for you, darlin'. You should have told me you wanted to go out. I'd have taken you to a better place than this. You've got no business being here without a man to protect you."

The warmth of her drink spreading slowly through her, Kat attributed the heat to the anger that was slowly starting to build in her veins. What did she have to say to get him to bug off? "I didn't tell you, Vince, because I'm not going to go out with you," she said in a low voice that was no less fierce for the fact that it didn't carry past their table. "Tonight or any other night. So if you don't mind, that chair is taken. Angela will be returning any second. Go find somewhere else to sit, okay?"

"Yeah," Jenny added coldly. "This is girls' night out. No men allowed."

Ignoring her, Vince reached for Kat's hand. "Dance with me and we'll discuss it."

"There's nothing to discuss!" Jenny snapped before Kat could open her mouth, her voice rising in frustration. "In case you missed it, she just told you to take a hike—"

"What I heard was you pushing your nose into something that's none of your business," Vince snarled. "Back off, green eyes."

Seething, Kat bit her tongue before she could yell at him that *he* was the one who needed to back off, not Jenny. But the situation was already getting out of hand and drawing interested gazes from nearby tables. There were more than a few Double R ranch hands there, but Kat knew if she lost her temper and started a shouting match with Vince, they wouldn't hesitate to come to her aid. Somebody would throw a punch and then all hell would break out. All because Vince Waters wouldn't take no for an answer.

"All right," she hissed. "I'll dance with you . . . on one condition."

"Just name it, honey." Satisfaction gleaming in his eyes, he practically beamed with goodwill now that he had gotten his way.

"You go away afterward and leave me alone. I mean it," she said sternly when he started to protest. "You give me your word or I can surround myself with Red and the rest of the Double R hands who are here tonight and you won't get anywhere near me. The choice is yours."

He didn't like the choices—that much was obvious from the ugly look in his eyes. But something in her fierce tone must have finally convinced him she meant business. Uttering a crude oath, he rose to his feet and held out his hand commandingly. "Okay. Let's dance."

Kat merely looked at him, not moving so much as an eyelash. "Your word, Vince, or I don't budge from this chair."

For a second, she thought she'd pushed him too far. Painful color flushing his cheeks, he scowled down at her with eyes that were cold and dangerous. Too late, Kat questioned the wisdom of making any kind of deal with him at all. He was a huge man, and powerful, with hands that could easily snap her in two. Everyone within a hundred miles knew just how volatile his temper was, and any woman crazy enough to think she could control him was deluding herself.

Suddenly realizing for the first time that this was a man she should probably actively fear, she started to tell him she'd changed her mind, but he didn't give her the chance. "You have my word," he said through tightly clenched teeth. "C'mon." His fingers closed around hers like a vise, and he pulled her out of her chair.

The minute she stood, the drink she'd foolishly allowed Jenny to talk her into taking hit her. Her head suddenly spinning, she knew she was in no shape to handle Vince. The second he realized she wasn't completely sober, he'd do everything he could to take advantage of her. The only problem was she'd given her word and there was no way in hell he'd let her go without giving him the dance she'd promised.

Stiff as a board when his arms went around her, she resolved to get through the experience as gracefully as possible. She did not, however, have to suffer through his groping in front of a roomful of cowboys. Cold fury burning in her eyes, she ignored the way the floor had a tendency to tilt under her feet and stopped abruptly, uncaring that other couples danced around them. "All I have to do is raise my voice and you're going to have more trouble than you can handle," she warned silkily. "So I suggest you put your hand back where it belongs."

"Aw, come on, Kat, don't be a prude—okay, okay," he grumbled when she opened her mouth as if to scream. "I was just having a little fun."

"Then we obviously don't agree on the definition of fun," she replied coldly. "If you want to maul someone, you need another partner."

"But I don't want anyone else," he murmured huskily. "I want you." His arms tightened around her, and he forced her closer, smiling down into her resentful eyes. The fact that she was as unbending as an iron fence post in his arms didn't seem to bother him at all.

"Then you're doomed to disappointment," she tossed back, "because this song's over." Her feet refusing to budge once the music ended, she pushed at the arms that banded around her like steel. "Let go, Vince. Now!"

"Just one more," he said in a voice that brooked no room for arguments. "After playing hard to get the last few weeks, it's the least you can do."

"Dammit, Vince, I wasn't playing—"

"Neither am I," he growled, jerking her close again. "I want another dance, and you're going to give me one."

The minute Lucas pulled into the parking lot, he spied the candy-apple red pickup that belonged to Kat's friend, Angela. So this was where they'd gone. Scowling at the windowless facade of the beer joint, he almost turned around and got the hell out of there. He wanted a beer, but he was in no mood for company. Especially Kat and her fast friends.

For well over an hour after they'd left, he'd thrown himself into his work with a vengeance, determined to get Kat out of his head. But she'd clung like a burr to his thoughts, the image of her dressed to kill in those tight black jeans and red peasant shirt driving him crazy. It didn't take a genius to figure out that she and her friends were on the prowl—why else would they have turned up at the local cowboys' favorite watering hole? And if he had any sense, he wouldn't come within miles of her when she was looking for that kind of trouble.

But it was a free country, and no one was ever again going to tell him where he could and couldn't go. His pride making the decision for him, he cut the engine. He would not, he promised himself, spare Kat Rawlings a second glance.

But the minute he stepped into the loud, smoke-hazed lounge, the first thing he saw was Kat on the dance floor in Vince Waters' arms. Surprised, he stopped short, jealousy punching him right in the gut, infuriating him. If that wasn't just like a woman, he raged, a muscle rippling along his rigid jaw. One week she's chewing the jerk out, practically ordering him off her property, and the next she's all but crawling in his shorts in front of half the county.

The first wave of fury rolling through him, he started to turn toward the bar and the double shots of whiskey he planned to keep ordering until he forgot the boss lady's name. But something...instinct, maybe...warned him that the situation just didn't smell right, and he glanced back toward the dance floor—just in time to get a good look at Kat's face. She was unnaturally pale, her beautiful mouth set in a thin line that could only mean one thing—she was mad as hell.

His black eyes narrowing, Lucas started toward her before he realized what he was doing. Fool! he berated himself. The lady had been wrapping cowboys like Waters around her little finger since she was old enough to put on lipstick. She didn't need him to come charging to the rescue...especially when she could take care of a jerk like Waters with one hand tied behind her back.

But the hand that should have been slapping the bastard's face was caught tight in a grip that had to be cutting off the flow of blood to her fingers. Lucas didn't wait to see more. He didn't care if she could take care of herself, she needed help.

"The lady doesn't want to dance, Waters," he growled, bringing his hand down hard on the other man's shoulder and gripping it fiercely. "Let her go."

Kat's knees almost buckled at the familiar sound of Lucas's voice. Later, that would bother her, but for now, all she could feel was relief. She was so dizzy, she almost stumbled when Vince suddenly jerked her behind him. "Dammit, Vince—"

Ignoring her, he glared belligerently at Lucas. "Get lost, cowboy. This is none of your business."

"Maybe not," Lucas agreed, and had the satisfaction of watching the overgrown gorilla blink in surprise. "But if you think I'm going to walk away and let you bully the lady, then you're dumber than I thought you were. Now get away from her before I forget I'm not a violent man."

Unimpressed, Vince smiled nastily. "So you want to fight? Let's go outside—"

His fist flew out so fast, Kat only had time to gasp in horror. But Lucas was ready for him. Quickly sidestepping Waters' punch, he grabbed his arm and jerked it up behind his back. When Vince swore and tried to jerk free, Lucas only shoved his arm higher.

"Listen, you son of a bitch," he gritted through his teeth, "in case you haven't figured it out yet, you don't want to mess with me. Other people around here might take your garbage, but you keep pushing it at me, and I'm going to stuff it down your throat. Now get out of here!"

The minute he was released, a smart man would have taken the hint and gotten out with his skin intact, but no one had ever accused Vince of being an Einstein. His face red with rage, he snarled an oath and whirled... only to run right into Lucas's iron fist. Knocked cold, he hit the deck like a fallen tree.

The silence was immediate; even the jukebox ran out of coin and stopped. Suddenly realizing that the ugly little scene had drawn the eye of everyone in the place, Lucas swore under his breath. He never should have come here, never should have gotten into a fight. Normally, he was smarter than that, but he'd only been able to think about one thing...Kat.

He turned, the harsh lines of his face carved in stone, and found Kat staring at Vince's prone body in disbelief. When her eyes lifted to his, she looked at him like he'd just slain a dragon for her. "Thank—"

"Don't say it," he said flatly and grabbed her arm. "Where's your purse?"

"At the table with Jenny. But—"

Not waiting to hear more, Lucas ignored the sudden tense mood of the crowd watching his every move and hauled her over to a wide-eyed Jenny. Snatching up her purse, he pushed it into her arms. "Say goodbye to your friends, boss lady. I'm getting you out of here before lover boy wakes up."

Chapter 6

Outside the cool night air did nothing to clear Kat's swimming head. Feeling as if she'd stepped into a sudden fog on a cloudless day, she frowned, trying to think straight, but the liquor she'd consumed and her low tolerance for it made everything fuzzy. Somewhere in the back of her brain she knew Lucas had just saved her from what could have been a very nasty situation and she had to thank him. Now. Because in the morning she just might not remember. Next time, she promised herself groggily, she was sticking with soda.

His fingers were tight around her arm, and she stumbled as he hauled her around the corner of the building, only to have him catch her lightning fast when her legs didn't want to work properly. Glancing up in surprise, she found him towering over her in the shadows, so close she could see herself reflected in the bottomless depths of his scowling eyes.

"Are you okay?" he demanded tersely.

Breathless, her inhibitions floating in liquor, she smiled up at him in bemusement. "Mmm-hmm. How 'bout you?"

She said the words clearly enough, but there was something in her slightly unfocused eyes that told Lucas something wasn't quite right here. His gaze sharpened, and he studied her more closely. "Are you drunk?"

He expected her to hotly deny it, but she only grinned, not the least perturbed. "Maybe. Did I thank you?"

He blinked at the sudden change in subject. "For what?"

"For beating Vince to a pulp."

"I didn't *beat* him—"

"He's such a worm," she continued as if he hadn't spoken. "A low-down, belly-crawling worm in the grass."

His lips twitching in spite of his best effort to appear stern, he said dryly, "I think you mean snake in the grass. How many drinks did you say you had?"

"Just one. You see, I have this little, teeny, weeny tolerance problem with alcohol. It makes me dizzy." Delighted that the world seemed to stop tilting under her feet as long as his hands anchored her to the ground, she smiled up at him guilelessly. "My hero." Giving into impulse without a thought to the danger, she rose up on tiptoe to press a kiss to his weathered cheek.

He moved so fast, she didn't even have time to gasp. The second her lips brushed his skin, he had her backed up against the rough outer wall of the building, his body, hard as granite, leaning into hers, his eyes hot with fury as they bore into hers.

"Don't think you can treat me like Waters and the other cowboys you jerk around on a string, boss lady," he growled in a low voice that flicked at her like a whip. "I've been through hell and lived to tell about it, so save your teasing little games for someone who appreciates them. When a woman kisses me, I'm damn well going to get more than a measly peck on the cheek." And with no more warning than that, he swooped down and covered her mouth with his.

He meant to scare the living hell out of her. The little witch deserved it, bussing his cheek as if he was some harmless old fool who wouldn't know what to do with a woman even if he had one. One of these days she was going to do that to the wrong man and find herself up to her sweet little rear in her worst nightmare. And it was no more than she deserved. Didn't she know men like him ate babies like her for breakfast?

Anger crawling through him at the thought of her naiveté, he hauled her flush against him, his arms trapping her close, his tongue deliberately rough as he forced it into her mouth. She stiffened, her protest a muffled cry caught between them. Dragging her closer, he tried to tell himself he was doing the right thing. She had to learn that some men were dangerous. And he was just the one to teach her.

But it didn't feel right. Didn't taste right. He'd lost count of the number of nights he'd dreamed of this moment, fantasized about it. The illusion had been so real, it had haunted him until all he'd been able to think about, dream about, was her sweetness wrapping around him, seeping into him, slowly washing away the hate and bitterness of prison that he would have sworn went bone-deep. But instead of losing himself in the honeyed wonder of her mouth, all he could taste was his own self-disgust.

He couldn't do this, he realized too late. He couldn't kiss her as if she was some two-bit little tramp. He couldn't act like the animal he'd been accused of being two years ago.

But he couldn't let her go, either. Not yet. He wanted, needed, burned for a kiss. Just that, nothing more. The anger draining from him, his mouth softened and his hands, which had been gripping her as if she might bolt any second, gentled.

She could have punched him in the gut then—he certainly deserved it—and he wouldn't have done a thing to stop her. But sometime between one heartbeat and the next, she stopped fighting him. The hands that had been pushing him away abruptly stilled in surprise, and then she was clinging to him, her mouth moving sweetly, hungrily, under his.

Lightning in a bottle. There was no other way to describe the feel of her in his arms. Dazed, entranced, he crushed her closer, seduced before he even thought to note the danger. With a groan that could have been a curse or her name, he took the kiss deeper.

The two cowboys who suddenly stumbled out the front door of the bar were drunker than skunks and complaining loudly about being thrown out of the joint. The fire raging in his blood threatening to flare out of control, Lucas heard them the minute they lurched outside and started around the corner of the building. Suddenly remembering where he was and who he was kissing like there was no tomorrow, he jerked back, cursing, his breathing far more ragged than he'd expected. What was he doing?

Flustered, her heart pounding crazily in her ears, Kat unthinkingly started to reach for him, only to have him swear and grab her by the arm. "C'mon," he said harshly, hustling her toward his truck. "I'm taking you home."

Her head was still fuzzy and her knees alarmingly starchless, but she found herself bundled into his truck and heading for the Double R before she could so much as draw a steadying breath. Heart beating unevenly in her breast, she clung to the passenger door, more shaken than she'd ever been in her life.

With a will of their own, her fingers lifted to her fever-ish mouth. He'd kissed her, she thought, more disturbed than she wanted to admit. He'd finally grabbed her and kissed her like a man pushed to the edge of his control. And she'd melted; there was no other way to describe it. Just like chocolate in the sun.

The silence that engulfed the cab was thick enough to swim in. She cast a quick look at him and was just able to make out the hard, uncompromising set of his jaw in the darkness. Her throat suddenly dry, she swallowed. She'd flirted with cowboys all her life, enjoyed their kisses, and had even given serious thought to losing her heart to one or two of them. But she'd always kept her head, always known what she was doing. Until tonight. Locked against Lucas's lean, hard length, intoxicated by the heat of his kiss, she'd been lost to everything but the all-consuming desire he'd so effortlessly stirred in her. Once he'd touched her, a freight train could have roared past and she wouldn't have noticed.

The thought horrified her, appalled her. He thought she was nothing but a flighty little girl who needed to be taught a lesson, and he'd kissed her for no other reason than to prove a point. Just that easily, he'd made her forget her name, then he'd put her from him as if she was nothing more than a nuisance to be dealt with. God, what he must have thought of her!

Mortified, hurt, her temper boiling, she stared straight ahead at the long road that stretched out before them. "You didn't have to cut your evening short because of me," she said coldly. "I'm not a child. I don't need a baby-sitter. There were plenty of cowboys from the Double R in the crowd. I'm sure one of them would have been happy to bring me home."

"Oh, yeah, I'm sure you would have had every man in the joint lining up to get you in their trucks," he replied shortly. "Especially if they thought you might kiss them the way you just kissed me. You're right, sweetheart—you don't need a baby-sitter. You need a keeper."

His words lashed at her, cutting deep. He saw her wince, the hot color sting her cheeks, and he steeled himself against the guilt that dripped like acid into his gut. *He* was the one who had come on to her like gangbusters, the one who would even now be kissing her like a man who had been too long without a woman if those two cowboys hadn't nearly tripped over them on their way to the parking lot. A fresh-faced kid with his first girl would have more control than he'd had, and he didn't like it one damn bit.

Like a VCR replaying a tape, his memory taunted him with images of Kat as he'd pushed her away, the heat in her eyes that had, for the span of a heartbeat, almost sent him to his knees. The lady could break him, he acknowledged grimly. Make a mockery of the resolves that he'd have sworn, after two nightmarish years in prison, were indelibly carved in stone. All it would take would be another kiss, another five minutes with her in his arms, moving against him—

No! Silently cursing his damn thoughts, his fingers tightened on the steering wheel and he increased his speed, unable to get back to the ranch fast enough. The lady wasn't ever going to catch him unawares again, he promised himself. He'd do what he had to, say what was necessary, to make her hate his guts. Then the next time he felt the urge to grab her and kiss her, she'd hopefully knock his head off. Maybe then he'd remember that Kat Rawlings wasn't his for the picking but a woman he intended to turn his back on just as soon as he'd saved enough money to get out of there.

"If you'll remember correctly," she said icily, "*you* grabbed *me*. Not the other way around."

If she'd expected to wound him with that paltry accusation, she failed miserably and only ended up sounding like a child. His hide thicker than leather, he took his eyes away from the road just long enough to arch a brow at her and taunt, "Are you bragging or complaining?"

She wanted to hit him, to cry, to get out of the truck and walk the rest of the way home in the dark, cursing him every step of the way. But she would be damned if she'd give him the satisfaction. Struggling to rein in her temper, she eyed him speculatively and decided to give him a taste of his own medicine.

Her mouth unconsciously seductive, she smiled slightly at the thought and shrugged. "That depends."

Something in her tone warned him he wasn't going to like what she had to say, but he couldn't stop himself from asking suspiciously, "On what?"

"On whether you're bragging or complaining that I kissed you back, of course," she retorted sweetly, her blue eyes just daring him to lie to her. "From where I was standing, it didn't seem like you were trying all that hard to fight me off. But then again, I wasn't thinking too clearly myself. Maybe I was mistaken."

He couldn't deny it and she knew it. Furious with himself, with her, with the whole damn situation, he wished like hell he'd never started the conversation. Didn't she know better than to admit to a man that she didn't think too clearly when she was in his arms? He didn't need to know that, didn't *want* to know that.

"Maybe you were," he growled. "When a man finds his arms full of a willing woman, he usually doesn't object.

But any female stupid enough to read something into that is a few sandwiches short of a picnic. In case you've forgotten, two years in prison without a woman is a long time."

If he hadn't glanced at her just then, he might have missed the sudden flash of outrage in her eyes, the hurt that was quickly masked behind feminine disdain. "So any woman with all the right working parts would have done. It that what you're saying?"

He nodded. "That about sums it up. I'm sorry if—"

She stopped him before he could go any further, the look she shot him in the darkness withering. "Spare me, Valentine. I'm not some little naive high school girl who gets her feelings hurt by the truth. So save your apology for someone who needs it. I understand completely."

"You do?"

"Of course. Lust isn't limited to just men, you know. You don't have to have testosterone to feel it." In the darkness, she caught just a hint of his clenched jaw but had no intention of stopping there. "And we are two civilized adults," she continued in a reasonable tone that should have set his teeth on edge. "You kissed me and I kissed you back. It wasn't any more important than a handshake, so what's the big deal?"

"You were the one who brought it up."

"Only because I didn't want you to misunderstand. If you're afraid I'm going to throw myself at your feet tomorrow or fall in love with you because of a single kiss, you can relax. I'm not that stupid."

"Good. I'm glad to hear it."

"After all, you're not the first man who's ever kissed me. Or even the best kisser," she lied airily, giving him an apologetic smile. "Not that I didn't enjoy it. But I doubt that the ground moved under your feet any more than it did under mine, so let's just forget it.''

His jaw rigid, he stared straight ahead, the tension so thick and cold in the cab of the truck it almost fogged the windows. ''I couldn't agree more,'' he replied shortly. ''It won't happen again.''

Her point taken, Kat stared blindly out the window at the darkened countryside and tried to take some comfort from the fact that she'd scored a direct hit right in his wounded male vanity. But that didn't ease the hurt she was too stubborn to let him see.

Miles passed, the silence that surrounded them throbbing like a stubbed toe. Turning off the main road, they bumped onto the rutted path that led to the cabin. Still refusing to so much as glance at him, Kat sighed in relief as it came into view; the light she'd left on was setting the windows aglow in the darkness. Before Lucas had even braked to a stop at the front porch, she was reaching for her door handle.

She would have given anything to just climb out of the truck without saying a word, but she couldn't be that rude, especially when she remembered the way he'd come to her rescue at the Crossroads. ''Thank you for the ride home,'' she said stiffly as she pushed open the passenger door and stepped down to the ground. ''And for taking care of Vince for me. He gave his word that he'd go away and leave me alone if I danced one dance with him. That's the only reason I went anywhere near him.''

She didn't owe him the explanation, but she'd hoped it might ease the tension between them. Watching him carefully, however, she realized she might as well have saved her breath. His expression stony, he only nodded in acknowledgment that he'd heard her and threw the truck into first, obviously anxious to be gone. Her heart bruised, she stepped back and shut the door. Seconds later, he was gone.

His jaw aching from the blow he'd taken and his pride badly damaged, Vince slouched against the bar and signaled the bartender for another shot of whiskey. Fury bubbling in his gut like hot oil, he contemplated his next meeting with Lucas Valentine. Because there would be another meeting, he promised himself savagely. And next time he wouldn't be the one knocked out cold on the floor. Oh, no. Next time it would be Valentine, and he wouldn't be getting up any time soon.

Downing the whiskey in a single gulp, he didn't wait for it to hit his stomach before calling for another. His mind filled with plots of revenge, he didn't see Aaron Fletcher, the deputy sheriff, take a seat next to him until he drawled, "Better watch the sauce, Vince. I know you're madder than hell, but getting drunker than a skunk isn't going to help matters. Why don't you take a walk outside and cool off?"

"Because I'd rather sit here and think about planting my fist in Valentine's ugly mug the next time I see him," he spat. "So lay off, Fletcher. I know my limits."

Aaron only shrugged and, as he was off duty, ordered himself a beer. "Have it your way. I just wanted you to know I know how you feel."

Vince's eyes narrowed suspiciously. "About what?"

"About Kat Rawlings, of course," he retorted simply. "I've had a crush on her since we were in high school, but she doesn't even know I'm alive."

His shrug philosophical, he reached for his beer and took a long swallow. It didn't help. "I can see why she wouldn't give me the time of day—I'm about as exciting as a mud fence. But you've got a hell of a lot going for you—certainly more than Valentine."

Vince, never one to lack for conceit, didn't hesitate to agree. "He's nothing but a damn drifter. I took one look at him and knew he was bad news. But do you think Kat listened to me? Hell, no. She was determined to hire him, she didn't care what anyone said."

"I don't understand it, either," Aaron grumbled into his beer. The drinks he'd had loosening his tongue, it was all too easy to forget what was privileged information and what wasn't. "You'd have thought she'd have sent him packing the minute she heard all about his trouble in Texas, but I guess she figured he was safe since they let him out of prison and cleared his record."

"Prison?" Vince echoed, jerking to attention. "Are you saying the bastard's got a record? For what?"

Too late, the deputy realized what he'd let slip. Suddenly uneasy, he quickly tried to backpedal. "Now, Vince, I wasn't supposed to mention that. The sheriff said Valentine's got a right to his privacy. A man's past is his own and nobody else's business. Anyway, it's not the kind of thing you go discussing over the supper table, if you get my drift."

"Tell me, Fletcher."

At the steeliness of his tone, Aaron tried not to squirm. "Dadblameit, Vince, haven't you heard a word I've said? The man's kept a low profile. As far as I know, he hasn't told anyone about his past except the sheriff and Kat Rawlings and her brothers. And maybe some of the ranchers he talked to about a job. But if he told them anything, that's between them and him, and they're keeping their mouths shut. And I need to do the same thing. If the sheriff gets wind that I've been wagging my tongue about privileged information, I can kiss my job goodbye. Riley's a real stickler about ethics.''

Vince merely gave him a scathing look, refusing to be put off. ''Don't give me that crap. You know I'm not going to tell anyone. So what's this garbage about a prison record? I knew the bastard was hiding something! It's written all over his face.''

Frowning, the deputy struggled with an answer that wasn't as simple as it should have been. ''Well, now, I don't know if you could exactly say he has a record since the girl claimed she was lying and they had to release him from prison—''

''What girl? Damn you, Aaron, quit rambling and get on with it! What did Valentine go to prison for?''

''Rape,'' he replied, resentment flashing in his eyes at the other man's criticism. ''At least that was what he was charged with and went to the pen for in Huntsville, Texas. Spent two years, there, too. But then the little girl that put him there—some big rancher's daughter—came forward and claimed that she'd lied and he'd never so much as touched her. She swore she was telling the truth this time, that she couldn't live with the guilt, and the authorities believed her. So Valentine walked.''

''Even though he was guilty as hell.''

''Now, Vince, we don't know that—''

''The hell we don't,'' he tossed back furiously. ''He was convicted of rape, dammit!''

''But the girl lied.''

''So she says now. How do we know that the real lie wasn't the one that got him released?''

''State prison officials aren't idiots,'' he argued, frowning. ''They hear sob stories every day, they don't mean a damn thing.''

''Then how did he get out?''

He shrugged. "Dunno. Sheriff Whitaker didn't say. But you can bet it would take more than a few tears from some poor little rich girl to get Valentine off a rape conviction. We're talking serious evidence here, Vince. Like a lie detector test or even some corroborating testimony from reliable witnesses who knew she was going to set Valentine up. Whatever it was, it sure convinced somebody he was innocent as a baby."

Not buying that, Vince merely looked at him. "Mistakes are made every day, and Riley Whitaker made a big one when he let that piece of trash into our county. I don't care if Valentine's story can be verified, he's trouble and he's got no business hanging around Kat. If she won't get rid of him, then I will."

Allen shifted uncomfortably at the threat. "Don't do anything stupid, man," he warned. "You know I'll have to bring you in if you do, and I don't want to do that. Okay? Let Kat handle Valentine. She knows what she's doing."

What Kat was going to have to handle was him, but Vince had no intention of telling the deputy that. Slapping Aaron on his thin shoulder, he forced a grin that was lethal with promise. "Did I say I was going to do anything illegal? You know me better than that. So lighten up, and let's have another drink. All this gossiping has made me thirsty."

Lucas arrived back at the bunkhouse to find it nearly empty. On a Friday night most of the men were out looking for trouble, and those that weren't only tossed a greeting at him and left him alone, which was just fine with him. Over the course of the week, he'd earned the respect of most of the hands by working his butt off for Kat, but he was in no mood for conversation. His mouth compressed, his rugged face set in harsh lines, he plopped down on his bunk and tugged his Stetson down over his eyes, determined to block out the world.

You're not the first man who's ever kissed me. Or even the best kisser.

Kat's husky voice whispered in his ear, taunting him, annoying the hell out of him. Little tease! he fumed. Didn't she know better than to throw that kind of sass at a man? She'd been all but begging to be taught a lesson, and for a hot moment there, all he'd seen was red. He'd almost reached for her then, almost hauled her into his arms and shown her just how much she knew about men and kissing. But if he had, he wouldn't be here now. He'd be in her bed, buried deep inside her.

His blood heating at the thought, he stiffened, the curses he wouldn't allow himself to utter ringing in his ears. He jerked his hat off his face, then tossed it onto the bedpost and snatched up the hot girlie magazine on the bunk next to his. It had been making the rounds through the bunkhouse for the past few days, but when he flicked it open to the centerfold, the nearly naked blonde who smiled invitingly at him didn't rate so much as a second glance. Her hair was too pale, her breasts too big, her eyes brown instead of blue.

Swearing, he slammed the rag shut and threw it on the next bunk for someone else to drool over. He could feel the walls closing in him, the silence that slipped under his skin and ate at his nerves until he thought he would go mad. A cold sweat broke out on his brow and he knew he had to find something to do. Glancing over at a young tawny-haired kid who sat at the poker table working on a damaged halter, he said, "Hey, Steve, you got any more of that tack that needs fixing?"

Not surprised by the request—Lucas had asked him the same question every night that week—Steve glanced up from his task and grinned. "You know I do. But if the boss ever finds out you're helping me with all this, I'm going to have some explaining to do. You're not on the Double R payroll."

Unperturbed, Lucas held out his hand. "I'm not doing it for the money, just to pass the time. Toss me one of those bridles."

Catching the worn tack that came flying across the room at him, he reached into the nightstand next to his bunk and pulled out the small collection of tools he'd stashed there. Within minutes, he was hard at work on the damaged bridle, Kat and the close confines of his surroundings completely pushed from his thoughts.

He worked until well after midnight, until his hands and eyes were tired from the work and the rest of the cowboys had called it a night. Even then, he would have picked up another bridle and started on it if someone hadn't grumbled at him to turn out the damn light. Reluctantly, he put away his tools and stretched out on his bunk.

His hands laced behind his head, he stared up at the darkened ceiling, willing himself to relax as the silence of the night drifted down over him. All around him men settled into their bunks, their snores soon stirring to life. Envying them the peace they found so easily, he silently swore tonight would be different. Tonight the bunkhouse wouldn't shrink to a prison cell in the darkness. Tonight the tormenting memories wouldn't creep out of the shadows like cold specters and seize him by the throat.

But the menace of the past was closer in the dark, less manageable than in the light of day. The tight rein he kept on his emotions slipped, and even as he cursed his lack of control, the air around him took on the closed, nostril-flaring stench of prison. Trapped. He felt the bars of his cell caging him like an animal as surely as if they sprang up out of the bunkhouse's wooden floor. Dread, cold and nauseating, swirled into his stomach.

Cursing the weakness, hating it, he fought it. The past was over; he was free. No one would ever again lock him up; he'd die first. Dragging in great gulps of air, he willed his pounding heart to slow and his stomach to settle. But the night was too black, too still, the terror that reached out to claw him too persistent. The air started to back up in his lungs, choking him, and he knew with sudden clarity that if he didn't get out of there, he was going to make a damn fool of himself.

His chest heaving, he bolted to his feet, only taking time to grab the well-used sleeping bag from under his bunk before he burst out the door, not caring that he was drawing the eye of every cowboy in the bunkhouse. By now they were used to him fighting his way outside every night soon after the lights were killed. Yesterday, he'd even heard them taking bets on what he would do when it rained.

Outside the air was clean and sharp and he couldn't get enough of it. Dragging in a deep breath, he lifted his face to the star-filled night sky. As usual, it only took a matter of seconds for the panic attack to pass, thanks to the wide open spaces surrounding him. But he couldn't go back inside. Not tonight.

Tossing his sleeping bag in the back of his truck, he damned the phobia that controlled him every bit as much as the guards had in prison. Tonight he'd stayed inside five minutes longer than he had the night before. And tomorrow, he'd damn well stay in that bunk five minutes longer than he had tonight even if he had to tie himself to it! Because if he didn't, he'd never be really free.

He should have dropped right off to sleep after that. But before he could even close his eyes, he found his thoughts wandering to the one other subject that was guaranteed to keep him wound tighter than a broken clock.

Katharine Hepburn Rawlings.

And a kiss that never should have happened.

In the blink of an eye, he was back at the Crossroads, holding the infuriating woman as if he would never let her go, kissing her senseless. God, the taste of her! Would he ever get it out of his head? He hadn't expected her to be so sweet . . . or so damn passionate. She should have pushed him away. Hell, she should have knocked his head off. He'd kissed her as if she was some kind of possession, and not a very valuable one at that, and he wouldn't have blamed her if she'd doubled up her fist and let him have it.

A good left hook he could handle, he told himself bitterly. It was the wanting that was killing him.

Overhead a shooting star blazed a path across the cloudless night sky. Caught up in his grim thoughts, Lucas wouldn't have noticed if the whole galaxy had lit up like a Christmas tree. How the hell had he let this happen?

He wasn't a randy kid trying to deal with lust for the first time, he reasoned. Before prison, he'd had his share of women, but none of them had ever shaken his control. Because when a man let his emotions rule him, he was vulnerable. And he hadn't let any woman get close enough to hurt him since his mother had walked out on him when he was twelve. For one fleeting moment outside the Crossroads, however, when there'd been no one around but him and Kat and she was so close he could feel the wild beating of her heart in her breast, she could have made him howl at the moon.

A woman who could do that to a man with nothing more than a kiss could wrap him around her little finger anytime the mood struck her.

He knew that, had known it from the moment he'd first laid eyes on her. If he'd been less desperate, he would have left right then. But beggars couldn't be choosers, and his stupid pride had refused to let him run from any woman, let alone one like Kat.

His mouth twisting cynically, he damned his own arrogance. He'd thought he was too jaded, too wise to the ways of conniving women to be taken in by an amateur like the boss lady. Whatever sizzled to life every time their eyes met could be controlled. The only problem was there were some things between heaven and earth that weren't meant to be controlled.

Cursing the philosophical mood that seemed to have overtaken him, he turned over on his stomach and buried his face in his arms. Almost immediately, Kat's scent, which still clung faintly to his shirt, rose up out of the night to subtly tease his senses. Groaning, he clenched his hands into fists, but there was no enemy to strike out at, only an insidious need that attacked him from the inside out.

He wanted her. So badly his teeth ached. So badly that if she'd somehow magically appeared in front of him then, he would have been in a hell of a lot of trouble. Disgusted, he tried to tell himself that it was only because it had been over two years since he'd been with a woman. After that kind of abstinence, a man wasn't too particular. Just about any woman would do as long as she was willing.

But Kat Rawlings wasn't just any woman. There wasn't a doubt in his mind that making love with her would be like spontaneous combustion. If he survived it, it would cost him more than he wanted to pay. She was a lady of

fierce passions. Sex would never be uncomplicated and
easy with her—he couldn't take her to bed, then just walk
away unscathed. Because she was the kind of woman who
got into a man's bloodstream, into his head, and refused
to get out.

And there was no way in hell he was letting her do that
to him. Spoiled and pampered, she might get everything
that struck her fantasy, but she wasn't getting him. He'd
had two long years to think about his future, to work on
the details of the small spread he would buy just as soon
as he'd saved up enough money for a down payment, and
nowhere in those plans was there a place for Kat Rawlings.

Chapter 7

The next morning was gray and overcast, the clouds that hung low in the sky thick and threatening. Rain wasn't forecast until much later that night, but anyone who knew New Mexican weather wouldn't have taken any bets that it would hold off that long. The heavy air was too still, too warm for October. Whatever breeze there had been had died during the middle of the night, and in its place was a hot expectancy that grated on the nerves like the coarsest grade of sandpaper.

Standing in the open doorway of the barn, Lucas glanced up at the too-dark sky, his brows knit together in a frown. "Red's volunteered to help me string some lights in here today," he called out to Kat, "so there's no use you sticking around. Why don't you go on into town and get the rest of the supplies we're going to need? If it doesn't rain tomorrow, we can get started on the corrals."

He spoke brusquely, not bothering to look at her, the edge to his words sharp and uncompromising. From the moment he'd arrived that morning, he'd been all business and hard as ice. Not once had he smiled or let his glance lock with hers. If Kat hadn't known better, she would have sworn he and the man who had kissed her so desperately last night were two completely different people. A stranger seeing him now would never guess there was any blood in his veins, let alone anything that faintly resembled desire.

She knew what he was doing, of course. He was showing her, telling her without words, that a kiss that had nearly exploded the stars in the sky for her had meant less than nothing to him. He'd turned his back on it as easily as if it had never happened, and if she was wise, she would do the same thing.

Her blue eyes glinted with anger, and she was so frustrated, she was practically grinding her teeth. Last night, she'd lain awake for hours—*hours, for God's sake!*— thinking about the man, mooning over him like a boy-crazy teenager who ached for something she couldn't put a name to. Hot, crazy, restless, she'd twisted her sheets in knots, walked the floor until she was so tired she could hardly put one foot in front of the other. And when she finally had drifted into an exhausted sleep, he'd been there to greet her in her dreams.

If she could have gotten her hands on him sometime between three and four in the morning, she would have killed him...or dragged him into her bed and never let him out—she still didn't know which sounded more inviting. But after the way he'd treated her this morning, she was leaning more toward the former than the latter, damn his handsome hide.

Because of him, she'd had what could only be described as a pitiful amount of sleep. Yet she'd woken to a single, all-consuming thought—to see him again. But instead of answering her tentative good-morning with any degree of civility when he'd arrived for work earlier, he'd just nodded stiffly. As cold and reserved as he'd been when he'd first shown up on her doorstep in answer to her ad in the paper, he hadn't said a single word since that hadn't pertained to work.

Don't get any ideas about me, sweetheart. I'm not interested.

The message was all but stamped across his forehead like a warning label for the unwary, there for anyone to see. If she hadn't been so irritated, Kat would have laughed. Couldn't he see it was too late? That it had been too late from the very beginning? She'd taken one look at him and something had shifted deep inside her, throwing her off balance so that she didn't know if she was coming or going. And working with him so closely for the past two weeks had only made it worse. Her mind sizzled with the kind of ideas she'd never had about a man in her life.

If he hadn't kissed her, she might have held her tongue— if for no other reason than because he was so good at masking his emotions, she could never be sure where she stood with him. But she'd been on the receiving end of that kiss. Lucas might be furious with her, she could even accept that he resented the tug of emotions between them, but there was one thing he wasn't, and that was indifferent.

At that moment he turned away as if the decision was his to make and he couldn't wait to get away from her, and something in her just snapped. Following him further into the shadowed depths of the barn, she stopped abruptly and planted her hands on her hips. "Yeah, I'll go to town, but it isn't going to change anything and you know it. We'll still have to deal with this when I get back."

For the flash of a second, she thought she saw him stiffen, but she couldn't be sure. As implacable as ever, he swung sharply around and lifted a brow at her as if she was speaking in riddles. "You want to tell me what the hell you're talking about? Because I haven't got a clue."

So he was going to make her spell it out. Frustrated, she snapped, "A kiss, Lucas. I'm talking about last night and a kiss that isn't going to go away no matter how much you want it to."

"We've already had this discussion," he reminded her. "Forget it. I have."

His words struck her like little darts, but she didn't so much as flinch. "Oh, really?" she replied, lifting a delicately arched brow. "Then why are you treating me as if I'm some kind of leper this morning? You haven't come within six feet of me since you got here."

She should have known that in a battle of wits, she couldn't beat him that easily. His eyes trapped hers, nailing her to the ground in front of him. "Do you have a complaint about my work?"

"No, of course not—"

"Have I been late? Quit too early in the day? Showed up drunk as a skunk?"

He practically threw the questions at her, but she didn't so much as blink. "I got to you last night, didn't I?" she taunted him softly, watching him like a hawk, her eyes searching his. "And it scared the hell out you. That's why you're so cold this morning. Admit it, Valentine. You haven't forgotten that kiss any more than I have."

"Nothing happened."

The hard look he shot her dared her to contradict him, but she had come too far to back down now. "Maybe not," she agreed. "But before we were interrupted, you didn't even know what planet you were on. And neither did I."

The silkily delivered accusation slid between his ribs like a well-placed dagger, striking far too close to his heart. Furious, feeling threatened, he stepped toward her and instinctively struck back. "If that's all it takes to send you into orbit, sweetheart, then you obviously haven't been kissed much. It was late, we'd both worked hard all day, and you'd had too much to drink. So don't make a federal case out of it, all right? It was just a kiss."

She was pushing him, playing with fire, and she knew it. But something was driving her, something she couldn't control. Refusing to examine too closely why it was so important for her to make her point, she moved until she was standing directly in front of him. Her blue eyes, bright with defiance, met his unflinchingly. "Are you thinking clearly now?"

"Of course I am. That's what I've been trying to tell you!"

"Good. So am I." And with no more warning than that, she reached out to grab his shirt, then hauled him close for a kiss.

Breathless from her own outrageousness, she felt his fingers close around her upper arms. Her heart fluttering frantically in her breast, she braced herself for his rejection. Any second now, he was going to push her away and tell her exactly what he thought of her brazenness.

But her heart beat out a ragged rhythm, marking time, and he only hesitated, his hands tightening convulsively. Then, just when she thought she couldn't wait another moment for some kind of reaction from him, he muttered a curse and slanted his mouth against hers.

He kissed her hard, not in anger, but in passion, a passion that seemed to come out of nowhere and sweep down over them with all the force and volatility of a tornado. Restraint fell away, control simply ceased to exist. Her head reeling and her knees melting, Kat clung to him. This was what she'd dreamed of, she told herself as her thoughts began to cloud over—Lucas, no holds barred, giving in to the desire she'd seen smoldering in his black eyes for days now.

Last night he'd warned her he was a man, not an unshaven boy who didn't know what to do with a woman when he was lucky enough to get one in his arms. He knew what to do, all right, and he didn't waste any time proving it. Murmuring her name like a hungry lover who had called to her a hundred times in his dreams, as if she'd been lost and was now found, he urged her closer. His hands stroking her, claiming her, he kissed her thoroughly and all but dared her to resist him. She couldn't. His tongue swirled into the dark wetness of her mouth, boldly tangling with hers, openly seducing her, and she could do nothing but whimper as her bones dissolved one by one.

The small revealing sound went through Lucas like a flash of heat lightning, streaking straight to his loins and trailing fire in its wake. Groaning, his hands clenched, molding her against him. His breathing turned rough. Wildfire burning in his veins, he knew he had to let her go. Now. Before he did the unacceptable and dragged her down to the barn's dirt floor.

But finding a way to step away from her wasn't easy. Not when he was this hard for her and hurting, his need gut-deep and staggering. With his body screaming for release, his hands ignored common sense and traveled slowly over her, blindly charting every curve. He'd worked side by side with her for nearly two weeks; he'd seen for himself how hard she pushed herself. She wasn't afraid to sweat, to get dirty. Considering the way she threw herself wholeheartedly into a project most women would have turned their nose up at, she should have been as hard as tempered steel and just as appealing.

Instead, she was soft, so damn soft he wanted to sink into her like a drowning man and never come up for air. Dragging his mouth from hers, he laced kisses down her neck and around her throat, unable to get enough of touching her, tasting her. Somehow her blouse came free of the waistband of her jeans, and the tender skin of her midriff beckoned. Unable to resist, he stroked the tempting flesh but couldn't find the strength of will to stop there. Within the blink of an eye, his hand had slipped beneath her shirttail and he had her breast firmly captured in his palm.

"Lucas!"

At the sound of his name on her lips, everything in him seemed to go still. He'd never heard any woman call to him quite that way before. Sharp with need, husky with pleasure, desperate for more. She could make him forget the long, tortured nights of his incarceration, he realized, stunned. With hot kisses and the maddening little sounds she made in the back of her throat, she could make him forget his resentment, the all-consuming anger that had got him through every day—and night—of the past two and a half years.

But he didn't want to forget . . . ever.

A muscle bunching in his jaw, his blood suddenly running cold, he jerked back abruptly, cursing fluently. "I don't know what you think you're doing, little girl, but I don't like being manipulated," he snarled, glaring at her as if he couldn't stand the sight of her. "You got that?"

"I wasn't—"

"Save it," he cut in. "I'm not blind or stupid. You're steamed because I won't join the crowd of idiots chasing after you, so you set out to prove you could make me want you.''

He made her sound like a spoiled brat determined to get the one thing she was told she couldn't have, and she didn't like the comparison... especially when it was right on the money. Lord, had she been that obvious? Heat flushing her cheeks, she retorted, ''What was I supposed to do? It's not exactly easy to stand here and listen to you say you never would have touched me last night if you hadn't been too tired to think straight. I do have some pride, you know.''

''So you proved your point. I want you.'' He spit the admission at her in disgust and dared her to take any pleasure in it. ''I wouldn't go patting myself on the back if I were you. I'm no Prince Charming, so if you're looking for someone to build a fairy tale with, you'd better keep looking. Happily ever afters are nothing but a crock.''

The conversation over, he turned his back on her. ''Don't hurry back from town on my account.''

''Fine.'' Biting off the single word between her teeth, she knew she was acting the child he considered her, but this time, she flatly refused to let him have the last word. ''Then maybe I'll meet one of my friends at the Sagebrush for lunch. I'm not sure when I'll be back.''

His grunt of acknowledgment was hardly the reaction she wanted. She stormed out of the barn, promising herself she wouldn't come home for hours. He wasn't the only one who could be indifferent.

The rain started halfway to Silver City and didn't let up all the way to town, the gloomy skies suiting Kat's mood exactly. Greeting other ranchers, who seemed to have come out of the woodwork with the soggy weather, she could have had her pick of friends to share lunch with. But contrary to her parting shot to Lucas, she wasn't looking for company. Before she quite realized how it happened, she found herself heading home, the supplies she'd bought neatly stacked in the back of her pickup.

Thirty miles from home, the rain stopped and the sun actually broke through the clouds for a few moments, but Kat hardly noticed. Unable to get Lucas out of her head, she told herself she wasn't a complete innocent. She knew what it was to want a man, to ache in the middle of the night, just to need to be held. But what she felt for Lucas was far more complicated than that.

Logic told her she was headed down a road that could lead to nothing but disaster. He could hurt her. The man was like a bear with a sore paw; he'd made it plain he wasn't letting her or any other woman get anywhere near his tightly guarded heart. So why wasn't she heading for the hills? Why was she so drawn to him that she was willing to blatantly chase him and risk rejection after rejection just to make him admit that there was something between them, something even she was afraid to put a name to?

Troubled, she knew she had some thinking to do, some decisions to make. She wasn't looking for a man; she hadn't been lying when she'd told Lucas that. She was just now stretching her wings, just now carving out some independence for herself and becoming her own woman. A man—any man—would threaten that. Yet there was still something about Lucas Valentine that tempted her to throw caution to the wind and just go with what felt good.

Bumping over the rocky road that led to the springs, she pulled up in front of the barn to find Lucas stringing an electrical wire from the cabin to the barn, while Red worked on the breaker box. Red waved, but as she waved back, it was Lucas who grabbed her attention. Taking advantage of the break in the weather, he stood on a ladder he'd rested against the side of the barn, working like a driven man.

Almost as if he couldn't get away from her fast enough and the work was the only thing holding him there, she thought resentfully. Hurt, rebellion, suddenly flashed in her eyes. She might be cutting off her nose to spite her face, but if he was going to walk away as if the kisses they'd shared were meaningless, she was going to make damn sure he wasn't going to forget her anytime soon.

By the time Lucas and Red finished wiring the barn, the skies had clouded up again, and they only had time to cover the supplies in the back of Kat's truck with a tarp before it started to pour again. The rain lasted all the rest of that day and the next, so it was Monday before Lucas could help Kat unload her truck.

Because of the rain and the forced time off, they'd both had a chance to cool off, and at first Lucas thought he had finally gotten through to Kat. All business, she kept her distance and would hardly look him in the eye. Then she touched him and he wasn't so sure. It wasn't an overt caress, just the brush of her hand as she helped him with a roll of barbed wire, but it could have been avoided. His skin heating at the contact, he threw her a suspicious look from under his lowered lids, but she was struggling to hold up her end of the barbed wire and didn't spare him a glance. Shaking his head at his overactive imagination, he helped her store the wire in the barn.

It didn't happen again... for nearly an hour. By then they'd finished unloading the truck, and Lucas had started digging postholes for the corral fence, thankful that it was a solitary job that wouldn't require her help. Concentrating on jamming the twin shovels of the tool into the wet dirt as deep as they would go, he didn't have any idea where Kat had disappeared until he stopped for a break and looked up to find her standing right in front of him with a glass of ice water.

"I thought maybe you could use a drink," she said quietly, holding the glass out to him. "You look hot."

Hot didn't begin to describe what he was feeling right then. He was sizzling, and not from the sun. She was close, so close that if he so much as drew in a deep breath, the glass—and her fingers—would graze his chest. His heart starting to pound, his brows snapped together in a scowl, but she only returned his survey with an innocence that would have done a virgin proud.

He knew immediately what the little witch was up to, but he only took the glass and drained it, handing it back to her with a muttered thank-you that was just short of surly. This time, however, when her fingers deliberately curled around his on the now-empty glass, there was no doubt that she was being deliberately provocative. She stood perfectly still, her eyes wide and guileless as they lifted to his.

Swearing, Lucas snatched his hand back and just barely restrained the urge to throttle her. "Your brothers should have paddled your backside good when you were little. What do you think you're doing?"

Undaunted by his hostility, Kat gave him a slow, inviting smile. "If I have to spell it out, I'm obviously not doing it very well. Maybe I need to be more obvious."

She started to reach for him, but his hand jerked up to capture her wrist in a steely grasp. Under his fingers, her bones were delicate, fragile, too sweetly feminine to be ignored. "Dammit to hell, woman," he grated, tossing her hand away before he was tempted to drag her closer, "you're not going to get away with this! Do you hear me?

I'm not interested, so lay off. Your little seduction scheme isn't going to work.''

For a man who wasn't interested, there was an awful lot of heat in his eyes. Delighted with her progress, Kat grinned. "If I were you, I wouldn't take any bets on that, Valentine. You said yourself that I was a spoiled brat, and you were right. So I'll give you fair warning right now...I always get what I want.''

Over the next few days, the battle lines were drawn, positions taken. All day, every day, a taunting game of cat and mouse was played, and it quickly became apparent that rules were for the fainthearted. And one thing no one could ever accuse Kat Rawlings of being was fainthearted. Her objective no secret, she teased Lucas with flirty glances, whisper-soft touches and long, slow smiles that were guaranteed to set his blood throbbing in his veins. And when he only set his jaw and stubbornly ignored her, she got that dangerous glint in her eyes that could mean only one thing...trouble for Lucas. Squared off like two old-time gunfighters, the tension coiling tighter with every passing day, each of them waited for the other to blink. Neither did.

But she was getting to him. She could see it in the tense lines that bracketed his mouth, in the way he'd go perfectly still for just a moment when she managed to catch him off guard with an unexpected touch. And in the way he watched her when he thought she wasn't looking. Practically stroking her, his quick, hot looks warmed her inside and out.

Surprised at times by her own brazenness, Kat wondered if Lucas realized she'd never been so bold with a man in her life. She'd flirted and teased and thoroughly enjoyed the cowboys she'd dated, but she'd never openly chased anyone, never wanted to. Except Lucas. And for the life of her, she didn't know what it was about him that made her dare just about anything to get his attention.

Her pride should have been in shreds, she ruefully acknowledged. She was making a fool of herself over the man, and for what? He didn't even see her when he looked at her. By accident of birth, she was too much like the conniving rancher's daughter whose lies had cost him two years of his life. Another woman would have cut her losses and run. But she wasn't a quitter, and she knew if she just hung in there long enough, she could make him see that he had no reason to distrust her.

"I don't know about you," she said as they finished the corral fence at the end of the third day, "but I'm starved. I put a roast in the slow cooker this morning—it ought to be good and tender by now. You want to stay for supper?"

Gathering up the tools, he shot her an exasperated look. "I told you no last night. I haven't changed my mind."

"But last night I only offered you soup and a sandwich," she said cheekily. "I didn't figure you'd be able to turn down roast and mashed potatoes and gravy."

Little flirt. Refusing to let her tempt him with food when her body was already driving him crazy, he said, "Then you figured wrong. I'll eat at the bunkhouse just as I do every night."

"Okay," she said with a shrug, "but if you change your mind, just come on up to the cabin. I made enough for an army."

Surprised that she gave up so easily, Lucas's eyes narrowed suspiciously on her slender back as she headed for the cabin. She was up to something; she had to be. She'd teased him all week, rubbing up against him like a little cat when he made the mistake of turning his back on her, unabashedly trying her best to seduce him. And she'd come damn close. Thankfully, she didn't have any idea just how close. The need to reach for her, to haul her into his arms and give her the kiss she was all but begging him for, was turning him inside out, infuriating him. If she touched him one more time, he swore he was going to give her the paddling she deserved.

Hot and sweaty, so edgy he felt like growling, he scowled at the cabin door, half expecting Kat to come back outside any moment with some new game she'd devised to torture him. But five minutes passed, and there was still no sign of her. For the first time in hours, the tension in his neck and shoulders eased slightly, but the fever she'd deliberately lit in his blood was hotter than ever. Cursing her and his own weakness, he shot one more glance at the cabin door to make sure it remained shut, then silently headed for the creek.

The sun had already slipped behind the rocky ridge to the west, leaving behind long shadows that quickly bathed the canyon in coolness. Back at the bunkhouse, the rest of the hands would be washing up for supper, but Lucas was in no mood for food. Stripping to the buff, he left his clothes scattered on the bank and dove into the springs.

The water was like ice, sucking the breath from him before he knew what hit him. Gasping, he shot to the surface, his muttered curses turning the air blue, goose bumps painfully skating over his bare skin. He'd known the water was cold, but no one had warned him it could freeze all his vital parts in a matter of seconds. Chilled to the bone, he started for the bank.

His hands briskly rubbing his upper arms, he didn't see Kat until he was hip deep, and even then he probably wouldn't have noticed her if she hadn't shifted her feet on the rocky ground. Startled, he stopped dead in the water at the sight of her standing by his clothes, her fingers already reaching for the buttons of her blouse.

"What do you think you're doing?"

"I'm hot," she said simply, her grin full of wicked mischief. "I thought I'd go for a swim."

"The hell you are! Dammit, woman, put your shirt back on right this minute!"

Defiant, she tossed her blouse down to the ground and prayed that he couldn't see how she was shaking like a leaf in a hurricane. When she'd glanced out the window and seen him heading for the springs, she'd hesitated, torn by the need to go to him and the fear that she was going to totally humiliate herself. There was a difference between openly flirting with a man and shamelessly throwing herself at one, and she didn't know if she was ready to cross that line. But she'd had days to deal with her feelings for him, nights to dream about him, long for him until she literally ached. She could have no more resisted going to him than the sea could stop churning.

Wondering how she'd ever be able to look him in the eye again if he rejected her now, she resisted the urge to cover herself and instead boldly flipped open the snap of her jeans. "Come out of there and make me," she teased, her smile slow and bewitching.

"I should," he told her tersely. "I should stuff you back into the damn thing, then turn you over my knee. Dammit, Kat, I'm warning you...."

She'd never seen him quite so rattled, and it thrilled her that she'd finally found a way to crack that cool control of his. Grinning, she unzipped her jeans with lingering grace and watched his features sharpen in reaction. Her knees were starting to shake, but her husky voice was remarkably steady when she said, "I like the way you say my name. Say it again."

His eyes locking on her hands as she started to slide her jeans down over her hips with agonizing slowness, Lucas swallowed a curse. What the hell was she doing to him? He was standing in ice water, for God's sakes, but any minute now, it was going to start boiling like a sauna. "I'll say whatever you want," he retorted. "Just put your clothes back on."

But it was too late. Her jeans hit the dirt, then her bra and panties. Desire slammed into Lucas's gut, hot and clawing, making rational thought impossible. All his objections turning to dust on his tongue, he could only stare at her, his mind nothing but mush. God, she was beautiful. He'd known that, of course, but he hadn't allowed himself, even for a second, to picture her bare and free in the twilight. Now he knew why.

Lord, she was something. Her skin was flawless in the dusky light, as pale as ivory. Shadows sculpted her, clinging to her as if she was some kind of exotic mistress of the night, giving him only teasing glimpses of the generous swell of her breasts and the dark curls at the juncture of her thighs. And her legs. Dear God, they seemed to go on forever. Lean and strong from hard work, they would hold a man and never let him go.

His loins hardening at the thought, he realized, too late, that while he'd been staring at her like a boy who didn't know what to do with his first woman, she'd started toward him and was already at the water's edge. Stiffening, he said hoarsely, "Stop and think what you're doing, you little nut. We're not on this ranch all by ourselves, you know. What are you going to do if one of your brothers decides to drop by without warning? They've done it before, you know. In fact, Gable's been out here just about every other day. He's due a visit."

"He's got better things to do at night than drive all the way out here to check on me," she said confidently. The second the cold water closed around her trim ankles, she gasped, but Lucas should have known it would take more than that to discourage her. Her chin set at a stubborn angle, she started toward him.

Clenching his jaw, he swore he wasn't going to touch her. But then she was right in front of him, slipping her arms around his neck as if she'd done it a thousand times before. Her bare thighs met his, her breasts came to rest against the hard wall of his chest, and suddenly it was all he could do just to breathe.

In the thickening darkness, her eyes met his from only inches away. "I want you."

"No!"

"Yes," she whispered fiercely. "Do you think I would dare this if I didn't?"

He wanted to believe that she was a woman who would dare anything with a man, but he only had to take one good look at the emotion darkening her blue eyes to midnight, the hot color he could now see stinging her cheeks, to know that she wasn't quite as sure of herself as she'd pretended. The heat warming his blood seemed to turn up another hundred degrees.

Alarm bells clanged loudly, frantically reminding him of what happened the last time he made the mistake of underestimating a woman who always got what she wanted, but he couldn't hear the warning for the roaring of the blood in his ears. His hands tangled in the seductive fall of her hair, anchoring her close, and he had no idea of how they got there. He just knew he had to have her...even if he lived to regret it. Some things were worth the risk, and he had a feeling Kat Rawlings was one of them.

"Be sure, boss lady," he growled roughly, deliberately reminding her of their working relationship. "I don't play games. If we start this, there's no going back. And no crying afterward. You don't cry over sex."

The warning was harsh, cold, nonnegotiable. Searching the black, bottomless depths of his eyes, Kat didn't doubt that he meant every word. If she wanted him, it would be on his terms. If she couldn't accept that, he would let her go so fast, he'd be dressed and on his way back to the bunkhouse before she could so much as blink. And he wouldn't touch her again come hell or high water…in spite of the very real strength of his arousal pressed against her.

Her heart squeezed at the thought, pain tearing at her. She didn't pretend to misunderstand him. This was no encounter in a fairy-tale romance. If she had sex with him hoping it might turn into something more, she would be the one who got hurt. Hesitating, her throat dry, she stared up at him, the decision hers to make. The only problem was the decision had been made the first time he'd held her. Nothing had ever been so right before or would be again if she walked away from him now.

More sure than she'd ever been of anything in her life, she went up on tiptoe, bringing her mouth even with his. "I'm sure," she said simply, and kissed him.

He said something against her mouth…a curse, a plea…but his arms came around her, clamping her tight against the hard, solid length of him, stealing her breath. Her heart slamming against his, she gave in to the longing that had stalked her dreams for nights, giving him hot, wet, openmouthed kisses guaranteed to slowly drive him out of his mind. And in the seducing, she was the one who was seduced.

Feeling as if she was floating, she didn't realize he'd carried her to dry land until the world tilted on its axis and she suddenly found herself being lowered to the clothes they'd left scattered on the banks of the springs earlier. The night was cool, the breeze whisper-soft, but when he sank down with her, never breaking the kiss, all she felt was heat. Toe-warming, bone-searing, all-the-way-to-her-soul heat.

And suddenly, she wasn't quite as sure of herself as she needed to be. The hot urgency of his kiss, the knowledgeable sweep of his hands touching her just where she ached to be touched, overwhelmed her. Her heart thundering, her senses swamped, she knew she was in over her head. He didn't believe in fairy tales. And she did.

Her breathing ragged, she struggled to find the right words in her passion-fogged brain, but he made the task nearly impossible. He moved over her like a dark force, heating her from the inside out with scattered kisses and wicked, knowing hands, touching, stroking, until she thought she would melt from the pleasure. Then, just when she thought she couldn't stand any more, his mouth closed over the sensitive crest of her breast, his tongue swirling around the tight bead of her nipple, sending a white-hot streak of need straight to her womb. His name a startled cry on her lips, she arched against him, clinging to him as if she'd never let him go.

"Please . . ."

"Oh, I will," he promised thickly, releasing one breast, only to tease the other unmercifully with teeth and tongue. "Tell me what you want."

The sheen of tears stinging her eyes, she looked up to find him watching her intently, and something she hadn't expected took hold of her heart. "You," she murmured.

"I just want you. But I'm afraid you'll be disappointed. I haven't done this much."

His gaze sharpened in the darkness. "How much is much?"

"Twice."

It was an admission he didn't want to hear, didn't want to think about. He didn't want to know that she wasn't nearly as experienced as he'd thought, didn't want to compare her to Melaney Kent. Not now, when he had her close and bare in the darkness and his body was strung tighter than barbed wire with need.

But it was too late. The words couldn't be taken back. She was trouble, just as he'd known from the start, and he should have kissed her goodbye, then left, this time for good. But staring down into her midnight blue eyes that were wide and vulnerable, he couldn't even think about leaving. Somehow she'd reached out and found a softness in him he hadn't even known he'd had, and already his hands were gentling on her.

"Don't worry," he rasped softly. "You won't disappoint me. I'll take care of everything."

His only thought to make her forget her insecurities, he clamped down on the need raging in his blood and focused all his attention on Kat and the pleasure he intended to give her. And Lord, she was easy to please. He only had to touch her to draw a sigh from her, only had to trail his fingers over the soft skin of her inner thighs to have her bucking toward him, reaching for him, her eyes dark and heavy-lidded with need.

"Easy," he murmured, nuzzling the warm skin of her neck as he captured her wrists and pinned them to the ground above her head. "Let's take it slow and easy."

It should have been that simple, but he hadn't counted on what the feel of her under him could do to him. He swept a hand down her tempting curves, loving the way her skin heated for him, and found his own blood turning hot in his veins. Her scent teased him, seduced him; the soft whimpers she made in the back of her throat drove him out of his mind. She moved under him, for him, and all he could think about was burying himself deep in her wet heat. Then he dragged one of her hands down to where he was hot and hard for her, and he couldn't think at all.

Kissing her roughly, he burned for her. Her touch was soft, sweetly hesitant, innocently teasing. Somewhere in the back of his mind, his conscience reminded him that she was fairly new to this; he wasn't supposed to jump her bones like a sex-starved lunatic. But he couldn't remember the last time he had wanted a woman this badly, and it was too late to pull back. The fire in his belly was out of control.

Jerking her hand back up to the safety of his chest, he groaned. "No more. Sweetheart, you're killing me. I can't stop."

His callused hands moved to her hips, her thighs, caressing her, readying her for his possession, stroking her until she was wild for him. He was big, rough, a man who came from a hard world where there was no softness. But he coaxed and fondled and whispered outrageous praise in her ears, and was so patient, in spite of his claims to the contrary, that she melted with tenderness.

Smiling, knowing that whatever else happened between them, tonight was right, she opened for him. "Then don't," she whispered, and drew him close, as close as a man and woman could be.

Perfect. They fit perfectly. As if they were made for each other. Later, he knew that would bother him, but for now the woman who held him so intimately was like wildfire in his arms. She moved under him, adjusting her hips to his and unconsciously drawing him deeper. His mind clouded, the world narrowed to Kat…her scent, the seductive hold she had on him, the pleasure she lit in him so effortlessly. She moved against him, with him, shattering what he thought he knew of passion. And when she came undone in his arms and pulled him with her over the edge of reason into paradise, it was her name he groaned like a prayer.

Chapter 8

Rolling over onto his back, his breathing still ragged, Lucas stared up at the cloudless night sky and felt he'd been taken apart and put back together again. Nothing was as it had been only minutes before. The stars were brighter, the breeze more seductive, the soft laughter of the springs as intimate as a lover's secret murmurings in the dark. Even the beat of his heart was altered. With no conscious effort on his part, it beat in time to the woman who lay next to him, snuggling up to him as if he was all she needed to make her world complete.

God, what had he done?

Savagely cursing his own stupidity, the answer was as clear as the infatuated smile curling up the corners of Kat's mouth. He'd let himself get caught up in her inexperience and dropped his guard, allowing her to see a side of himself that he'd have sworn was beat out of him in prison. Tenderness, caring, softheartedness...she'd pulled the unwanted emotions from him effortlessly and made him love every minute of it.

And now she thought she was falling in love with him.

He wanted to deny it, but one look at her dreamy expression and his gut clenched. Cinderella had that same look on her face when she tripped over Prince Charming. And he knew only too well what happened with that fairytale heroine... she got her man.

Panic slammed into him then like an out-of-control freight train. Sick dread spilling into his stomach, he forgot the incredible satisfaction he'd found in her innocent arms, forgot the way she'd made even his teeth ache for her. She was just another conniving woman willing to go to any lengths to get what she wanted. And what she wanted was him. If he didn't like it, that was just too damn bad.

Well, not this time, he thought grimly. Spitting out a curse, he sat up abruptly and reached for his clothes. She was looking for a hero and he didn't have the qualifications for the job. Even if he had, he wasn't looking for a woman of any shape, size, brand or color.

"Where are you going?"

Her voice was husky with confusion and lingering passion, and for just a moment, it was all he could do not to turn to her. His mouth pressed flat, he jerked on his jeans. "Back to the bunkhouse," he retorted. "It's late."

"But I thought—"

"What?" he demanded harshly, whirling so fast she gasped. "That I'd spend the night? That I wouldn't be able to tear myself away from you? Sorry, sweetheart, but I don't stick around for the morning after no matter how good the sex is." He knew he was being deliberately cruel, but he had to get that enchanted look out of her eyes, had to make her see that he was nothing but a callous jerk she had no business wasting her tears on.

"And don't you dare cry," he snarled when he saw her eyes mist. "I warned you, dammit, and you're not going to pull a guilt trip on me now. So save the waterworks for someone who appreciates them."

Her chin came up at that, the defiance he'd hoped for there in the ramrod-straight set of her spine. "Bastard."

The insult struck home, but he didn't so much as flinch. "I never claimed to be a saint." Reaching down for her blouse, he tossed it at her. She was shivering. "Get dressed before you catch pneumonia."

But her fingers were shaking—he hoped with anger instead of hurt—and she couldn't manage the task. Swearing, he hunkered down in front of her and took the blouse from her. It was a mistake. She was naked, her breasts beautifully bare, and all he could think about was cupping her, tasting her. A muscle bunching in his jaw, he held the shirt up so she could slip her arms in it, determined not to let his gaze slip below her neck. By the time she was decently covered, he was hot and hard and furious with himself.

"There," he growled, snatching his hands back as if he'd been burned. It didn't help. Sitting on her bare feet, the tails of her shirt just reaching midthigh, she was sexy as hell. And if he didn't get out of there right then, he was going to do something incredibly stupid... like strip that damn blouse from her and lose himself in her all over again.

Steeling himself against the temptation, he shot to his feet. "I'm out of here." His boots in his hand, he hurried toward his truck, never once looking back, uncaring that he looked like a man who was running for his life. Because he was.

* * *

Hours later, when the lights finally went out in the bunkhouse, he promised himself he wasn't going to lie there and torture himself with images of Kat and how good it had been between them. And just to be sure, he deliberately dredged up the memory of Melaney Kent, the way she walked—as if the world was her oyster—that feline smile that told anyone who cared to look that she got what she wanted or else. And the lies. Could he ever forget the ugly accusations and the trial that followed, the twenty-year sentence that had been pronounced without inflection? Caught in the web of a black widow spider, he'd been trapped, helpless.

The recollections swirling against the back of his closed eyelids, he waited for the walls to close in on him the way they always did when he thought of Huntsville, the cold sweat that made it impossible for him to tolerate the close confines of the bunkhouse in the dark. But all he could think of was Kat. The taste of her, the hot sweetness of her mouth, the feel of her taking him into her, holding him.

Suddenly hot, he tensed, a need he'd have sworn was assuaged pooling in his loins. Shifting restlessly on his bunk, he silently cursed, damning himself for an idiot. He couldn't let himself start to get ideas about Kat Rawlings. Not now, not ever. She was too fresh, too sassy, too untouched by the harsh realities of life to be satisfied for long with a man who had suffered indignities she couldn't begin to imagine. If she was fascinated with him now, it was only because he wouldn't let her wrap him around her little finger the way she did the other men in her life. He was a challenge, nothing more, one she would soon tire of.

He never should have touched her, never should have made love to her, never should have tasted what he couldn't have. He'd known he was playing with fire; now he was the one who burned. And it was his own stupid fault. From the moment he'd met her, he'd made one mistake after another, but he was breaking that habit first thing in the morning. As soon as he could pack his gear and collect what she owed him, he was hitting the road.

The hand that clamped on his shoulder and shook him just before dawn was rough and callused and definitely didn't belong to the little cat he was dreaming about. Startled, he came awake abruptly to find Red leaning over him. One of the oldest cowboys on the Double R, Red's face was weathered and lined and grimmer than Lucas had ever seen it.

His heart jerking to a stop in his chest, he stiffened, on guard instantly. "What's wrong?"

"The sheriff's here. He needs to talk to you. He's waiting for you in the mess hall."

Every muscle in Lucas's body seemed to freeze. The law didn't come calling before the sun was even up unless there was trouble. "I'll be right there," he said tersely, and reached for his jeans.

The mess hall was attached to the bunkhouse by a covered walkway, and at that hour of the morning, it was the most popular spot on the ranch. A dozen or more cowboys had already finished breakfast and were lingering over coffee, while others were just starting on the sausage, eggs and biscuits that were the usual morning fare. What little conversation there was stopped the second Lucas walked through the door.

Unable to believe he'd overslept—and inside, no less!—Lucas felt his stomach drop sickeningly, the scene all too reminiscent of the last time a law enforcement officer had paid him a visit. No one said a word, but they didn't have

to. He could hear their whispered comments, their specu-
lations, clearly in his head.

Fighting the sudden need to run, it took all his self-
control to stand his ground and search out Riley
Whitaker. It didn't take long to find him. Alone in a corner, a cup of coffee caught between his hands, the sheriff
watched him like a hawk, his shuttered eyes missing little.
Whatever he'd come to tell him, it wasn't good news.

Crossing to him, Lucas straddled the bench across the
table from Whitaker, his shoulders rigid as he felt the eyes
of everyone there stabbing him in the back. His gaze locking with Riley's, he didn't waste time on pleasantries.
"You wanted to see me?"

"Last night, an eighteen-year-old girl was raped about
five miles from here," he said without preamble, his low-
pitched voice carrying to every corner of the silent room.
"You know anything about it?"

The words struck him like a blow. *No.* This couldn't be
happening. Not again. "No," he said flatly. "Why should
I?"

"She was home alone when a man slipped in through the
back door and grabbed her. He wore a mask, so she didn't
get a look at his face. But he was tall—about six-four—and
lean. And she's pretty sure he had dark hair." His gaze
lifted to the brown hair Lucas had taken time to wet and
comb before presenting himself in the mess hall. When he
returned his eyes to Lucas's, they were steely. "You want
to tell me where you were between seven and eight o'clock
last night?"

Stunned, Lucas didn't even have to think to answer that
one. He'd been with Kat, making love to her like a man
possessed, uncaring that they were out in the open and
anyone could have driven up. She was his alibi. All he had
to do was open his mouth and tell Whitaker and every

Double R cowboy within shouting distance that he'd had Kat Rawlings naked and in his arms at the time that girl was being raped, and he could walk.

The alibi shriveling to dust on his tongue, he returned the sheriff's hard gaze with one of his own. "Are you saying I'm a suspect?"

"That depends," he said shortly, irritation flickering in his eyes. "Where were you between seven and eight?"

"I don't remember. It was a long day."

"Damn it, man, don't be a fool! I don't like this any more than you do, but a girl's been raped, and you're going to answer my questions or I'm going to haul your ass in. So what's it going to be? Make it easy on yourself."

The rugged lines of his face set in granite, Lucas rose to his feet. "Then I guess we'd better be going. You want to use the cuffs or do you trust me not to knock you over the head and make a run for it?"

Riley swore, long and fluently. Valentine was determined to make things hard on himself. Muttering under his breath about proud fools, he set his coffee cup down on the table with a thud. "I don't need the cuffs to stop you from knocking me over the head, Valentine. Let's go."

The second Lucas turned toward the door, the cowboys who had avidly watched the entire scene glanced quickly away, not able to meet his eye. It wasn't the first time men he had worked with had him tried and hung before they ever heard the facts; it had just been so long, he'd forgotten what it felt like. His face set in implacable lines, he told himself he didn't give a damn. But as he strode outside with the sheriff right on his heels, fury churned in his gut.

All business, Riley motioned for him to take the passenger side of the front seat, but just as he started to jerk the door open, Gable drove up and braked to a jarring stop in a cloud of dust. Jumping out of his truck, he advanced on them with long, angry strides. "Dammit, Riley, what the hell do you think you're doing? When Red called the house and said you were out here on official business, I couldn't believe it. What's going on?"

Drawing himself up to his full height, Riley shot him a narrow-eyed look that warned him to back off. "Stay out of this, Gable. It doesn't concern you."

"It does when you start hauling in cowboys from this ranch without so much as a by-your-leave," he snapped. "If you're arresting one of my hands, I've got a right to know why."

Surprised that one of Kat's brothers was standing up for him when he didn't even know what he'd supposedly done, Lucas refused to feel appreciative. Gable would change his tune fast enough when he heard the details. "There's been a rape," Lucas said coldly. "He's taking me in for questioning."

Caught off guard, Gable's protests sputtered and died as Lucas turned without another word of explanation and climbed into the patrol car. Slipping behind the wheel, Riley gave him a terse nod, then drove away, leaving Gable standing there, wondering how he was going to break the news to his sister. She wasn't going to like it, he thought, swallowing. Not one little bit.

Exhausted from a night of tossing and turning, Kat had barely been asleep two hours when a sudden loud pounding jerked her awake. Startled, her heart jumping into her throat, she bolted up and grabbed the first thing she could find to cover the skimpy chemise she'd worn to bed—the shirt Lucas had dragged on her last night after they'd made love. Wincing at the unfortunate choice, she started to drop it and find something else, but the pounding started at the door again.

"Dammit, Kat, open up!" Gable thundered. "I know you're in there!"

"I'm coming. Just a second." Alarmed, she struggled into the shirt and hurried to the door. The second she threw the lock, her three brothers swept in like a storm surge after a hurricane. She took one look at their fierce frowns and paled. They knew. Somehow, some way, they knew she and Lucas had made love and they were here to rake her over the coals. Outraged at their daring—she was twenty-six years old, for God's sake!—she scowled right back at them. "If this is about Lucas—"

"So you know?" Cooper cut in, the frown that wrinkled his brow deepening. "How the hell did you find out? They just left."

Whatever Kat had expected him to say, it wasn't that. Confused, she swept the tangled cloud of hair back from her face and pulled out a chair from the kitchen table. "I obviously missed something. Let's start over. Who just left?"

The three men exchanged glances, but there was never any question of who would break the news to her. "Riley Whitaker paid a visit to the bunkhouse a little while ago," Gable said stiffly. "He wanted to talk to Valentine."

What color there was in Kat's face completely drained away. "About what?"

He hesitated, but there was no avoiding the truth. "There was a rape last night—"

"Oh, God."

"I wasn't there when Riley questioned Valentine about it," he continued, "but Red overheard the entire conversation—"

"I don't care what he heard," she said fiercely. "Lucas didn't rape anyone."

"Then why didn't he say that?" Flynn retorted. "All he had to do was tell Riley where he was last night between seven and eight. But according to Red, he wouldn't say a word in his own defense."

Because he'd been with her. Horrified, Kat's heart dropped to her toes. He could have used her as an alibi, but for some reason she wouldn't let herself guess at, he'd gone to jail rather than mention her name to Riley Whitaker. "I've got to get him out," she murmured, jumping to her feet. "God, where are my clothes?"

"What the hell do you mean *you have to get him out?*" Gable roared, following her to the bathroom, where she shut the door in his face.

"She's lost her mind," Cooper said with a shake of his head. "I knew it was a mistake to let her move out here by herself. It's the springs. The constant gurgling is enough to get to anybody."

"Something's gotten to her," Flynn said ominously. "And I've got a feeling it's Valentine." Glaring at the closed bathroom door, he yelled, "Dammit, Kat, the man's a convicted rapist! And don't give me that bull about how he was wrongfully accused. Maybe he was, but it's a hell of a coincidence that he hasn't even been here a month and a woman's already been raped."

Dressed and steaming, Kat opened the door abruptly, her blue eyes flashing. "He was vindicated in Texas, Flynn, so drop it. I told you . . . he didn't rape anyone."

"How do you know?" he demanded. "He won't even tell Riley where he was."

"Because he was with me."

That little announcement fell like a bomb in the sudden silence, drawing muttered curses, just as she had known it would. She wanted to assure her brothers that they had nothing to worry about—she knew what she was doing.

But she didn't have time. "I can't talk about this now," she said, grabbing her purse and hurrying toward the door. "I've got to get to town."

An hour later, she slammed into Riley's office, the indignation that had built with every passing mile burning in her middle. "He didn't do it, Riley. Let him go."

In the process of writing up a report on his latest fruitless interrogation of Lucas, the sheriff leaned back in his chair to study her with shuttered eyes. "Who didn't do what?"

If he'd wanted to get a rise out of her, he'd pushed just the right button. Jamming her hands on her hips, she looked ready to explode. "Don't you pull this crap with me, Riley Whitaker! How many men have you arrested today? You know I'm talking about Lucas."

Kat Rawlings in a temper was something to see, but Riley was more than capable of handling her. His face impassive, he motioned for her to take the chair across from his desk. "If you want to talk about Valentine, we will, but don't stand there glowering at me. I haven't arrested anyone."

That took the starch out of her. Confused, she dropped into the chair he'd indicated. "But you brought him in."

"For questioning," he explained. "He wouldn't cooperate, so I had no choice. I've got him in an interrogation room right now, but the man's as closemouthed as a CIA agent. He won't say a word."

"Because he was with me."

She'd thought that would be enough to get Lucas released—he had an alibi now and couldn't possibly be a suspect. But Riley only stared unblinkingly at her. "You sure about that, Kat? I know Lucas hasn't been staying at the springs. According to Red, he's usually back at the bunkhouse in time for supper."

"Well, yes, he is—"

"Then what was he doing at your place so late? He couldn't have been working—it was already dark."

Telling her brothers wasn't nearly as difficult as telling a law enforcement officer, even if he was a friend. Heat climbing into her cheeks, she met his hard gaze head-on. "We were making love." She saw his eyes narrow slightly and had the horrible feeling he didn't believe her. "It's true! If you don't believe me, give me a lie detector test and I'll prove it."

"What time was this?"

She shrugged. "Seven... seven-thirty, somewhere around there. We were outside by the springs, and when I came inside after Lucas left, it was a little after eight." Her blue eyes dark with entreaty and a wealth of emotion she hadn't admitted to herself yet, let alone anyone else, she said softly, "He didn't tell you where he was because he was trying to protect my reputation, Riley, not because he had something to hide. You've got to believe me. He didn't rape anyone."

Under other circumstances, if Kat Rawlings had told him the moon was blue, he would have believed her—she was that honest. Just as her brothers, she didn't lie or cheat, and her word was as good as money in the bank. But anyone with eyes could see that she was crazy about Valentine, and she came from a long line of family that fought for what was theirs. How far would she go to protect her man?

"Have you heard the description of the rapist?" At the shake of her head, he said, "He wore a mask, so the victim didn't see his face. But he was tall, lean, dark-haired."

And so was Lucas. Her blood chilling at the thought, she lifted her chin defiantly. "Half the men in the county fit that description. Have you questioned them to see how many of them have alibis?"

The taunt struck home, though she never would have known it if she hadn't been watching his eyes. They sharpened suddenly, but his tone was even as he said, "There hasn't been a rape around here in more than ten years, so there's a good chance that whoever did this is an outsider."

"But you can't be sure of that, can you?"

That was a point that had been nagging at Riley all morning. "At this point, I can't be sure of anything except that I can't hold Valentine if he has an alibi." Rising to his feet, he headed for the door. "Sit tight. I'll be right back."

Lucas was pacing the confines of the interrogation room like a death row inmate whose time was running out when the sheriff suddenly opened the door and walked in. Stopping short, Lucas warned, "You can let me stew until the cows come home, Whitaker, but I've said all I'm going to say. So cut the fun and games and either book me or let me out of here. I don't care which, just make up your damn mind."

Standing tensely, he expected Whitaker to throw him in a cell, if for no other reason than to prove to him that he could, but his surly words slid off the other man like water off a duck's back. Amusement flashed for a second in his ice blue eyes before he turned abruptly serious. "You're free to go...for now."

Leery of strangers bearing gifts, Lucas just looked at him. "Why?"

"Because I'm pretty damn sure you weren't anywhere near that girl last night. But with a rapist on the loose, I can't afford to be too careful. You're an outsider, and the second some of our fine upstanding citizens find out about your past, they're going to be screaming for your blood. So until I have another suspect, I'm going to have to ask you not to leave the county. It would only make you look guilty, and that's the last thing you need right now."

Motioning to the open doorway, he said, "Go on, get out of here. Your ride's waiting in my office."

His ride? Lucas thought, frowning. Suddenly not liking the suspicions flicking at him like a whip, he went looking for Kat...and found her just where Whitaker had told him he would—in his office.

Stopping in the doorway, his breath seemed to lodge in his throat at the sight of her. She stood with her back half turned to him, her expressive face pensive as she stared out the window behind Whitaker's desk. She looked like she'd dressed in a hurry...her hair was a dark mass of tangled curls, her jeans wrinkled. And unless he was very much mistaken, she was wearing the shirt he'd covered her with after they'd made love.

Emotions hit him, tearing at him like the wild winds of a storm. Hunger, delight, a need so strong it almost brought him to his knees. And frustrated anger. What they'd shared last night was over, done with, a dream that had vanished the second he'd turned his back on her and walked away. He'd acted like a first-class bastard and left her with tears in her eyes, damn her. She should have hated his guts.

Instead, she'd raced all the way to town the minute she heard he was in trouble. She'd told Whitaker everything, he realized, stunned. That was why he was free to go. Not because the sheriff believed in his innocence, but because she'd confided the intimate details of her love life so he'd have the alibi he needed to get out of jail.

Something twisted in his heart at the thought of her doing that for him, something he refused to see as anything but resentment. He didn't want her help, didn't need it, didn't want to think of her anywhere near the ugliness of a jail. If he'd wanted Whitaker to know about last night, he would have told him himself.

Tempted to shake her until every tooth she had rattled in her head, he said tightly, "You shouldn't have come. I don't want you here."

Surprised by the harsh greeting, Kat blinked. Frantic to get to him, she hadn't allowed herself to think about how he would react to seeing her again after the way he'd left last night, but she certainly hadn't expected the cold fury burning in his eyes. Hurt, her temper stirring to life, she retorted, "What was I supposed to do? Leave you here to rot when I knew you were innocent?"

"You don't know anything. I haven't been innocent since the day I was born."

He practically threw the words at her, as if he actually *wanted* her to think he was guilty. And for Kat, it was too much. If he wanted a fight, she was just in the mood to give him one. After crying over him for hours last night, racking her brain to figure out what *she* had done wrong, she was spoiling to lock horns with him. "Don't give me that bull. You can play the hard ex-con with everybody else, but I know you, cowboy. Oh, I can't tell you what your favorite color is or how you like your steak, but I know that last night you liked it when I kissed you and touched—"

Swearing, Lucas didn't wait to hear more. Whitaker's deputy and secretary were both within listening distance and he didn't doubt that they were hanging on every word.

Closing his fingers around Kat's slender wrist, he hauled her outside, cursing all the while.

"And I know enough to know that you didn't rape that girl," she finished defiantly as he tugged her over to her truck, "because you were with me."

His jaw set in granite, he took the keys from her and jerked open the passenger door. "Don't take any bets on that," he advised her mockingly, stuffing her into the cab. "You don't know what I did after I left you."

He slammed the door in her face, but if he thought she was letting him walk away from that low blow, he was badly mistaken. As soon as he stalked around the pickup and climbed behind the wheel, she said tartly, "Save it for someone who wants to believe the worst of you. I don't."

Heading back to the springs, he shot her a dark look before turning his eyes back to his driving. "Then you're living in a fantasy, sweetheart, because there are plenty of others who will eat this up with a spoon...especially when word gets out about my past. And it will get out now," he warned her. "Too many people know Whitaker took me in, and they're going to want to know why he was suspicious of me in the first place. By defending me, you've only made yourself look like another good woman who foolishly threw her cap over the windmill for a loser."

Her throat tight, Kat wanted to tell him he was wrong. But his words rang with a brutal honesty that cut to the bone. Suddenly wanting to cry, she imagined the sick dread that went through him when he found himself being questioned about another rape.

She ached to reach out to him, to hold him, but she knew she didn't dare. He was as touchy as a lion with a sore paw, distrustful and resentful and ready to bite off the head of anyone who tried to comfort him. "Riley's a good sheriff," she said quietly, breaking the cold, unfriendly silence. "He'll find whoever raped the girl. You've just got to give him a little time."

"And I'm Prince Charming," he snorted cynically. "Grow up, boss lady, and smell the coffee. I'm the perfect suspect, and if Whitaker's pressured to make an arrest, you can bet the ranch he'll come after me."

"But he knows you were with me!"

He laughed at that, but there was no humor in the sound. "Haven't you figured it out yet, little girl? The system doesn't care about guilt or innocence. The law just wants somebody to blame. So if I'm the lucky bastard Whitaker and the DA decide to hang this on, the alibi you gave me won't be worth cow chips. No one will believe that the high-and-mighty Kat Rawlings would ever give herself to an ex-con like me."

"But that was all a mistake!"

He gave her a pitying look. "Don't you get it? When people find out about my past, they'll think my *release* was a mistake, not my conviction. It's much more interesting to believe the worst, and as soon as the word gets out on this, I'll be tried and convicted without a trial."

She didn't want to believe him, couldn't accept his cynical viewpoint. After what he'd been through, maybe he had a right to expect the worst from people, but she couldn't believe her friends and neighbors would condemn him when she was willing to stand up in front of the whole county and swear to his innocence.

"You're wrong," she said flatly, but she might as well have saved her breath. His expression was closed, his eyes hard. He'd made up his mind, and nothing she could say was going to change it. Sighing in defeat, she decided to back off. He'd find out soon enough that he was wrong. Until then, all she could do was give him the space he so obviously needed.

Leaving him two hours later for an auction in Tucson, however, was probably the hardest thing she'd ever done. In no mood for company, he'd refused to go with her and Gable to look over some longhorn calves now that the barn and corral were finished; and short of holding a gun to his head, she'd had no choice but to go without him.

Walking through the cattle barns before the auction, she was hardly aware of the calves her brother pointed out to her. All she could think of was Lucas and how alone he'd looked as she'd driven away with Gable. She shouldn't have left him, she realized too late. Not today.

"Hey, there's Bud Sawyer," Gable said suddenly, breaking into her musings. "And John Fleming's with him. Let's go talk to them and see what's going on. I've been so busy, I haven't seen them in months."

The two men, old school friends of Gable's, were discussing a couple of bulls they were each thinking about bidding on when Gable walked up behind them and slapped each on the shoulder. "Save your money," he teased. "I've got a couple of tough old bulls that will put those in the shade, and I'll sell them to you cheap. Scout's honor."

Surprised, Bud glanced over his shoulder and grinned. "Gable! You old goat roper!"

"Where the hell you been?" John demanded, turning to return the slap on his shoulder. "The last time I saw you—" Suddenly spying Kat, he broke off abruptly, his smile vanishing. His hand falling to his side, he nodded stiffly at her, and Bud didn't even do that.

Since they'd been akin to two more older brothers when she was growing up, their sudden coolness was a slap in the face. Stunned, she frowned in confusion. "Hi, guys. Is something wrong?"

"You're damn right something's wrong," Bud retorted. "I thought I knew you, but the Kat Rawlings I know wouldn't lie for no damn rapist."

Kat paled. "I didn't—"

"You damn sure did," John cut in resentfully. "Did you think no one would know about it? That poor girl's daddy started asking questions the minute he heard a suspect had been released, and the whole damn county's been buzzing about it ever since. Jesus H. Christ, girl, I can't believe you did something so stupid!"

Gable scowled at that and stepped close to his sister's side. If he and his brothers chewed her out, that was one thing. But no one, not even a friend, was going to take her to task in front of him for something that was none of their business. "That's enough, John," he said coldly.

"The hell it is! That girl was raped less than a mile from my house, and now the scum bag who did it is back on the streets. How do you think that makes my wife feel?"

"That *scum bag,* as you call him," Kat lashed out, "didn't rape anyone. I know because he was with me at the time the rape occurred."

"You don't have to lie for him," Bud scolded her. "For God's sake, Kat, he's an ex-con! How can you stand here and defend him?"

"Because he didn't rape anyone... *ever!*" Struggling to hang on to her temper, she dragged in a calming breath, but it didn't help much. "Lucas's conviction in Texas was nothing but a terrible mistake," she said quietly. "If you don't believe me, ask the sheriff. Lucas told him the whole story the first day he came to town, and Riley checked it out."

She told them the rest of it, how Lucas was the victim of a vicious lie and a powerful family's need for revenge, how no one would believe him until the girl he supposedly raped couldn't live with herself anymore and finally admitted the terrible thing she'd done. But as the words tripped over themselves in her haste to defend Lucas, she knew they were falling on deaf ears. Their faces carved in stern, unrelenting lines, the two men obviously didn't believe a word she said.

Chapter 9

Spitting mad, Kat slammed out of Gable's truck the second they returned to the springs, hot color flying high in her cheeks. "Damn them," she raged, stomping back to the stock trailer hooked to the back of the pickup. "Hypocritical, judgmental jackasses! Who died and left them judge and jury of the world?"

Moving to help her, Gable had listened to her rant and rave all the way from Tucson. She'd worked up a full head of steam, and he knew from experience she wasn't going to wind down anytime soon. He couldn't say that he blamed her. He'd been just as disturbed as she by his friends' attack, but he had to admit he shared some of their concerns.

It wasn't what she wanted to hear, but he said it, anyway. "They did act like a couple of jerks, but you can't blame them for being worried, honey. They've got wives and daughters to think about."

"Then maybe they should quit condemning an inno-cent man and help Riley find the monster who did this," she returned crossly, refusing to be pacified. "He's out there, Gable, walking around free, without a care in the world because everyone suspects Lucas. As far as we know, he could be a pillar of society, and as long as he's loose, every woman in this county is in danger."

She spoke nothing less than the truth, and just the thought of someone he knew, someone he might call friend, forcing himself on an eighteen-year-old kid, turned Gable's stomach. "Riley will catch him," he said grimly. "He's damn good at what he does, and he'll track the pervert down like the miserable dog that he is if he has to."

She desperately wanted to believe him, but she could still see Bud's and John's closed faces, the obstinate set of their jaws as they refused to hear a word she said. She'd never felt so frustrated in her life. For the first time, she under-stood the source of Lucas's anger and bitterness, the help-lessness that must have choked him when he'd known he was innocent and no one had given a damn. Dear God, how had he stood it?

"What happened?"

Lost in her rage, she hadn't seen Lucas working on the pasture fence when they'd driven up, hadn't seen him start toward them. Suddenly he came around the corner of the barn, his sharp gaze taking in the fire in her eyes, the flaming color in her cheeks. Too late, she struggled to get her temper under control, her heart squeezing just at the thought of telling him what had happened at the auction. She couldn't do it, she realized, couldn't stand to see that cold look come into his eyes when he learned that he'd been right all along about how people would condemn him no matter what she said.

Forcing a smile a blind man could have seen through, she quickly turned toward the stock trailer. "Nothing," she fibbed. "I've just been talking Gable's ear off about starting my herd. Come take a look at what we got."

Standing back, she watched him and Gable unload the longhorn bull and pregnant cow she'd bought at the auction, and for a few minutes, it was easy to forget the ugliness that had tainted the day. Excitement danced through her, making it impossible for her to stand still. It seemed she had been waiting forever for this moment, planning it down to the last detail, her expectations higher than a kite. Not even her dreams, however, could touch the emotions that swept her at the sight of the longhorns grazing on Double R land.

With only a little imagination, she could see the magnificent animals as they'd been a century ago, roaming Texas wild and free. They'd been cursed and maligned and wrongly accused of being stringy and tough, but they'd made a place for themselves in history with the legendary spread of their horns and the fact that no two had the exact same coloring. They'd almost been lost forever in the cattle drives of the 1800s, but they were making a comeback and finally coming into their own as a breed.

"Those are prize cattle," Lucas said, knowingly studying the quality lines of the animals as they slowly explored their new home. "They didn't come cheap."

It was a statement, not a question, and Kat didn't bother to deny the obvious. "It was money well spent. I plan to have one of the best herds in the country, and to do that, you've got to start with quality from the very beginning."

She spoke with the ease of a woman who had never known want, never known what it was like to be out of work and broke, without a prospect in sight. He didn't begrudge her the fact that she could make her dreams come true simply by writing a check, but neither did he intend to forget it.

Turning, he faced her squarely. He didn't spare her brother a glance, didn't care what Gable read into his words. "Are you going to tell me what happened at the auction or do I have to guess? And don't tell me 'nothing,'" he warned her before she could open her mouth. "I can read you like a book, lady, and you were madder than a wet hen when you got back here. Somebody said something to you, didn't they?"

"No—"

She was a lousy liar and didn't help matters by not meeting his gaze. Glancing at her brother, Lucas wasn't surprised to find Gable watching him like a hawk. "Spit it out, Rawlings. You can't hurt my feelings. By this time, I've heard it all before."

Gable had to respect a man who didn't flinch from the truth. Giving him a condensed version of the conversation with Bud and John, he told him exactly what happened. "They're usually fair-minded men," he finished, "but Kat got hot and so did they, and nobody was listening to reason."

Not surprised, Lucas took the news impassively, but inside, something twisted at the thought of her standing toe-to-toe with men she considered friends, arguing with them, defending *him*. He told himself he didn't want her in his corner, didn't need her support. But he could practically see her raking those men over the coals, and the image clutched at his heart, warming his blood in a way he hadn't expected.

She was getting to him in a way no woman ever had, he admitted somberly. And all he had to offer her was heartache. "I never meant to cause problems between you and your friends," he said tightly. "The sheriff asked me not to leave the county because he felt that would only make me look guilty as hell, but he never said anything about not finding somewhere else to stay. I'll be out of your hair within the hour.''

"What?" Kat exclaimed. "You can't be serious! You can't leave! Gable, tell him—"

Gable frowned, his first instinct, like Kat's, to insist that he stay. The Double R was his and his family's, and no one, least of all a couple of so-called "friends," dictated what he thought about another man's guilt or innocence. But he hadn't missed the tension between Valentine and his sister, the current that sparked between them like a power surge. When Kat had confessed earlier that she had *been* with her hired hand, he hadn't wanted to believe that she meant intimately, but seeing them together now, there was no doubt about it.

Disturbed—how could she have grown up without him noticing?—he readily acknowledged that Valentine wasn't the type of man he would have picked for her. But then again, he wasn't consulted in the matter, which was probably for the best. As far as he was concerned, no man was good enough for her.

Deciding it was time he got some answers, he studied the other man shrewdly. "Did you rape that girl?"

"Gable, for God's sake! I told you he was with me!"

Neither man spared Kat so much as a glance. His eyes locked with Gable's, Lucas knew he didn't have to answer. Rawlings wasn't a cop or his boss and he didn't owe him any explanations. But Gable hadn't condemned him as his friends had, and the least Lucas could do was tell him the truth.

"No, I didn't," he said coolly. "I've done some things in my life I'm not particularly proud of, but mistreating a woman isn't one of them."

Gable prided himself on being a damn good judge of character, and if Valentine was lying, he'd eat his shorts. "Where'd you go when you left here last night?"

"The bunkhouse. If you don't believe me, ask Red or one of the others. I was there by eight-fifteen and didn't even go outside again until the sheriff showed up this morning."

There was no doubting his sincerity. His frown easing somewhat, Gable nodded, satisfied. "Then what's all this garbage about leaving?"

Just that easily, he was accepted, no more questions asked. Bewildered, Lucas tried to remember the last time anyone had taken him at his word, but the memory escaped him. "People will accuse you of harboring a rapist," he warned. "It could get ugly."

Gable only shrugged, amusement lighting his eyes. "Kat obviously hasn't told you the family history, or you'd know that we can handle just about anything. So relax, man. Nobody tells us who can and can't stay at the Double R."

Lucas had learned a long time ago that there was no substitute for hard work to make a man forget his troubles, so he returned to the pasture as soon as Gable left and spent what was left of the afternoon attacking the post holes that needed digging for the next fence. With the sun beating down on him, his shirt clinging to his back and his palms starting to sting because he'd misplaced his work gloves somewhere, he had plenty of things to think of besides the possible rape charge hanging over his head. But every time he looked up, his eyes fell on Kat, who had stubbornly refused to leave his side.

He didn't understand her or her family. He had a history that scared most people witless, and by now, he liked to think that it didn't bother him when that all-too familiar uneasiness crept into strangers' eyes the second they learned why he'd spent time in prison. The coldness, the blatant rudeness, he could handle. The Rawlingses, however, Kat included, were something else.

In the eyes of just about everyone in the county, he was a condemned man. Now that the truth was out about him, he wouldn't have been able to find work anywhere else even if he'd wanted to and it had been available. But Gable, who had every right to object to him being anywhere near his sister, hadn't given a damn what his friends and neighbors thought. He'd listened to the facts and accepted Lucas's story with an ease that still stunned him.

In Lucas's world, that kind of acceptance was unheard of. Oh, the cowboys he'd worked with in Texas had called him friend easily enough, but they accepted anyone who did his share of the work and didn't get drunk and bust up the bunkhouse on Saturday nights. No one had cared about his past or future as long as he continued to carry his share of the load. They worked alongside him every day for months, sweated in the heat, cursed the cold and laughed over jokes with him. But when trouble came calling in the form of the sheriff, they'd turned their backs as if they'd never seen him before in their lives.

That's what Gable should have done. And Kat. Watching her take a turn with the posthole digger, her hair falling into her eyes and the sheen of sweat dotting her nose, he couldn't take his eyes off her. He'd never met a woman like her and didn't have the slightest idea how to deal with her. She had everything going for her—looks, money, family. She could have had any man in the state, but she wanted him. And she wasn't shy about letting him know it. Last night, she'd taken him apart and put him back together in her arms, then charged to his defense this morning with blue eyes blazing. Any other woman would have consigned him to the devil. But not Kat. She never did the expected. Dammit, what was he going to do with her?

Brushing her hair back with her forearm, Kat looked up to find him studying her as if she were some strange new breed he couldn't quite figure out. Her arm fell to her side and she smiled, arching a brow at him. "What's the matter? Have I got dirt on my face or what?"

He didn't smile in return, but she hadn't expected him to. He hadn't said two words to her since Gable had left. If she hadn't known better, she would have sworn the closeness they'd shared last night had never happened. He was withdrawn, cold, silent. He hadn't said the words, but she knew he just wanted to be left alone to brood in private.

She almost gave in. But she'd seen the surprise he hadn't been able to hide when Gable had believed him, and it had broken her heart. A man who didn't expect to be believed when he told the truth had been alone, with no one in his corner, for far too long. She was going to change that, she promised herself. Because he needed her, whether he knew it or not, and somehow she had to make him accept that.

But the day was gone, and before she could find a way to reach him, the daylight was gone and she was exhausted. Pretending his coldness didn't hurt took a lot of energy, and as she dropped him off at the bunkhouse and watched him disappear inside, all she wanted to do was go home and crawl into bed. But there was a family meeting at Cooper and Susannah's to discuss the final preparations for the family's annual Halloween party, and she'd promised to attend.

The rest of the clan was already there when she arrived. Susannah opened the door to her, saw the exhaustion she couldn't hide, and immediately hustled her inside. "Tough day, huh? Come on inside and sit down before you drop. Cooper, get Kat a drink.''

"I'm okay," she began, only to have Flynn gently push her into Cooper's favorite chair.

"You're a whipped puppy and you know it," he scolded, his blue eyes, so like hers, playfully teasing. "So shut up and let us baby you."

She grinned, unable to help herself. "Thank God Tate and Josey are the doctors in the family. Your bedside manner stinks."

"Drink up, brat," Cooper said, handing her a glass of iced tea. "Would you rather have some wine? You look like you could use it."

"We're trying to make her feel better, Coop," Gable said dryly, "not knock her out. If you give her alcohol when she's this tired, we'll have to pour her into her truck to get her home."

Laughing along with everyone else, Kat blinked back sudden foolish tears before anyone noticed her eyes were flooded. She knew Gable had told them about Lucas's encounter with the sheriff earlier—he wouldn't keep something like that from the rest of the family—and she had braced herself for the heavy weight of their worry and disapproval. But instead of the questions she'd expected, they wrapped her in teasing laughter, which was just what she needed. Her tiredness drained away, and for a little while at least, she was able to forget the ugliness of the morning.

Supper was ready, and they all trooped into the large kitchen for the stew and biscuits Susannah already had on the table. The house had once been the home of Susannah's father, who had made no secret of the fact that he hated the three Rawlings brothers. But Joe Patterson was dead and gone, and the old wounds had been healed with

Cooper's marriage to Susannah. As comfortable at the old Patterson homestead as they were at the Double R, the family lingered over the meal, laughing and talking and teasing.

But when apple pie and coffee were brought out, it was time to get serious. "Okay," Gable said after a mouthful of pie, "how do we stand for next week?"

"I've got the men lined up to clean out the barn Saturday morning," Cooper said. "As soon as they're ready, the girls can start decorating."

"What about the beer?"

"It's all taken care of," Flynn replied promptly. "I talked to Stan Larson in Silver City just this afternoon and gave him directions. He promised he'll have the kegs out here by three on Saturday. *Guaranteed.*"

"That's what that guy you lined up last year said," Josey reminded him, grinning. "And we ended up with no beer."

"Yeah, but he was a damn liar and I didn't know it until it was too late," he defended himself. "Stan's one of the biggest distributors in the state. He may charge a little more, but he's dependable and he offered a written contract without my even asking for it. Don't worry, he'll be here."

"Did anyone remember to talk to Riley about being one of the judges for the costume competition?" Tate asked. "The five-hundred-dollar grand prize is going to bring people out of the woodwork. Even the hands are talking about entering this year."

Unlike some other ranches in the county where ranchers didn't socialize with their cowboys, Double R hands were considered part of the family and always invited to the Halloween party. Which brought up a possible problem Kat hadn't thought of until now. Lifting her eyes from her untouched pie, she said, "Speaking of the hands, I assume Lucas is also invited."

Her brothers, bless their hearts, didn't even hesitate. "Of course."

"Why wouldn't he be?"

"All the cowboys are invited."

Kat smiled, wanting to kiss them. "I know. But Lucas isn't your average ranch hand."

"Do you think he'll come?" Susannah asked, moving around the table to refill coffee cups. "After all he's been through, you could hardly blame him if he didn't. This morning couldn't have been pleasant."

"It wasn't."

"Gable told us what happened at the auction," Cooper said quietly. "If you're worried about that kind of crap happening here, honey, don't. This is our ranch, our party. Anyone who has any complaints about our guest list can leave."

The rest of the family nodded in agreement. Deep in her heart, she'd known she—and Lucas—could count on their support, but she hadn't realized just how much she needed to hear the words. Relieved, she felt the knots in her stomach unravel. Suddenly the party she hadn't even allowed herself to think about facing earlier in the day sounded like fun.

The meal broke up soon after that and Kat headed home, feeling more relaxed than she had all day. The cabin was less than a mile from Cooper and Susannah's as the crow flies, but because of the canyon that cradled the springs in its belly, it wasn't that easy to get to. She had to take the Patterson drive to the highway, then head cross-country on one of the ranch roads that crisscrossed the

Double R. By the time she turned into the entrance of the canyon, it was after ten.

Driving the route by heart, she easily maneuvered between the rocks, her headlights cutting a wide swath in the darkness that was blacker than pitch. The canyon was just as it always was at night...silent, still, its large boulders like old friends sculptured in deep, black shadows. She was at home here, comfortable. Out of all the nights she'd been there by herself, she couldn't remember once being afraid.

But as the cabin came into sight, an unexpected uneasiness crawled up her back, sending goose bumps scattering across her skin. Suddenly chilled, she frowned. But the cabin was just as she'd left it, the porch light casting a soft yellow glow to guide her home. Heading straight for it, she shrugged over her strange jitteriness and pulled up next to the porch in her regular parking spot. It wasn't until she reached for the key in the ignition that she saw the fences.

They were downed, the posts lying on the ground like fallen soldiers all in a row that stretched into the darkness past the reach of her headlights, the barbed wire that Lucas had just started to string that afternoon cut and twisted.

"No!" she cried, throwing open the door and stumbling out of the truck. But there was no one to hear her cry except the faint breeze that whispered through the tops of the trees. Helpless, all she could do was stand and stare at the mindless destruction. Nearly a full day's work had been viciously, needlessly wiped out. And for what? Who would do this? Why?

Caught up in the questions that slammed into her from all sides, she didn't know how long she stood there before she suddenly remembered her longhorns. "Oh, God!"

Whirling, she ran for the pasture that joined the corral, her heart in her throat. How could she have forgotten about them? If the fence had been destroyed here, too—

But the tan-and-white bull and russet cow were there in the darkness, calming watching her wild approach with sharp eyes that missed nothing. Relief sucked all the air right out of her lungs. Her legs suddenly boneless, she dropped to the dirt and buried her face against her knees, the tears she hadn't felt stinging in her eyes suddenly streaming down her face. Muttering curses at the weakness, she sat up to impatiently dash them away, only to freeze as her gaze lifted to the barn.

RAPIST. CONVICT.

Written in white paint, the words leapt out of the darkness at her like a thief in the night, stabbing her right in the throat. Gasping, she jumped to her feet, eyes wide. Obscenities were sloppily painted all along that one side of the barn, words that she'd never seen printed, let alone spoken. And all of them attacked Lucas.

It was then the anger hit her, white hot and savage. Shaking with fury, her blood boiling and her eyes burning with the light of battle, she ran for her truck. Whoever did this wasn't going to get away with it.

She never thought to run to her brothers. Later, after she'd had time to calm down, that would stun her. In the past, they'd always fought the dragons she couldn't handle alone, and turning to them for help when she needed it was as instinctive as breathing. But there was only one man she wanted now, only one man's arms she needed to feel around her. Throwing her truck into gear, she headed for the bunkhouse.

She'd made the fifteen-minute drive dozens of times in the last couple of weeks—that same ranch road led to the family homestead—but tonight it seemed to take forever.

Alone in the darkness, the first rush of her anger started to fade, and before she could stop it, sick fear spilled into her stomach. She could have been there, she thought, clutching the wheel in a death grip, when the bastard slipped into the canyon to do his dirty work. Or worse yet, come home early and surprised him in the act.

The blood draining from her face, she started to shake, making it nearly impossible for her to keep her truck on the rough path. But the desert surrounded her on all sides, so it didn't matter—there was nothing to hit.

She pressed down on the accelerator, quickly putting more miles between her and the barn, but it didn't help. She could still feel the raw fury emanating from the obscenities scrawled across its surface. And now that the initial shock was starting to wear off, she no longer had to ask herself who would do something like this; the answer was obvious. Someone who hated Lucas with a passion. Someone who resented him and saw him as a threat. Someone who wanted him gone.

Yesterday, she'd have had a hard time coming up with anyone other than Vince Waters to hang that description on. Today, however, the list wasn't nearly that short or obvious. For all she knew, it could include just about everyone in the county but her immediate family.

It was a sobering, daunting thought. This wasn't the first time the Double R had been vandalized by unknown enemies, but always before the attacks had stemmed from some resentful neighbor's jealousy. Her brothers had tried reasoning with them, and when that hadn't worked, had defended themselves and the ranch. That type of dispute she could understand. But how could anyone reason with people who refused to accept the word of an innocent man?

The bunkhouse came into view then, and she raced toward it with a sigh of relief, the need to feel Lucas's arms around her almost more than she could bear. But when she pulled up next to the other pickups that were parked in front of the no-frills dormitory-style building and cut the engine, there wasn't a light on anywhere. A glance at her watch told her it was still fairly early, but that meant nothing on a ranch where the cowboys were up by dawn and hard at work before most city people crawled out of bed.

Hesitating, she stared at the darkened windows and seriously wrestled with the idea of going back to the cabin and dealing with the problem herself. She was twenty-six years old, for God's sake! She didn't need a man to hold her hand while she called the sheriff, or, worse yet, take charge and handle the whole problem for her. She wasn't some little helpless bimbo who fell apart in a crisis. She knew what to do and how to do it.

But her heart slammed painfully against her ribs just at the thought of returning to the springs by herself. She needed Lucas. Now. Even if she had to go from one bunk to the next to find him. Carefully opening her door, she eased out of her pickup and found herself suddenly teased by the absurdity of what she was about to do. Grinning, she could just see Red's face if he woke up to find her searching his bunk for Lucas in the darkness. The other hands would rib him about it for years to come.

For what seemed like an eternity, she just stood there, wanting to laugh. But soon the memory of the vile words painted on her barn sobered her and she started making her way through the haphazardly parked trucks toward the darkened doorway.

Trying to make as little noise as possible, she was so focused on what she would do once she got in the bunkhouse that she didn't see Lucas's pickup until she almost passed it. Absently glancing over at it, she stopped so suddenly that her feet skidded slightly on the gravel covering the parking area. A large lump, bathed in deep, concealing shadows, lay in the bed of the truck. Frowning, she moved closer, her breath catching in her throat. It was Lucas, stretched out in a sleeping bag, his face half buried in his bunched-up pillow. What was he doing sleeping outside?

Horribly afraid she knew, she melted at the sight of him—there was no other way to describe it. When had he come to mean so much to her? she wondered, blinking back tears. She'd been so sure that she was in control of her emotions, so sure that her pursuit of him was something she could stop at any time. But seeing him so relaxed, his face looking surprisingly boyish in the shadows, she could no more stop the longing his mere presence stirred in her than she could stop the bubbling of the springs with a snap of her fingers.

Needing, aching, to touch him, she climbed into the bed of the truck and knelt next to him on the cold metal. Her fingers shaking ever so slightly, she reached out to gently shake his shoulder. "Lucas?"

Caught up in the depths of a dream that had descended on him the second he'd closed his eyes, Lucas heard her calling to him and warned himself not to be taken in by how close she sounded. She was in his dreams, hiding in the fog, teasing him, daring him to catch her, making him ache just as she did every night. She got a kick out of driving him crazy, but this time he wasn't going to play her little game. He'd stand perfectly still and make her come to him. Then he'd have her...for always.

"Wake up, cowboy. I need to talk to you."

She touched his shoulder, just that, and still managed to make him burn. His whole body starting to throb, he murmured her name and rolled toward her, unable to resist her seductive call.

Relieved, Kat smiled tentatively at him as he slowly lifted heavy-lidded eyes, an explanation already forming on her tongue. But before she could say a single word, he reached for her, lightning quick. "Lucas!"

He had her in the sleeping bag and under him in the blink of an eye, his mouth hot and hard and hungry on hers. Stunned, she tried to stop him, but all she could manage was a squeaky "wait!" before his lips settled on hers, his tongue seducing, and his arms wrapping her close.

He was naked.

The knowledge first registered on her fingertips as her hands instinctively flew to his chest, the feel of his hair-roughened torso setting her nerve endings atingle. Her heart pounded, and she told herself she must be mistaken. But then one of his roaming hands trailed down the base of her spine to press her intimately into his arousal, and there was no doubting that the man didn't have a stitch on.

Heat scorched her all the way to her toes. Her breathing ragged, her blood suddenly hot and thick in her veins, she felt her brain start to cloud and found it increasingly difficult to remember what she'd raced over there to tell him. Blindly, hungrily, she kissed him back.

His blood on fire, Lucas wrapped her closer until every sweet inch of her was molded against him. Too real, he thought dazedly, wrenching his mouth from hers to press his lips to the pulse pounding at the base of her throat. His dreams were becoming so real he could actually taste her on his tongue, feel the tempting fullness of her breasts rub against his chest, driving him out of his mind.

Then she moved against him, her low moan vibrating in his ears, and he froze. No dream, no matter how good, was that lifelike. Opening his eyes, he drew back abruptly at the sight of her lying under him—in the sleeping bag!—her mouth looking crushed and just-kissed in the darkness, her hair a dark tangled cloud on his pillow, her eyes midnight blue with desire.

Needs screaming through him, clawing at him, he almost leaned down and snatched another kiss, damn the consequences. But there was a whole bunkhouse full of cowboys sleeping less than a stone's throw away, and it wasn't unusual for one of them to step outside for a smoke when sleep just wouldn't come.

Muttering a curse, he hissed, "What the devil are you doing here? And how the hell did you get in this sleeping bag without me waking up?"

Her eyes sparking with outrage, she gasped as if he'd slapped her. He made it sound as if she was some kind of seductress who'd waited until he was asleep to take unfair advantage of him! "Because you grabbed me the minute I touched you," she whispered hotly. "As to why I'm here...well, excuse me for disturbing your beauty sleep, but I thought you might want to know that someone vandalized the barn tonight. Now that you know, I'll get out of your hair. And your damn sleeping bag!"

Too furious to care that she was wearing her heart on her sleeve, she started to fight the restrictive folds of the jumbo bag only to suddenly find herself flat on her back again with Lucas leaning over her, pinning her under him. "Dammit, Lucas, let me up!"

"Are you okay? What happened? If anyone touched you—"

He didn't finish the threat, but he didn't have to. His eyes were like dark coals in his harshly lined face, his hands incredibly tender as they swept over her. Caught in the heat of his gaze, Kat's anger suddenly vanished, tears coming out of nowhere to flood her eyes. This was why she had raced to the bunkhouse, why she'd needed so desperately to see him. "No," she whispered thickly. "I was at Cooper's when it happened."

She couldn't bring herself to ask him to hold her, but the need must have been reflected in her eyes. Murmuring her name, he rolled to his side and gathered her close. "Come here," he said gruffly.

He settled her against him, her head tucked under his chin and his arms wrapped snugly around her. With his heart pounding reassuringly in her ear, Kat could have stayed there forever. Dear God, how could she have gone all of her life without him? He only had to draw her into the warmth of his body and she felt like nothing could touch her as long as he was holding her. When had she come to need that kind of protection from a man? *This* man?

"Okay, what happened?" he asked into her hair. "Tell me everything."

She didn't want to, would have given anything to spare him the obscenities that had labeled him the lowest scum on earth. But she couldn't shield him from the truth, not when he had an enemy he couldn't even put a face to, and the words just came tumbling out. "As soon as I saw the barn, I jumped into my truck and drove over here," she finished. "I didn't realize everyone would be asleep."

Black rage filled him—not for the potshots taken at him, but for the attack on Kat's property and the fear she had suffered just because she believed in him—but he kept his touch deliberately soothing as he repeatedly ran his hands down her back. Promising himself that whoever had done this would pay, he murmured, "You didn't call your brothers?"

She shook her head, the movement unconsciously seductive against his naked chest. "I just wanted to get to you."

If he'd been standing, she could have knocked him to his knees with that admission. His hands tightened on her, and for just a moment, all he could think of was finishing what he'd started when he'd awakened to find her in his arms. But they had bigger problems to handle than the fire that roared between them whenever they were this close.

"Then we'd better go wake them," he said, pushing the sleeping bag back so she could crawl out. "They're going to want to hear the whole story."

Chapter 10

The minute Gable opened the door to them, he took one look at Kat's pale face and Lucas's stony expression and immediately jerked the door wider. "What's wrong?" he asked sharply, his narrowed eyes locked on his sister. "Why aren't you home in bed?"

"I'm all right," Kat said quickly, recognizing that tone. As overprotective as an old hen, he was all set to jump on whoever had upset her. "So just chill out until you hear the rest of the story. I'm fine."

"What happened?"

Stepping into the entrance hall with Lucas right on her heels, she winced at the biting edge of Gable's voice. So much for remaining calm. "You're not going to like it."

"That's obvious or you wouldn't be beating around the bush the way you are. Just spit it out and get it over with."

She hesitated, her stomach twisting at the memory of the cold, deliberate destruction she'd stumbled across at the cabin. "Someone paid a visit to the springs while I was at

Cooper's," she said stiffly. "Fences were knocked down, and the barn was vandalized."

A muscle worked in his granite jaw, but he only asked curtly, "Vandalized how?"

"Some reflections on my character," Lucas said without inflection, speaking for the first time. "Rapist. Convict. Just the usual comments from someone exercising freedom of speech."

Gable bit out a short, terse oath that said what he thought of that garbage. "If someone wants to express their opinion, let 'em write it on their own barn or take out an ad in the paper." Scowling, he turned and strode into his study. "I've got to make some calls, get some of the boys together, then get out there and see just how much damage has been done," he told them as he reached for the phone on his desk. "If we're lucky, whoever did this left some kind of calling card so we'll be able to identify him."

In a matter of minutes, he called Cooper and Flynn, the bunkhouse, and the sheriff. When he finally hung up for the last time, he had the satisfied look of a man who was used to calling the shots and getting his way. "Everyone's going to meet us at the springs," he said, pushing to his feet. "Let's go."

The group Gable had called together looked like an army convoy reconnoitering at the canyon as it arrived en masse at the darkened cabin. Red and a handful of other trusted hands pulled up behind the family vehicles and spilled out, their faces grim as they took in the malicious words scrawled on the side of the barn. Someone cursed, muttering that he'd like to get his hands on the foul-mouthed bastard who did his dirty work in the dark like a damn coward. The others silently agreed.

Unlike the rest of the cowboys, Lucas had known what to expect. His thumbs hooked into the back pockets of his jeans, he stood at the back of the group and read the ugly words, his face impassive. They weren't new—he'd heard them all before. But he'd never seen them splattered over something he'd sweated and labored over and built with his own two hands. Rage twisted in him, tying him in knots.

Kat, sensing his fury, moved closer to his side. "They're just words," she said quietly. "Sticks and stones and all that jazz. Don't let them get to you."

"She's right," Flynn said, joining them. "Only a small mind could come up with something this low. Don't worry. The jerk'll pay for this."

Riley Whitaker arrived then, the flashing lights on the roof of his patrol car casting a red-and-blue glow over the canyon. Already apprised of the situation, he took one look at the barn and started throwing out orders. "We need to check the cabin and the interior of the barn. Red, take some of the boys and see how the fence was knocked down. And be careful! Whoever did this was in a rage and probably careless. Look for empty spray cans, tire marks, anything that might give us a clue to his identity. Has anyone checked out those longhorns?"

"They seem to be okay," Cooper said. "They don't act spooked, so I doubt the jackass bothered them. Since he did all this in the dark, he probably didn't even notice them."

Riley nodded, his eyes swinging to Kat. "Start from the beginning and tell me what happened from the time you took Lucas to the bunkhouse, then went to your brother's. What time was it? Did you see anything unusual? Anyone hanging around that didn't belong on the Double R? Maybe a truck you didn't recognize?"

"No, nothing." Step by step, she went over the events of the evening, leaving out nothing. "I really wasn't paying any attention," she said regretfully. "I was thinking about the incident at the auction—"

"What incident?" Riley asked, his eyes razor sharp. "What happened?"

Gable told him about Bud and John, his tone disgusted as he added, "They acted like a couple of jackasses, but they're not vandals. They might talk a tough line, but they would have never done something this stupid."

"I don't think so, either," Riley said, "but at this point in the investigation, it's too soon to rule out anyone."

"Hey, sheriff, I found something!"

The call from one of the cowboys who was going over the corral area brought them all running. "I don't know if you've had anyone out here recently who smokes cigars," the young, fresh-faced ranch hand told Kat, "but this cigar butt looks like it was just tossed here." With the high-powered flashlight he carried, he pointed to the tail end of a cigar lying in the dirt.

Hunkering down on his haunches, Riley lifted the butt with the tweezers he pulled out of his shirt pocket, then dropped it into a clear plastic evidence bag. The pickups were still parked facing the barn and downed fence, the sharp glare of their headlights stripping away the darkness and painting the whole scene in stark white light. Holding the evidence bag up to the light, Riley revealed the cigar piece and the ivory plastic holder attached to it.

Kat caught her breath at the sight of it, drawing a steely-eyed gaze from the sheriff. "Do you know anyone who smokes cigars like this, Kat?"

She nodded, her throat suddenly as dry as toast. "Vince Waters," she finally managed to say after she swallowed. "He's been smoking them for years."

The hands, gathered around them in a semicircle, exchanged sharp glances, and more than a few cursed. Vince had never bothered to hide the fact that he considered himself superior to the hardworking ranch hands, and they despised him for it, considering him a condescending jerk.

Ignoring the hostile mutterings, Riley pushed to his feet. "Has he been out here since you moved into the cabin?"

"Once," she replied, and explained the circumstances. "But the barn wasn't built yet, and we talked over by the cabin, anyway. He wanted me to fire Lucas."

As far as evidence went, it was only circumstantial, and damn thin at that. But it was all they had to go on. Further investigation of the scene turned up nothing, and since most of the cowboys were at the bunkhouse at the time the damage was done, there were no witnesses. With the cabin so secluded and miles from the rest of the ranch, that wasn't surprising. The Double R was crisscrossed with dirt roads that anyone bent on mischief could use to avoid the house and bunkhouse.

An hour after they'd arrived to help search the canyon, the ranch hands were thanked and sent back to the bunkhouse. Soon after that, the sheriff left, too, promising to contact Kat when he had more information. Within minutes, everyone was gone but Lucas, Kat and her brothers.

In the sudden silence that fell, the isolation of the canyon was more apparent than ever. Gable took one look at the darkened cabin that sat all alone in the clearing and told Kat, "Go pack a few things. You can stay at the house with me and Josey tonight."

Before the words were out of his mouth, she was shaking her head. "Vince has already done his dirty work. He won't be back tonight."

"You don't know that," Cooper argued. "You don't even know for sure that Waters is the one who did this."

"No, but I wouldn't put it past him. He's made no secret of the fact that he hates Lucas, and I've seen him smoke that same brand of cigar a hundred times. He did it, Coop," she said quietly. "He had to have. I don't know anyone else who would dare."

"If that's the case, he's capable of doing just about anything," he replied. "Including coming back here to cause more mischief. *If* he's as guilty as you think he is."

"So go pack a bag, brat," Flynn said irritably, at the end of his patience. "It's getting late and I don't like leaving Tate at home by herself."

Her own patience at a premium, she straightened all five feet ten inches of her slim frame. "The hell I will! This is my home now and I'm not letting Vince Winters or anyone scare me away from it."

"Dammit, you're not staying here alone—"

"I'll stay," Lucas said suddenly, stepping into the middle of what was quickly escalating into a knock-down-drag-out. On the way out to the canyon, he'd had Kat drop him off at the bunkhouse to pick up his truck so no one would have to drive him back later. Parked halfway between the barn and cabin, it still had his sleeping bag in the back. All he had to do was crawl into it. "Most nights I sleep in the back of my pickup, anyway, so it wouldn't be a problem. It's already here."

Cooper and Flynn were in no mood to compromise, but Gable wasn't ready to take such a hard line. Like Kat, he was convinced Lucas hadn't raped anyone, but that didn't mean he wanted him sleeping right outside his sister's cabin. The chemistry between them was almost visible and so volatile that the two of them could hardly stop looking at each other. And Lucas was fighting it every step of the way.

Suddenly amused, Gable had to fight to hold back a grin. He could have told Valentine he was wasting his time—if Kat had decided they were made for each other, it was a done deal. Valentine might as well go out and buy the ring—he was going to need it.

Still, he hesitated at leaving the two of them there alone, even if one of them was inside and the other out. Glancing at his sister, he arched a brow at her. "It's your call. Just don't feel like you have to stay here because you're all grown-up and you're not supposed to get scared. You don't have to prove anything to anybody."

Kat smiled; she couldn't help herself. *Finally!* Cooper and Flynn were grumbling under their breath, but she was obviously making some progress with Gable. Without too much insistence on her part, he was actually letting her make a decision. Would wonders never cease! "Quit worrying," she said softly. "I'll be fine."

He wanted to argue, but he knew a lost cause when he saw it. "All right. If that's the way you want it. But if Waters comes back or anything unusual happens, you'd damn well better call."

She saluted snappily, her grin sassy. "Yes, sir. Anything you say, sir. Will that be all, sir?"

"Brat," he said, laughing, giving her hair a teasing tug. "I know it's hard, but try to behave yourself."

The less-than-subtle warning hung in the air long after he'd dragged a frowning Cooper and Flynn away. Her heart starting to pound, unexpected anticipation pumping through her veins, Kat stood at Lucas's side and watched their taillights disappear in the darkness and tried to convince herself that tonight was no different from any other night. But butterflies were already swarming in her stomach, and she couldn't stop remembering what it had felt like to lie in his sleeping bag with him, his big, hard, naked body surrounding her.

"You'd better go inside," he said in a low voice that skated over her nerve endings like a caress. "It's late."

"Oh, it's not that late. Anyway, I'm not tired."

"You will be when the adrenaline wears off. All this will hit you like a ton of bricks, and you'll be glad you had the sense to go to bed."

She knew she should go, but she hated to leave him. Cocking her head to the side, she asked suddenly, "Why do you sleep in your truck? I meant to ask you at the bunkhouse but—"

He'd been too busy kissing her.

In the blink of an eye, the image was there between them, heating the night breeze like a summer wind. His blood suddenly hot, his heart hammering, Lucas couldn't drag his eyes from hers. "The walls close in at night," he said without thinking, the admission he'd never intended to make slipping out before he could stop it. "I can't breathe inside."

He saw her start of surprise, the concern he told himself he didn't want that warmed him inside and out, and knew if he didn't convince her to go inside soon, he was going to have her flat on her back in his sleeping bag before she could do anything but sigh his name.

"Get inside," he growled. "Now."

He braced himself, expecting her to defy him as she had her brother. But something in his tone must have warned her his control was precarious at best and nothing had changed from the previous night, when he'd made love to her, then left her in tears. He wanted her, but he didn't want to want her, and that made all the difference.

Too proud and stubborn to let him see the hurt clouding her eyes, she turned away. "I guess I'll turn in, then," she said huskily. "Good night."

Telling himself it was the right decision, Lucas didn't wait to see her shut the cabin door behind her before climbing into the bed of his truck and slipping into his sleeping bag. Silence settled like a shroud over the canyon, the only sound the steady, soothing rhythm of the springs. It had been a long, chaotic day, and he was bone weary. He should have dropped right off to sleep, but the minute he buried his face in his pillow, Kat's familiar, intoxicating scent twined around him in the darkness as sweetly as if she were there beside him. Groaning her name, he cursed himself for sending her inside.

Call her back, a voice in his head urged. *That's all it would take.*

But he couldn't do it. Aching for her, he drew her scent in with every breath and spent the rest of the night wishing she were there in his arms.

Early the next morning, they began repairing the damage done during the night. It was infuriating work considering that they'd already done it once, and by the middle of the afternoon, they both would have strung Vince up by his thumbs if they could have gotten their hands on him.

"At least we don't have to dig the postholes again," Kat said through her teeth as she helped him restring the barbed wire. "As soon as we finish here, all we have to do is paint over Vince's handiwork, and everything'll be back to normal. Or at least it will be as soon as Riley has the jackass behind bars."

"Don't hold your breath," Lucas warned her as he swept his hat off to wipe his sweaty brow with the back of his hand. "Waters isn't some two-bit cowboy on the street. He's probably bought his way out of trouble for years."

Kat bristled at that. "He did before Riley became sheriff, but not anymore. Riley's as honest as a judge. He would never take a bribe."

Lucas only shrugged. He'd had that kind of faith in the law once, too. But the sheriff was an elected official, and politics and justice made strange bedfellows. When John Kent, seeking revenge, had reminded the sheriff of Dallas county that he never would have gotten elected without Kent power and money, the lily-livered coward had folded like a deck of cards and done what he was told. The sorry excuse for a lawman had sold him down the river, tampered with evidence, and paid off so-called witnesses who had testified to Lucas's volatile temper without ever revealing that they'd never seen him before in their lives.

Then, after he'd been tried and convicted and condemned to hell, the bastard had had the gall to apologize. No, Lucas didn't want to hear about honest sheriffs. He would have to reserve judgment on Riley Whitaker until he saw how he dealt with the rape and Waters, but as far as he was concerned, lawmen that were as straight as an arrow were a rare and dying breed.

Considering that, it wasn't surprising that he didn't view Whitaker's arrival an hour later with much enthusiasm. Standing patiently at Kat's side, he waited for the other man to cut through the pleasantries. He didn't have long to wait.

"Vince claims he was in Tucson all day yesterday and last night on family business," he said without preamble. "And he's got a hotel receipt to prove it."

Not surprised, Lucas swore. "Those slick rich boys always cover their butts, don't they?"

Stunned, Kat cried, "But that's impossible! You know he did this, Riley. We all do! And what about the cigar butt? Doesn't that count for anything?"

Riley, no happier than they were with the situation, scowled. "I wish to God it did. Waters has been a thorn in my side ever since I was first sworn in as sheriff, brawling and cussing and tearing up joints all over the county. But every time I think I've finally got him, he pays off the witnesses and I'm left with no case."

"Are you saying he paid off someone this time?" Lucas asked sharply.

"I don't know. Hell, I don't know anything except that he's got a legitimate alibi, and the only thing I've got against him is the speculation of people who know and despise him and the butt end of a fancy cigar that just about anyone in the country could have smoked. It's not enough for an arrest, let alone a conviction."

They were at a dead end and there wasn't a thing they could do about it. Furious, Kat could have spit nails. "So you're going to let him walk."

"I have to," Riley retorted. "I just can't go around arresting people because I *think* they're guilty. The system's not perfect, but it's the only one we've got, and until Vince makes a mistake, he's a free man."

"Then you'd better warn him to stay away from the Double R," she said tersely, "or he's going to have more trouble than he can handle. Cooper was out here earlier, and he said the hands are fighting mad. Vince may have bought himself an alibi, but they won't give a damn if they see him."

Riley understood about loyalty, especially on a ranch. An attack on one was an attack on all, and he couldn't really blame the Double R hands for wanting revenge. "Just make sure they don't make the same mistake the rest of the folks are doing around here with Lucas," he replied. "It's easy to jump to conclusions, but that doesn't mean you can try and convict a man without knowing the facts. Last I heard, a man was still innocent until proved guilty." Seeing by their somber faces that the point was well-taken, he touched the brim of his Stetson in a silent goodbye and left them with a lot to think about.

In spite of the sheriff's words of caution, tensions escalated over the next three days until everyone from the family to the newest ranch hand was as jumpy as a grasshopper on a hot rock. Vince may have cleared his name with Riley Whitaker, but the sheriff was about the only one willing to give him the benefit of the doubt.

Personally, Lucas didn't trust the bastard as far as he could throw him, but if Waters didn't vandalize the barn, someone else did. And Lucas had a gut feeling that whoever did it would be back. Because there was still a rapist walking around free, and until he was caught, there were a good number of people in the county who still thought he was guilty as hell and should be behind bars. For all he knew, any one of them could have left that message scrawled on the barn.

Still, when he stretched out in his sleeping bag each night and watched the lights go out in the cabin, it wasn't the list of possible suspects he thought of. It was Kat.

He was playing with fire, teasing—no, *torturing* himself with something he couldn't have. But he still couldn't make himself leave. She spent all day, every day, at his side, insisting on doing her share of the work as usual, their conversation restricted to the work, Waters, or the sheriff's lack of progress in the rape case. Neither of them mentioned the time they'd spent making love by the springs or the hot kiss they'd shared in his sleeping bag in the back of his truck.

But they weren't forgotten.

Every time their eyes met, every time the work brought them together, they remembered. Hearts pounded, time itself seemed to stop, and the need grew. Then one of them would blink or a breeze would whisper through the cottonwoods lining the springs and the moment would be lost.

But if the days were difficult, it was the nights that were the worst. Every evening when he crawled into his sleeping bag, he swore he was too tired to lie awake half the night brooding over the woman who was only twenty feet away behind a closed door she didn't keep locked half the time. But his mind and body had different ideas. She haunted him. And yet, if she was having trouble sleeping, he'd seen no sign of it—she was bright-eyed every morning, up at dawn and ready to work, so beautiful she stole his breath. It was damned irritating.

Still, he wouldn't, couldn't, allow himself to touch her. The last time, he'd hardly been able to make himself let her go. Next time . . . hell, there couldn't be a next time.

With any other woman, keeping that vow would have been a piece of cake. But Kat had already proven that she would never be like other women. Even when she wasn't trying, she pushed his buttons and made him as hot as a randy teenager. And with every passing day—and night— she made it harder and harder for him to keep his hands to himself. There was a storm building, burning in his gut hotter than the fires of hell. He didn't want to think about what was going to happen when it hit.

Bone weary, he settled himself more comfortably in his sleeping bag, only to stiffen when he heard what sounded like one of the longhorns moving restlessly in the corral.

Instantly alert, he sat up and peered into the darkness, listening.

The cattle settled down, however, and nothing moved. Without a sound, Lucas reached for his clothes and boots. He was pretty sure Waters wasn't hiding out there in the dark, waiting to ambush him—according to the sheriff, who had dropped by just about every day, the jerk was keeping a low profile and staying out of sight. But the other rancher wasn't the only threat out there, especially to the cattle. The mountain lion he'd come face-to-face with a couple of weeks ago hadn't been seen since and had probably headed north, where the food supply was more abundant. But there was no way of knowing that for sure.

Grabbing his shotgun and flashlight, both of which he'd started keeping within reach in the back of his truck since the attack on the barn, he jumped to the ground and cautiously made his way over to the corral, where they'd been keeping the pregnant heifer. Sweeping the light over her, he took one look at her and tensed, immediately recognizing the signs of labor. Her tail was sticking straight out and she was restless, lying down as he watched, only to get right back up again.

Lucas swore. It was too soon. He'd been checking on her four or five times a day and had decided just that afternoon that she'd probably go another month before she calved. So much for knowing what he was talking about, he thought grimly. But calving-out heifers was never predictable, especially when you had a new one you didn't know all that much about.

Watching the obviously uncomfortable animal lie down again, he knew there was no help for it; he was going to have to wake Kat. Longhorns were known for their fertility, and after centuries of roaming the west wild, survival of the fittest had taken care of any calving problems. But this heifer was young—she'd been accidentally pasture-bred while she was still with her momma—and he knew Kat wouldn't want to take any chances with her. She was counting on the heifer to add to her herd every year for years to come. If she lost her to a complicated premature birth, Kat would be devastated.

Taking time only to turn on the barn lights, he quickly crossed to the cabin and pounded on the door. "Kat? Wake up! We've got a problem out here."

Cocking his head, he listened for any sounds of movement on the other side of the sturdy wooden door, but there were none. Muttering a curse, he doubled up his fist and hit it again. Damn the woman, she slept like the dead! "Wake up, woman! Do you hear me? You've got to get up!"

The door was jerked open so suddenly his raised fist almost caught her on the forehead. He started to growl at her for taking so long, but then he got his first good look at her and the hot words stuck in his suddenly tight throat. No woman had a right to look that good when she'd just crawled out of bed. Barefoot, her hair tumbling down her back and the ruffled flannel nightshirt she wore just grazing the middle of her bare thighs, she was mussed, soft and so damn tempting he couldn't think straight.

She was also mad as hell. Her blue eyes narrowed in irritation, she pinned him to the weathered floor boards of the porch. "This better be good, Valentine. In case you hadn't noticed, I don't like being dragged out of bed in the middle of the night."

"You will for this," he said in a voice that was as rough as sandpaper. "Your heifer's gone into labor. I thought you'd want to know."

"What?" Her gaze flew past him to the barn and the lights that were already burning there. "But it's too soon! I thought you said another month."

He shrugged. "Obviously Mother Nature decided otherwise."

"Is she okay? God, I've got to get out there!"

"No!" Staring after her, Lucas cursed as she flew across the cabin, snatching up clothes on her way to the bathroom, unaware of how much thigh she revealed as she bent to grab her boots. His breath lodging in his throat as need slammed into him, he whirled and headed for the barn. He never should have woken her, never should have let himself come anywhere near the damn cabin. Now he was going to have to spend hours with her, possibly the rest of the night, and only God knew how he was going to keep his hands to himself.

Her pulse racing with a mixture of excitement and worry, Kat jerked on a faded navy sweatshirt, then hopped from one foot to the other as she tugged on her jeans. It was cold out—the first really cold night of fall—but she couldn't find her jacket and didn't want to take time to look for it. Impatiently brushing her hair back from her face, she rushed outside less than ten minutes after Lucas had appeared at her door with the news.

"Where is she? Is she okay? Maybe I should call Doc Taylor just in case there's a problem." Even before she reached the small holding pen in the barn where Lucas had moved the prize heifer, Kat was throwing questions at him. "He's been the family vet for years, and he'd come in a second."

Casually seated in a metal folding chair outside the pen, Lucas pushed it back on two legs as if he didn't have a care in the world. "He won't thank you for calling him all the way out here for nothing," he retorted. "The calf's in the right position, everything's fine. All we can do now is wait."

Her heart pounding fit to beat the band, Kat looked at him as if he was crazy. "Wait? What do you mean *wait?* I've been waiting for this moment for as long as I can remember. You can't just expect me to sit around on my hands at a time like this. There's work to be done!"

With a nod of his head, he motioned to the items resting on the ground next to the holding pen gate. A plastic bucket of warm water and antiseptic lubricant were all prepared and ready, and hanging on a nail on the door to the pen were calf-pulling chains and a set of come-alongs. "It's already been done."

Kat's eyes widened at the sight of the chains. "Oh, God, do you think we'll have to use those?"

"Hopefully not. Longhorns usually have easy births, but since she's a heifer, I felt it was better to be prepared." Glancing at the animal who was much calmer than Kat, he continued quietly, "She's doing fine. In fact, I think she'd going to make you a good brood cow."

Turning to follow his gaze, Kat propped her arms on the top railing of the pen. She *was* a beautiful animal, she acknowledged. Kat had been taken with her from the moment she'd first seen her in the auction barn. And although the cow was restless—and who could blame her?—she wasn't panicking and didn't appear to be in any difficulty. Some of her own anxiety draining away, Kat dropped to the ground next to Lucas's chair and crossed her legs Indian-style, prepared to sit there as long as it took.

Time should have dragged, but the quiet of the night slipped down around them, enveloping them in a silence that was somehow comforting and intimate. Seldom taking her eyes from the heifer, Kat settled into a comfortable position and found herself telling him about the first time she'd seen a longhorn in the flesh, how after that she'd read everything she could get her hands on about the breed in the hopes that she would one day have her own herd.

Listening to her murmured confidences in the stillness that surrounded them, Lucas allowed himself to forget, just for the moment, why he couldn't drop his guard with her. There was no past or future, just the two of them in a barn that still smelled of new lumber, talking about an animal they both loved. The tension gradually easing from his shoulders, he told her about his own experience with longhorns, how he'd cursed their stubbornness and come to admire their intelligence and finally accepted the fact that there was no other breed he wanted to work with. And all the while, he never realized just how much he was revealing about himself. But Kat did, and she hugged every word to her as if it was more precious than gold.

They were still talking an hour later when a beautiful tawny bull calf tumbled to the ground without any assistance from anyone but its mother. Sucking in its first breath of fresh air, it blinked owlishly and immediately bawled for its mama.

Her heart crowded with emotion, Kat laughed in delight, her blue eyes welling with tears as the heifer claimed her calf and began to lick him clean. "Look, isn't he gorgeous?" she murmured, and unconsciously reached for Lucas.

If she hadn't touched him, if her big blue eyes hadn't been swimming when she looked up at him, he might have been able to keep things light and friendly between them. But the minute her fingers settled on his sleeve, the need that had been hammering at his iron control for days finally broke through.

Groaning, he snatched her close for a hot scorching kiss, telling himself it would be the last time. The last time he would kiss her, the last time he would make love to her. Because he *was* going to make love to her...nothing in heaven or hell could stop him.

"I want you," he whispered roughly. "I can't stop wanting you."

Capturing her face in his hands, he devoured her like a man possessed, the wet, hot heat of her mouth burning him alive. It had been so long...days that seemed like years, decades. She was in his head, in his blood, making him ache in a way no woman ever had. God, how was he ever going to get enough of her in just one night?

Wrenching his mouth from hers, a shudder racked him as she melted against him, boneless, her breath as labored as his, her hands already fighting his clothes. "The cabin," she breathed against his neck while her fingers tore at the buttons of his shirt. "Let's go to the cabin."

But he couldn't make it that far, couldn't make it past the pile of hay in the corner. He wanted her too badly, would explode if he had to wait any longer to have her. Sweeping her up, he carried her over to it and dropped to his knees with her still in his arms.

"Lucas!"

"I've got you," he rasped, lowering his mouth to hers again as he came down on top of her. "And I'm not letting you go. Not tonight."

He kissed her until neither of them could breathe, until thinking even the simplest thought was impossible, until they were both smoldering and ready to go up in flames. Then he touched her. Everywhere.

His name a startled cry on her lips, she arched against him, feeling as if she'd shatter any second. She'd expected his hands to rush over her, to push her over the edge before she could even catch her breath, but instead they lingered, teased, caressed. Gasping, she pushed his unbuttoned shirt off his shoulders like a woman possessed. "Hurry!" she whispered frantically.

But he only laughed, the warm, surprising sound delighting her. Refusing to be rushed, he slowly peeled her clothes from her layer by layer, as if she was a surprise, gift wrapped just for him. And when he was finished, she was naked in his arms, and still he didn't stop touching her. He cupped her breasts, the curve of her hips, the liquid heat between her thighs.

Whimpering, feeling like she was bathed in fire, she moved under him, *for* him, aching. "Oh, Lucas!"

Her cry went through him like a lance, destroying what was left of his control. His lungs straining, his heart slamming against his ribs, he tore at the fastenings of his jeans. But his hands were shaking, and he was cursing by the time he got them off. Tossing them aside, he came back down to her, a sigh ripping through him as she opened her arms to him.

Silk. She was like silk, inside and out. She drew him in as if she would take him into her very soul, then held him as if he was the dearest thing in the world to her. Emotion welled in his suddenly tight throat. She made him forget . . . everything. The ugliness of the past, the years he'd lost and could never get back, the innocence he hadn't even known he'd had until it was gone. Who he was, what he was, didn't matter.

Dangerous. God, he'd known the moment he first laid eyes on her that she was a woman to be wary of. But he'd never stood a chance. Shaken, feelings he couldn't put a name to choking him, he murmured her name, wishing for a moment that they were both anybody but who they were. Then he could tell her how she slayed him with her smile and how being with her like this was something out of a dream. But fate had dealt his hand a long time ago, and she wasn't a part of his future and never would be.

This was all he could give her... a pleasure that shattered time itself. His mouth slanting across hers, he kissed her with everything he had in him, as if he could do it forever and never come up for air. He felt the tension building in her, the fever crawling through his own blood, and he slowly circled his hips against hers, seducing her, wooing her. But she moved with him with a grace that threatened to destroy him, her legs tightening around him and her arms holding him close. He couldn't take it slow, couldn't draw out the pleasure. She started to come undone in his arms, and just that quickly, he was lost. Groaning, he buried himself deep in the slick heat of her and spilled his very soul into her.

Chapter 11

With the coming of dawn, Lucas knew he had to leave. Sometime during the night, he'd carried her to the cabin, to her bed, where he'd made love to her time and time again, unable to get his fill of her. Wrapped in each other's arms, miles from another human being, they hadn't spared so much as a thought to the outside world.

But it couldn't last—fantasies never did. With the rising of the sun, reality came crashing down on him like a ton of bricks. Cynicism turning his dark eyes to ebony, he looked down at Kat's sleeping face and acknowledged that he was living in a dream world if he thought things had changed. She was a Rawlings, for God's sake! The only daughter of one of the wealthiest and most respected families in the state. He could make love to her until neither of them knew their own names, but when people looked at him, they saw only one thing—an ex-con. So the best thing he could do for both of them was get out of her life for good.

Carefully easing himself out of her bed so as not to wake her, he stood for a long moment staring down at her, unable to tear his eyes from her. She slept on her stomach, her tousled hair half concealing her face, her bare skin soft and creamy in the early morning light. He knew he only had to touch her to rouse her, to make her want him again even after a night of loving, but his hand never moved from his side. His face as stony as granite, he forced himself to walk away.

Leaving, however, turned out not to be quite as easy as he'd expected. Kat slept another hour, and just as she came outside looking for him, Gable drove up. For just a moment, Lucas could have sworn she would have liked nothing more than to consign her brother to the devil. Then she smiled. "Gable! What are you doing here?"

Her face was like an open book, though, and she just couldn't hide the fact that she wasn't exactly thrilled at the thought of company. Hesitating, Gable shifted his eyes from Kat to where Lucas stood in the shadows of the barn, and then back again. "I just thought I'd stop by and have some breakfast with you." He held up a brown paper sack. "Alice sent you some cinnamon rolls."

The mouth-watering treat, dripping in icing, was one of her downfalls, and he knew it. "You rat! Just wait. I'll get you for this." Promising to make some coffee, she started to turn back to the cabin, only to suddenly remember the unexpected surprise that had arrived last night. "Oh, God, how could I have forgotten?" Whirling to face him, she grinned, her blue eyes dancing with excitement. "I've got a new baby! Come look." Grabbing his arm, she hauled him off to the barn.

After that, the news spread like wildfire. If Lucas had ever needed proof of just how supportive the Double R ranch hands and Kat's family and friends were of her and her dreams, he had it over the next eight hours. The Halloween party was that night, and there were dozens of last-minute details to still be taken care of, but everyone took time out of their busy day to drive out to the springs to see the new bull calf and congratulate her with hugs and kisses. The dust hardly settled after one visitor left before another one arrived to stir it back up again.

And Kat wasn't the only one who received pats on the back. Lucas hadn't been back to the bunkhouse since the barn had been vandalized, so the last time he'd seen any of the other ranch hands was when they'd shown up that night to check out the damage and help the sheriff look for clues. They'd seen the vicious words on the side of the barn, and he'd half expected them to blame him for bringing trouble into Kat's life. She was like a little sister to all of them, and they were nearly as protective of her as her brothers were.

But instead of giving him the cold shoulder when they dropped in to see the new addition to Kat's herd, Red and the others greeted him with a smile and a slap on the back and talked to him as if they'd been friends for years. Just that easily he was accepted, and he didn't quite know how to take it. They hadn't been exactly unfriendly before, but he'd never quite felt like he belonged, either, and he couldn't for the life of him find a reason for the sudden change.

Needing some time to himself to think, he headed for the springs after lunch, but he'd hardly taken two steps when Cooper, Susannah and Flynn arrived to see the new calf. Cursing under his breath, Lucas stopped to greet them. "Kat's over at the corral," he told them gruffly. "With the calf."

"I bet she hasn't let it out of her sight for longer than five minutes at a time," Susannah said, her smoky gray eyes alight with amusement. "Has she?"

"Nope."

"I knew it!" Flynn retorted. "She's going to be as bad after it as a kid with a new puppy. She's named it, hasn't she?"

Lucas nodded, unable to hold back a grin at his indignant tone. "She's been calling him Tiny all morning." At Cooper's wince, he added, "I know. It's a heck of a name for an animal that's going to eventually outweigh her by a thousand pounds, but she's made up her mind. . . ."

"And nobody's as stubborn as our baby sister when she decides to dig in her heels," Flynn finished for him. "Believe me, man, we know. After that garbage the other night, she wouldn't even be staying here if we had our way."

Unexpectedly, Cooper held out his hand for a shake. "It might not have sounded like it the other night, but we really do appreciate you volunteering to stay here overnight with Kat. Short of hog-tying her, there was no way we were going to get her to leave, and we know no one's going to get close enough to her to hurt her as long as you're here."

Stunned, Lucas shook his hand, then Flynn's, not sure what to say. Obviously sensing his awkwardness, they said something about finding Kat and headed for the barn. Susannah, who had watched the entire scene with interest, laughed softly when he stared after them, frowning. "I know how you feel. Just when you think you have these crazy Rawlingses figured out, they turn around and jerk the rug out from under your feet. You'll get used to it."

"I don't think so," he said with a shake of his head. "They've done nothing but surprise me from the moment

I got here. Considering the circumstances, you'd think they wouldn't want me anywhere near their sister."

"Why?"

"Because I'm an ex-con."

"No, you're a man a terrible injustice was done to. You shouldn't have to pay for that for the rest of your life when you were the victim."

"I don't think some of your neighbors would agree with you," Lucas replied dryly.

"Some of our neighbors are judgmental fools who wouldn't know the truth if they stepped in it," she tossed back without missing a beat. "If you stick around long enough, you'll learn that the Rawlingses have never given a damn about what anyone says. As far as Cooper and his brothers are concerned, you're protecting Kat and that makes you as much a member of the family as any cowboy on this ranch." Her smile was rueful. "So no matter what anybody else says, in our eyes you're one of the good guys. Get used to it."

Leaving him that little bit of advice, she went to join the rest of the family at the corral. Frowning at her slender back, Lucas warned himself not to be taken in by her tempting words. He knew from experience just how quickly acceptance could turn to rejection. In Texas, his boss had had nothing but praise for his work with his prize longhorns and had even talked of making him foreman...until his vindictive brat of a daughter had come running to him with lies of rape. Flying into a rage, Kent had refused to listen to the truth, refused to acknowledge that he himself had often commented on his daughter's deviousness when she was in a snit. He'd fired Lucas, then called the sheriff. And in the awful weeks that followed, the man he'd come to think of as a trusted friend had proved his daughter came by her spitefulness honestly.

As Lucas turned his back on the barn and on any future with the Double R, he knew he had to leave. He'd put it off for too long, and like a fool who had forgotten where he came from, he'd overstayed his welcome. But no more. Once the big Halloween blowout started later that evening, Kat and everyone else would be too busy to give him a second thought. He would collect his horse and stock trailer and leave. No one would know a thing about it until he was miles down the highway.

Just like a rat slinking off in the dark, he thought distastefully. But there was no help for it. He had worked side by side with the woman, held her, kissed her, made love to her until they were both too exhausted to move, and he knew her better than he'd ever thought he'd want to. She was falling for him . . . hard. He wanted to deny it, but she was the type of woman who would never give herself to a man unless she cared for him. No words of love were spoken, but he didn't need to be hit over the head to be aware of the tenderness that had been inherent in her every touch.

Refusing to allow himself to dwell on last night, on the emotions she'd drawn from him with just a whisper of a sigh, he told himself that while he might not be taking the honorable way out, he was doing the right thing. Regardless of what he said to her when he left, she was *going* to be hurt, and this would save them both the uncomfortableness of an awkward goodbye.

The night, however, never seemed so far away. The visitors left, and Kat made a quick trip into town for a few forgotten items for the party. Hoping she would go directly from town to the Double R headquarters to take care of any last-minute preparations, Lucas threw himself into working on a new fence for the next pasture Kat wanted staked off from the family holdings. He wouldn't come close to finishing it, but the task would help to pass the time. The next cowboy Kat hired could finish it.

At the thought of someone else taking his place, some lean and hungry cowboy recognizing a good thing when he saw it and moving in on Kat like a thieving coyote on a rabbit, his jaw hardened to tempered steel. He grabbed the posthole digger and jammed it into the hard ground. He was still working on the fence when Kat drove up two hours later.

Swearing under his breath at the sight of her pickup pulling into the canyon, he straightened to wipe the sweat from his brow as she parked and started toward him. "I thought you'd be over at the main house helping get ready for the party," he said by way of greeting. "Doesn't it start in a couple of hours?"

She nodded. "As soon as I change into my costume, I'll be ready. I thought we'd ride over together. What are you wearing?"

Surprised, his brows snapped together in a frown. "I'm not going."

"But all the hands are invited. In fact, just about the whole county's invited. It's going to be great!"

"It won't be if I go," he said flatly. "Just because you and your family think I'm innocent doesn't mean the rest of your friends will. They won't want to socialize with the likes of me."

"Then they can leave," she returned promptly, her chin jutting stubbornly. "We'll never miss them."

She had that defiant look on her face, the one that warned the world she was ready and willing to fight for what she believed in. And for the moment, at least, she believed in him. Swallowing a groan, Lucas knew if he made the mistake of going to the damn party, she'd stick to his side like glue and just dare anyone so much as to look at him crooked, let alone say something to his face. And tonight of all nights, he didn't want her that close. He'd never be able to leave if she was constantly at his side.

"I don't have a costume," he said quickly. "And I overheard you telling Susannah earlier that nobody was getting in the door this year without a costume."

Recognizing a lame excuse when she heard it, she dismissed it with a wave of her hand. "You can tie a bandanna around your face and go as Butch Cassidy. In fact, I think I've got one in the cabin. I'll go look for it while you clean up."

Scowling after her, Lucas didn't know whether to swear or laugh. He'd never met a woman so good at getting her way. Like it or not, it looked like he was going to the damn party. He'd just have to find a way to slip away when she wasn't looking.

Forty minutes later, Kat applied the finishing touches to her makeup, then stepped back to observe herself in the cabin's small, totally inadequate bathroom mirror. She had, she thought gleefully, totally outdone herself this year.

The woman who stared back at her from the mirror was an exotic stranger. She'd straightened her hair as much as possible with the curling iron, then parted it down the middle. Secured with a strip of shimmering gold cloth that banded her forehead and was tied at the back of her head, the dark strands fell past her shoulders in a long, graceful sweep that was a far cry from their usual wavy style.

But it was her makeup and costume that were going to knock people for a loop. Using a plain white sheet, she'd fashioned herself a simple sheath that covered her from her neck to her ankles, then topped it off with a homemade circular cardboard collar that was literally covered with different colors of glitter glued on in Egyptian designs. Her eyes dramatically outlined with eyeliner and her high cheekbones emphasized by more blush than she normally wore, she was a far cry from the Kat Rawlings who could count on one hand the number of times she wore makeup in a month. Cleopatra had never looked so good.

Her pulse skipping with excitement and her eyes dancing, she opened the door at Lucas's knock, only to laugh as his eyes widened in shocked surprise. The sudden ragged breath he drew in was more flattering than a dozen words of praise. Flashing her dimples at him, she grinned. "If that's a compliment, I'll take it. Are you ready?"

He nodded, unable to force a single word through his suddenly tight throat. Lord, she was gorgeous! And she knew it. He could see the knowledge in her sparkling eyes, in the slow, inviting smile that curved her sensuous mouth, and it went to his head like a dozen shots of white lightning. His blood starting to heat in his veins, all he could think about was hauling her off to bed.

"One last finishing touch, and then we can go," she teased, and held out the bandanna she'd promised him.

He eyed it with a sudden frown. "Are you sure that's necessary?"

"It is if you want to get in the door. Here, turn around and let me tie it for you." In the blink of an eye, she had the cloth settled over his nose and cheekbones and tied at the back of his head. When she turned him back around to face her, it was her turn to stare. He looked like an outlaw, the kind in old westerns who had an air of danger about them that even good women found hard to resist.

Her heart pounding crazily in her breast, she said huskily, "There. Is it too tight?"

What was too tight was the sudden fit of his jeans. Wanting to hold her, knowing if he did they'd never make it to the party, he muttered, "It's fine, but I feel like a damn fool."

The sexual tension broken, she teased impishly, "I could take a sheet and tie it into a toga if you'd rather wear that. It'd look real good with your cowboy boots."

The hard look he gave her dared her to try it. "It would take someone bigger than you to get me into a dress, sweetheart, so don't even think it."

Laughing, she took his hand and tugged him outside. "Somehow I had a feeling that was what you'd say. Shall we take my truck or yours?"

They took his, and if some of the amusement faded from his eyes as they drew closer and closer to the ranch headquarters, Kat was too distracted to notice. Guests had already started to arrive, and pickups of every make, model and description were parked haphazardly in the yard. "Oh, look," she said as he found a clear spot to park. "There's Riley in the skeleton costume. And that's Mary Springfield with him in the Little Miss Muffet outfit. Don't they look great? C'mon, let's go inside."

Just as Kat had promised, everyone was in costume, some more elaborate than others. Feeling more than a little odd with his face half covered by the bandanna, Lucas followed her into the barn and told himself that he wasn't drawing any more strange glances than anyone else. But he could almost feel hostile eyes boring into him, and he didn't like the feeling one damn bit. Stopping in his tracks, he surveyed his surroundings like a wolf scenting the air for unseen enemies.

The barn, complete with wickedly grinning jack-o'-lanterns and enough food to feed an army, had been turned into the perfect setting for a good old-fashioned Halloween party. Yellow-and-black crepe paper hung from the rafters in long streamers, and up in the hayloft, a band was already playing Alan Jackson's latest hit. The crowd on the dance floor was shoulder to shoulder and getting larger by the moment. And the party wasn't scheduled to start for another thirty minutes.

Standing in the shadows, Lucas searched the masked faces, recognizing a few of the ranch hands, but not many of the other guests. Gable and Josey were there, appropriately dressed as Rhett and Scarlett, while Cooper and Susannah had chosen to go as Tom and Jerry. There was no sign of Flynn and Tate yet, but Lucas didn't doubt that they were somewhere in the crowd, circulating in their Annette and Frankie getups. Everyone was having a good time and didn't seem to be paying the least attention to him or Kat.

Shrugging off his uneasiness, he started to ask Kat if she wanted a drink from the bar set up in the corner, only to freeze as his eyes locked with Vince Waters' across the length of the barn. Even at a distance, he could see the hate that burned in the other man's eyes.

"What the—" Swearing under her breath, Kat spied Waters at almost the same time. "I can't *believe* that man! I knew he was invited, but that was before he wrote his filthy messages all over my barn! Who the hell does he think he is?"

She started toward the other man before Lucas realized her intentions. Muttering a curse, he grabbed her. "Whoa, boss lady, what the hell do you think you're doing?"

"Getting rid of him. I don't care if he was invited, he's not welcome here anymore."

Lucas would have liked nothing better than to let her throw the jerk out, but he'd be damned if he'd let her sink to Waters' level. "The sheriff checked out his alibi," he reminded her. "I don't like it any more than you do, but it looks like he's in the clear."

"Tell that to someone who doesn't know him," she tossed back, scowling beneath her headband. "Dammit, Lucas, the man's a sneak with money—which is the worst kind. That alibi of his isn't worth the receipt it's written on."

"Maybe not, but until we've got proof of that, you've got to give him the benefit of the doubt." Guiding her out on the dance floor before she could protest, he turned her into his arms. "Relax," he murmured huskily. "You're here to party, not worry about that jerk."

He expected her to argue, but she was already snuggling against him with a sigh of contentment that knocked his heart from its moorings. Lord, she felt good in his arms! She fit against him as if she was made for him, uncaring that anyone might be watching as she hugged him to her and closed her eyes. Her scent wrapping around him as surely as her arms, Lucas caught her tight and took full advantage of his last chance to hold her.

For one timeless moment, the rest of the world faded away and it was just the two of them, moving to the slow, lingering melody of the love song being played by the band. Hips brushed, hands stroked, whisper-soft, hearts beat in time to a rhythm that they alone could hear. And if anyone noticed how close they were dancing, how they gazed into each other's eyes like new lovers, they neither knew nor cared.

It couldn't last, of course. There were too many friends waiting to talk to Kat, too many men wanting to dance with her. Lucas took one look at her slumberous eyes and knew she didn't give a plugged nickel about anyone else but him. But her family was hosting the party and she was supposed to do her fair share of circulating and seeing to the guests.

Reluctantly accepting a dance with someone else, she squeezed his hand and said huskily, "I'll be back soon. Wait for me."

She slipped away with another man, and it cost him more than he'd expected to let her go. Jealousy clawed at him, surprising him with its strength. Retreating to a dark corner where he had an unrestricted view of the dance floor, he told himself to get used to it. After tonight, he'd never see her again and she wouldn't pine for him forever. There would be other men.

A muscle ticked in his clenched jaw. Suddenly realizing that he couldn't stand there and watch her dance with one cowboy after another without wanting to throw something, he decided it was the perfect time to leave. The crowd had swelled until the barn was full to overflowing. By the time she finished with her hostess duties, it would take her a good hour to search the throng and discover that he was nowhere to be found. And even then, she wouldn't believe it.

She was going to hate his guts. The Lucas Valentine who had walked out of prison a little over two months ago wouldn't have given a damn what she thought. That cold bastard would have figured that if his leaving hurt her, that was her problem, not his. He wasn't responsible for her feelings. But as he deliberately turned his back on the dance floor and pushed his way through the party-goers to the wide-open barn doors, the sick knotting of his stomach told him he was no longer the unfeeling felon who'd walked out of Huntsville hating the world.

Outside, the night was refreshingly cool compared to the heated closeness of the barn. Tempted by the breeze that usually kicked up after dark, other guests had also wandered outside, but Lucas was in no mood to socialize. Jerking the bandanna from his face, he nodded curtly at those who spoke to him but never checked his pace as he headed for his truck. Now that he'd made the decision to leave, there was no use hanging around.

"Well, if it isn't everybody's favorite ex-con," a familiar voice drawled coldly from the shadows surrounding his pickup. "Where you running off to, lover boy? Got another eighteen-year-old to rape?"

The moon broke through the clouds then to reveal Vince Waters casually leaning against the fender of Lucas's truck as if he owned it, but Lucas didn't need the extra light to identify him. He'd recognized the bastard the second he had opened his mouth. "Where I go is none of your business, Waters," he said coldly. "Get away from my truck. You're tarnishing the paint."

"Well, ain't that too damn bad. Why don't you come over here and make me?" he challenged, straightening with a swiftness that had him stumbling to catch his balance. His cheeks flushed and his eyes more than a little blurred, he glared at Lucas in acute dislike.

Unimpressed, Lucas stood his ground. "You're drunk," he said, his mouth curling contemptuously. "I should have known. A man like you hasn't got any guts unless he's got a few beers in him first."

"That's a lie!"

Lucas stiffened at that, his eyes as hot as black fire in the darkness. He was willing to take a lot of bull off creeps like Waters to avoid coming to blows, but there was one thing he just couldn't swallow whole and that was being called a liar. "I don't lie," he said flatly. "Ever. So unless you want those fancy capped teeth of yours knocked down your throat, I suggest you apologize, then go soak your head in a horse trough somewhere. Maybe it'll sober you up."

A man who was used to intimidating anyone who had the misfortune to run into him when he was in a foul mood, Vince didn't take that kind of taunt from anyone. His face contorting with rage, he snarled an oath and charged Lucas like a mad bull.

Lucas was ready for him. Had the jerk been in full control of himself, Lucas would have liked nothing better than to teach him a much-needed lesson. But he wasn't going to take advantage of a drunk, no matter how badly he deserved it. His hand clenched in a rock-hard fist, he waited until Waters was close enough that he could see the whites of his eyes. Then he raised his fist, braced himself and simply let the other man run into it.

It happened so fast, Waters didn't have a chance to check his speed. With all of his weight behind him, he hit Lucas's fist like a train running into a wall. Muttering an oath, Lucas could have sworn he heard the crack of his knuckles. But Waters took the blow harder than he did, on a chin that was obviously made of glass. Without a sound, he crumbled to the ground.

Not trusting him, Lucas studied him suspiciously, half expecting a trick. But Vince was down for the count. Disgusted, Lucas bent and grabbed Waters under the arms, dragging him away from the parking area to a tree near the large Victorian house that dominated the desert landscape for miles around. Leaving the rancher in a heap, he retraced his steps through the jungle of parked vehicles to his truck.

No one tried to stop him, but Lucas didn't fool himself into thinking the scuffle had gone unnoticed. There were too many people milling around outside, and Waters hadn't exactly kept his voice down. Some of the cowboys grabbing a smoke in the fresh air had to have seen the whole thing, but none of them had chosen to come to Waters' defense. Considering what a creep the man was, that wasn't all that surprising.

Dismissing the rancher from his mind, Lucas turned his attention to getting out of there. A single glance at the pickups haphazardly blocking him in told him it wasn't going to be easy. With everything else that had needed to be done for the party, no one had thought to assign one of the hands to parking, and the guests had parked wherever they wanted. The clear escape route Lucas had allowed himself when he and Kat had arrived was now barricaded by a little foreign pickup, so the only way out was to back out of a very tight space.

Glancing over his shoulder, he swore. It was close, too damn close. But time was running out, and by now, Kat had probably started to look for him. If he was going to leave, he had to do it now. Putting the truck in reverse, he carefully started to back up.

It took him a good ten minutes to maneuver out of the tight spot and finally break free. Ten minutes after that, he braked to a stop at the bunkhouse. The windows were dark and there wasn't another soul in sight, which was just what he'd been counting on. With all the hands at the party, there was no one there to ask him what the hell he was doing.

Hurriedly hooking his stock trailer to the back of his truck, he strode over to the pasture where the horses used by the cowboys were kept. Sticking two fingers in his mouth, he gave a sharp whistle that was immediately answered by a distinctive whinny. A slow grin melted the harsh lines that carved his usually serious face as a second later a large beast of a horse stuck his head over the fence and gave him a curious look.

"Yeah, it's me, you old softy," he said with a laugh, giving the gelding a scratch behind his ears. His name was

Thunder, but he was as gentle as a lamb. "I came to break you out of this joint. It's time to hit the road again."

For an answer, Thunder only butted him in the chest, drawing a soft laugh from Lucas. He hadn't had much chance to work with him over the past few weeks, and he'd missed him. He'd actually been thinking of bringing him over to the cabin so he could at least exercise him once in a while, but now, of course, that wouldn't be necessary.

His smile dying, he gave the horse the apple he'd brought him, then led him into the stock trailer and slammed the gate behind him. Seconds later, he was headed for the springs and the personal items he hadn't been able to store in the truck without drawing Kat's suspicions.

The canyon, as usual, was as dark as the bowels of hell and silent as a tomb except for the bubbling of the springs. The breeze that had just barely stirred the air back at the party was stronger here, setting the leaves in the cotton-woods to whispering secrets in the dark. It was an eerie sound that raised the fine hairs on the back of Lucas's neck, but the days when he was afraid of boogeymen in the night were long since gone. He'd run up against the real thing in prison and lived to tell about it.

Pulling up next to the darkened barn, he cut the engine and hurried inside, flipping on the lights. The longhorn heifer and her calf, restricted to the connecting corral for a week until they were both stronger, blinked at him without expression. He had a few tools to collect, his shaving kit, the clothes that he'd brought over from the bunk-house when he'd started spending both his days and nights at the canyon.

Everything was just where he'd left it, and it took him all of five minutes to gather it up. His arms full, he checked to make sure he hadn't forgotten anything, a fist closing around his heart as his gaze took in the barn construction and the work he and Kat had done together. They'd made a good team, which was something he'd never expected when he took the job. But she was the boss lady and he was everything that a good woman didn't need. And that was never going to change. He was bad news all the way around, and it was better that he hurt her now than break her heart later.

But damn, he hadn't expected to feel like such a low-life, especially when he was doing the right thing.

His eyes black and hard, he stood in the wide-open doorway, bathed in light, and reached for the switch. But before his fingers found it, he heard a faint click in the echoing silence. It could have been anything—the cracking of a tree limb in the wind, a night animal on the prowl—but Lucas knew the sound of a gun being cocked when he heard it. And he was a sitting duck.

His blood turning to ice, he dropped like a rock and hit the ground hard, the items in his arms flying in all directions. But he was still caught in the light like a deer in headlights. Muttering a curse, he started to throw himself toward the protection of the concealing darkness, but just as he moved, a shot rang out.

The hit knocked him backward, away from the darkness, the pain as the slug tore through his upper arm immediate and hotter than hell. Blood poured out of the wound, soaking his sleeve in seconds, but he didn't have time to look at it. His arm hung useless at his side, but if he didn't move, and damn quick, it wasn't the bullet in his arm he'd have to worry about but the one in his head.

Flinging himself between the back of his truck and the horse trailer, he rolled to safety only seconds before another shot whizzed by, this one landing in the dirt in the doorway where he'd rested only a heartbeat before.

"Son of a bitch," he hissed, grabbing his throbbing arm and quickly examining the wound. He was bleeding like a stuck pig. Gritting out curses between his clenched teeth, he tugged at the handkerchief that still hung around his neck from where Kat had tied it earlier, then awkwardly wrapped it around his upper arm one-handed. With a tug of his teeth, he tightened the makeshift tourniquet as tight as he could and watched the blood flow slowly to a trickle. It would have to do.

Only then did he take stock of his situation.

The lights in the barn were still on, bathing the yard and his truck and trailer in yellow gold. Out in the darkness, nothing moved, but he wasn't fooled. The gunman was still out there, safely hidden in the deeply shadowed cliffs of the canyon walls, and it didn't take a genius to figure out that it was Waters. Lucas had known Waters would be madder than hell when he came to; he just hadn't expected him to come after him.

And that slight miscalculation could end up costing him big time, he decided, searching for a way out of his predicament. The barn, as well lit as a death chamber, was too far away for him to throw himself behind its protective walls without being an easy target for even the poorest marksman. That left his truck. But the shots had come from the rocky outcropping directly in front of the pickup. He wouldn't be able to make a move toward the cab without the gunman seeing him.

Swearing, he collapsed against the horse-trailer hitch at his back and faced the inevitable. He was trapped and unarmed. And whoever was out there in the darkness gunning for him wanted him dead.

Chapter 12

Wincing as her latest partner stepped on her foot for the third time, Kat forced a smile and thanked him for the dance as the band finally took a break. Heaving a sigh of relief, she quickly slipped away, searching the crowd for Lucas. The barn was packed to the rafters, but Lucas was so tall, she'd spied him easily a few minutes ago when she was dancing with the sheriff. Now, however, there was no sign of him.

Her head starting to throb and her feet aching, she told herself he was probably just outside where it was quieter and cooler. She'd steal a few moments with him in the dark, then come back inside and see how the food was holding out.

But she couldn't take two steps without someone stopping her to compliment her on her costume or tell her how wonderful the party was this year. Finally making the excuse that she had to get some more ice from the kitchen, she escaped outside with a sigh of relief. As soon as her

eyes adjusted to the darkness, however, she could see that
Lucas wasn't among the cowboys who had gathered in
small groups to smoke and swap stories out under the trees
where they could hear themselves think.

Where was he?

Her hands on her hips, she frowned out at the night, not
liking the uneasiness that suddenly curled in her stomach.
Before she could stop herself, she found herself thinking
of the one dance they had shared before someone had cut
in and she'd been whisked away. He'd held her so tight, as
if he couldn't bear to let her go. As if he had to and he was
fighting it every step of the way, she thought, stricken, the
blood suddenly draining from her face. Dear God, had he
been telling her goodbye?

No! she almost cried aloud, fiercely refusing to believe
it. He wouldn't just slip off like a thief in the night. After
all they'd shared, he wouldn't walk away without telling
her goodbye. He'd probably just gotten his fill of the
crowd and the music and gone back to the cabin for a little peace and quiet. She was panicking for nothing.

Needing to see him, to feel his arms around her, she
started for his truck, only to stop when she came to the
now-empty spot where it had been parked. Her heart
pounding heavily in her chest, she fought back panic. If
he'd returned to the cabin, of course he'd have taken his
truck. She would just take Gable's. He always left his keys
in, and he wouldn't mind.

As usual, Gable had parked his truck at the back of the
house, next to the pump house and away from everyone
else. And the keys were under the front mat on the driver's side, just as they always were. Releasing the breath she
hadn't realized she'd been holding, she grabbed them and
climbed into the pickup. With a flick of her wrist, she
started the motor and shifted into first, her thoughts al-

ready jumping ahead to the springs and the excuse she would give Lucas for following him.

Fighting the urge to press the accelerator all the way to the floorboard, she turned onto the gravel ranch road that led to the bunkhouse and springs. If Lucas had passed that way, the dust had already settled and there was no sign of his taillights in the distance. Her hands tightening on the steering wheel, she couldn't stop herself from speeding up.

The truck that was suddenly racing toward her at right angles on an intersecting ranch road caught her by surprise. Hoping it was Lucas and knowing there was no logical reason for it to be, she braked to a stop and rolled down the window as the driver turned and pulled up next to her, his front bumper headed back toward ranch headquarters.

Recognizing Bobby Martinez and Hector Johnson, two of the younger hands, she frowned. "Where are you guys off to in such a hurry? I thought you'd be at the party."

"We drew guard duty tonight, Miss Kat, and it looks like we got trouble. We just heard shots coming from the springs—"

"What?"

"Gable was afraid something like this would happen with the beer flowing like water. We started to go check it out ourselves, but we don't have any guns with us—"

Kat didn't need to hear more. If someone was shooting at the springs, it wasn't a drunk guest. "Get my brothers and some more men and tell them to bring their guns," she cut in harshly, throwing the truck into first. "Lucas is in trouble."

Easing up off the clutch, she took off, ignoring the shouts of alarm from the cowboys as she raced toward the springs. Afraid they would follow her and try to stop her, her eyes flew to the rearview mirror. In the cloud of dust her tires had kicked up, she could just barely make out the other truck speeding away from her.

Lucas would be all right, she told herself fiercely. He had to be. Nothing else was acceptable.

Her heart lodging in her throat, she flew into the canyon and prayed she wasn't too late. The night was darker here, the high cliff walls menacing shadows that seemed to tower over her in the truck. Shivering, she gripped the wheel tighter and pressed on, bouncing over the rutted lane.

Her eyes straining to pierce the darkness, she rounded the last bend before the cabin and caught her breath at the surreal scene that suddenly appeared before her. The barn was lit up like a Christmas tree, the light that spilled through the open doors falling on Lucas's truck and the horse trailer attached to the back. But there was no sign of Lucas. Or the gunman Bobby and Hector had heard squeezing off rounds.

Where were they? she wondered wildly. Had Lucas managed to escape and go on foot for help? Or had the gunman killed him, then slipped off in the dark to hide? Her blood turning cold at the thought, she charged unthinkingly into the yard and threw open her door before she'd even braked to a stop next to Lucas's truck. "Lucas?"

Still trapped between the back end of his truck and the horse trailer, Lucas froze at her call. When he'd heard the other vehicle drive up, he'd hoped against hope that someone had heard the shots and sent help. It had never entered his head that it might be Kat. Horrified, he scrambled up on his knees, knowing if he lifted his head another inch, he would get it shot off. "Get out of here!" he yelled. "Now!"

A bullet whined overhead, but instead of slamming into the ground just inches from where he was pinned behind his truck—as a half-dozen others had—this one crashed into Kat's windshield, shattering it. At her shriek of alarm, his heart stopped. "Kat? Oh, God, sweetheart, answer me!"

Dropping to the dirt, her heart in her throat, she cried shakily, "I'm okay." But a second quick glance at her position showed her she was anything but all right. The light from the barn spilled under Lucas's truck to where she cowered on the ground, clearly revealing her hiding spot between the two pickups to the lunatic hiding somewhere in the rocks fifty yards in front of her. "Hold on a second and I'll be right there."

"No!"

But she couldn't stay where she was, not when she could almost feel the gunman taking a bead on her. Goose bumps crawling over her skin, she suddenly rolled to her left under Lucas's truck...just as another shot rang out.

"It missed me," she called quickly before Lucas could do anything but snarl an oath. "I'm fine."

"What you are is certifiably crazy," he raged. "An idiot! Why didn't you get out of here when you had the chance? If you get hurt, how the hell do you think I'll be able to live with myself?"

Keeping her head down so she wouldn't knock herself silly on the transmission of the truck, she wriggled toward him on her belly in the dirt. It seemed to take forever to reach him. Tears of relief flooding her eyes at the sight of him, she hadn't realized until that moment just how afraid she'd been of losing him. "I'm not going to get hurt," she told him in a thick voice. "Not as long as I'm with you."

He swore, even as he reached for her one-handed. "Dammit, you've got to get out of here—"

"You've been shot!" Horrified, she drew back abruptly, her widened eyes locked on his blood-soaked sleeve and the makeshift bandage he'd managed to tie around his arm. "Oh, God! Let me look at it."

She lifted her hand to him, only to have her wrist caught tight in his left hand. "No. We haven't got time for that. Just crawl back under my truck and get the hell out of here while you still can."

"Don't be ridiculous. I'm not going anywhere."

"The hell you're not! You're leaving, sweetheart, even if I have to stuff you into the damn truck myself and take another bullet for it."

Unable to believe he actually thought she would just drive off at a time like this, she glared at him in growing fury, promising herself she was going to give him a good hard shake once he had two good arms she could grab on to. "Just try it, cowboy!" she said through her teeth. "Get this and get it good. *I'm not leaving you!* I don't care if there is some kind of nutcase out there taking potshots at both of us. I love you, dammit!"

Stunned, Lucas could only stare at her, but she was wound up and hardly noticed. "Get out of here, indeed," she snorted. "What kind of monster do you think I am? You're so weak right now, you can't even hug me properly!" Impatiently dashing away the hot tears that trailed down her cheeks, she glared at him, daring him to say a single word. "So you can forget it, buster," she said fiercely. "I'm not going anywhere without you."

Not missing a beat, she pulled her dirty skirt up to her thighs and grabbed the hem. An instant later, she ripped it, tearing off a wide strip across the bottom.

Lucas jerked as if she'd just torn a strip off of him. "What the hell are you doing?"

—

"Fixing you a bandage," she retorted just as a bullet ricocheted off the tailgate of his truck right above their heads. Swearing, they both instinctively threw themselves to the ground, their breathing ragged as they waited for the next shot. When it didn't come, Kat shot a furious glare toward the dark outcropping of rocks where the gunman hid out. "Bastard!" she muttered, helping Lucas sit up. "He'd better enjoy this while he can. I sent two ranch hands back to the party for help, and my brothers should be here any second."

"You should have gone yourself," he growled.

"Stuff it, Valentine," she bristled, her blue eyes narrowing dangerously. "I don't want to hear it. Now, let me see that arm before you bleed to death."

She had the bandanna he'd tied around his arm off and the sleeve of his shirt torn away from the wound before he could do anything but grumble, "Stubborn woman, don't you realize your brothers are going to have my hide for this?"

Her eyes on the ugly wound, Kat felt her fingers start to tremble. It was worse, much worse, than she had imagined. Pain squeezing her heart, she swallowed thickly. "They're not going to lay a hand on you," she promised huskily. "Brace yourself. This'll probably hurt."

Sucking in a sharp breath, Lucas closed his eyes and held himself perfectly still as she folded some of the material from her dress into a thick bandage and placed it over the wound. Gently taking his free hand, she placed it on the bandage. "Hold this in place while I wrap it," she said softly.

In the sudden silence, he heard her rip her dress again, then she was tightly wrapping the wound and within seconds had the bandage neatly tied in place. But it wasn't until Lucas felt her hand come to rest against his cheek that he opened his eyes.

She was close, too close, her blue eyes dark with worry, her cheeks pale in the light that spilled from the barn. The Egyptian collar that had looked so elegant on her earlier was slightly awry and dirty, and she'd lost her headband somewhere, probably when she dove under his pickup. She looked like she'd been playing in the dirt and her dress was now scandalously short, exposing a good bit of thigh, but as far as he was concerned, he'd never seen her look more beautiful.

Needing to hold her, he drew her against him, his good arm tightening around her as he felt her start to shake in reaction. "It's okay," he whispered, pressing a kiss to her hair. "We're going to get out of this. I just don't know if we can wait for your brothers."

"They should be here any second—"

A shot rang out, but this time, instead of aiming at where they huddled behind Lucas's truck, the gunman trained his rifle on Gable's pickup. And hit the gas tank. With a loud whoosh, it went up in flames like a firebomb.

Kat screamed, and back in the horse trailer, Thunder whinnied in alarm as he tried to break free. The heat was intense, the flames reaching nearly to the tops of the trees. Swearing, Lucas grabbed Kat's hand. "We've got to get out of here," he yelled over the roar of the flames and Thunder's frantic cries. "Stay here until I get Thunder out of the trailer—"

"No!"

"Yes, dammit! The minute he's out, stay low and run for the barn. I'll be right behind you." Giving her a fierce kiss before she could argue more, he ducked around behind the horse trailer, diving for the dirt as another bullet ripped through the night.

Her heart pounding in her chest, Kat shrank against the front end of the horse trailer, her widened eyes locked on her brother's burning truck less than six feet away. He was going to kill her...just as soon as he assured himself she was okay.

The flames that lit the canyon like a bonfire stripped away the concealing darkness. The heat so intense she was already starting to sweat, Kat frantically searched the rocky cliffs that were less than fifty yards away, half expecting to see Vince lining her up in his sights. But there was no sign of him anywhere. Praying he'd tired of the game but knowing that the worst was probably yet to come, she fought back the mortal terror that wanted to send her screaming into the night.

In the trailer behind her, Thunder restlessly shifted his feet, refusing to be calmed by Lucas's soothing murmur as he worked to get the animal free. Feeling eyes on him, Lucas didn't dare take time to look around, but simply flung the back gate open. Thunder, wild with fear, backed out and immediately raced off into the night.

They had seconds, maybe less, before the gunman realized they weren't on the horse's back. "Now!" he yelled hoarsely at Kat, then ran after her toward the barn.

It was only fifteen steps away.

It might as well have been a hundred. They'd barely moved when a masked man suddenly stepped out of the darkness at the edge of the corral. "Hold it right there," he rasped. To enforce the order, he lifted his rifle...and aimed it right at Kat's heart.

Lucas froze, swearing as Kat paled and skidded to a stop beside him. "You son of a bitch! You hurt a hair on her head and I swear you won't live to see another sunrise."

"You'll be dead before you can blink," the other man taunted in a hoarse voice he'd obviously disguised. "If you don't believe me, try it."

It wasn't Vince. The knowledge rippled through Kat like the aftershocks of an earthquake, shaking her to the core. The man behind the rubber Frankenstein mask was thinner than Vince and not quite as tall. And even though he clung to the shadows, his eyes were brown instead of blue and filled with a rage that horrified her. Who was he? she wondered wildly. And what had she and Lucas done to him to make him hate them enough to kill them?

"No!" she cried when Lucas tensed as if to spring. Stepping in front of him before he could stop her, she glared at the monster behind the mask. "Damn you, who *are* you? What do you want?"

"You," he snarled. "I wanted—"

Suddenly, without warning, a shot rang out from the cliffs surrounding them, and the gun in the man's hand went flying. Spitting out a curse, he turned to run.

But it was too late. Before he could disappear into the darkness, the Rawlings brothers and their ranch hands glided out of the shadows with their guns drawn, just daring him to try to get away. Still dressed as ghosts and goblins, their shrouded faces taking on a golden hue from the roaring flames that had once been Gable's truck, they looked like a commando group straight out of the "Twilight Zone."

"Hold it right there, Frankenstein," Gable said coldly. "You're not going anywhere."

"Thank God!" A nervous giggle rising in her throat like a helium balloon, Kat nearly laughed, but her eyes were suddenly brimming with hot tears. Feeling as if she was about to shatter, she whirled and walked straight into Lucas's one-armed embrace, not giving a damn who was watching as she buried her face against his neck.

Frowning at his usually unflappable sister shaking in Lucas's arms, Flynn waited only until Riley Whitaker had emerged from the shadows to slap a pair of handcuffs on the criminal before asking, "Is she okay?"

Tightening his hold protectively, Lucas nodded. "Yeah," he said gruffly. "Just give her a minute. That was a little too close for comfort."

"What about you?" Cooper demanded, nodding at the bloodied bandage wrapped around Lucas's arm. "Looks like you need to get back to the house and have Josey or Tate clean that up for you."

Lowering his gun now that Riley had the prisoner in cuffs, Gable snapped out an order for some of the hands to put out the fire before it spread to the cabin or barn, then told Cooper dryly, "I imagine he wants to see the face of the man who shot him first. I know I sure as hell do. Somebody owes me a damn truck and I've got a feeling it's him."

"He deliberately shot the gas tank," Kat confirmed in a voice that was still none too steady.

Not surprised, Gable arched a brow at the sheriff. "You want to do the honors or shall I?"

"Oh, no," Riley fairly purred. "This one's all mine." And with no other warning than that, he jerked off the gunman's mask.

Only to find himself staring back at the defiant eyes of Aaron Fletcher, his own deputy.

"Son of a bitch!"

Stunned, Kat jerked out of Lucas's embrace with a gasp, unable to believe her eyes. Aaron Fletcher was a friend, or at least she'd always thought he was. He'd gone all the way through school with her—he'd sat next to her in first grade, for God's sake!

Hurt, she cried, "Why, Aaron? Why did you do this? What have I ever done to you to make you hate me?"

"Don't give me that crap," he retorted contemptuously. "Like we were such buddy-buddy friends or something. I've loved you for years and you didn't even know I was alive."

Loved? He *loved* her? "But you never asked me out, never gave any sign—"

"I was going to now that you're home to stay, but then *he* came riding into town." With a jerk of his head, he motioned to Lucas. "I couldn't believe you hired him. He was prison trash—it stuck out all over him. You should have sent him packing that first day, when you found out what a loser he was."

"So you decided to do it for her, didn't you, Fletcher?" Lucas said silkily, the softly spoken words carrying like a shout in the sudden, tense silence. "You told Vince Waters all about my past, hoping that when he ran to Kat and her brothers with the story, they'd kick me out on my ear. Only it didn't work."

"She wouldn't listen," the younger man cried. "Vince told me nothing he said made any difference. She didn't care what you were."

"So you had to find another way to get rid of me, didn't you?"

"I didn't have any other choice—"

"You don't have to answer that," Riley Whitaker told him hurriedly. "As much as I'd like to hear you spill your guts, you're under arrest and you have the right to have an attorney advise you before you say anything else."

"I don't need an attorney. My butt's already fried."

"For God's sake, will you just shut up!" Riley roared. "Whatever you've done, you were once a hell of a good deputy and I can't just stand here and listen to you dig a deeper and deeper hole for yourself."

Caught up in a guilt that nearly flayed him alive, the deputy sheriff only shook his head helplessly. "It doesn't matter. Nothing's ever going to matter again. Dammit to hell, don't you understand? I raped that girl!"

Riley swore, but it was too late.

Aaron never noticed. "I thought he'd be blamed," he said, half to himself. "It seemed so perfect. But then Kat came forward with an alibi." He shot her a venomous look. "You ruined everything. The whole county was screaming for his arrest, but there was no way the D.A. was going to get a conviction with you claiming he was with you the whole time."

"So you vandalized the barn and the fences," Lucas said in disgust, "to try to drive me away. And when that didn't work, you decided to kill me. And Kat."

"No, dammit! Never Kat!"

"Don't give us that," Flynn snapped in disgust. "When we drove up, you were taking potshots at them both like they were ducks in a barrel."

His eyes nearly black with fury, Cooper took a step toward Fletcher and told him tersely, "It's a good thing you didn't hurt her, you bastard."

"Get him out of here, Riley," Gable cut in quietly. "The rest of us have a party to get back to."

Taking charge, he had Red make sure the fire was completely out, had one of the men check on the longhorns to make sure they'd been unharmed by all the shooting, then ordered everyone back to the party. Kat was too shaken to drive and Lucas was in no shape to, so Gable drove them back to the ranch headquarters in Kat's truck.

The party was still going strong, with few if any of the guests realizing that there'd been any trouble at all. And Kat wanted to keep it that way. Cringing at the thought of answering questions from curious guests, she said quietly, "We'll wait in the study while you find Josey or Tate."

"Good idea," Gable said. "Go on inside and sit down. You both look like you could use some peace and quiet."

Kat didn't need a second urging. Feeling as if she'd been through a war, she was still trembling on the inside, and her eyes had an alarming tendency to flood with tears at the least provocation. Blinking rapidly, she led the way inside to the study, then shut the door as soon as Lucas followed her in. The silence was immediate and unbreakable.

Her heart suddenly thundering in her ears, Kat watched Lucas ease down into the leather seat across from Gable's desk, his face ashen and gaunt with pain. Her fingers curled into fists to keep from reaching for him. Now that the crisis had passed and her every thought wasn't centered on just surviving Aaron's attack, she found herself dwelling on little things she hadn't had time to think about when she'd first arrived at the springs. Like Lucas's horse trailer hooked up to his truck, with Thunder already loaded inside. And his tools and personal items scattered haphazardly at the entrance to the barn, as if he were in the process of collecting the last of his things when Aaron had suddenly surprised him and he'd had to dive for cover.

He'd been leaving, just as she'd feared. Without a word.

Pain closed like a fist around her heart. Why? she wanted to cry, but the single word never left her tongue. Josey swept in then with her medical bag, her eyes wide with distress in her pale face, and the moment was lost.

"Gable told me what happened. Here, Lucas, sit on the desk and let me take a look at that arm." She helped him get his shirt off, then carefully untied the bandage. Silently, she examined the wound before suddenly looking up at him with a smile. "Well, you lucked out," she told him, then had to laugh at the rueful look he shot her. "Considering the damage that bullet could have done, you got off easy. It missed the bone and just went clean through the fleshy part of your arm. It'll hurt like hell for a while, but at least you won't have any lasting damage."

Giving him a shot for the pain, she quickly cleaned both the entrance and exit wounds, then efficiently began to stitch them up. Glancing over at her sister-in-law, who restlessly paced on the other side of Gable's desk, Josey frowned at her ashen face. She hadn't missed the tension crackling in the air when she'd walked in, and instinct warned her it wasn't totally a result of the nightmare Kat and Lucas had just survived.

"Are you okay, Kat?"

"Fine."

Her answer was short and succinct and didn't encourage further discussion. Knowing when to take a hint, Josey returned her attention to her work and rattled on about the party and some of the more imaginative costumes. Someone had come as a hot dog in a bun, and Laura Zucker, one of Kat's oldest friends, had come as a steaming cup of coffee.

"She had to use dry ice and water to make the steam," Josey said with a grin as she finished binding the wound. "I think I'm going to have to treat her for freezer burn by the time the party's over. There. How's that?" she asked Lucas. "Feel better?"

He nodded. "Yeah, thanks."

"If I were you, I'd take it easy the rest of the night, though I'm sure I don't have to tell you that. After everything you've been through and the blood loss on top of that, you probably don't feel like partying much. And you shouldn't be driving, either," she added, suddenly remembering that Gable had said he'd driven Kat and Lucas back to the house. "You're going to have to give that arm time to heal before you can work with it any."

"I'll drive him back to the cabin," Kat said quietly. "I'm not much in the mood for partying, either."

Josey could have told her she didn't look like she was in any shape to be driving, either, but she wisely held her tongue. Her chattering about the party hadn't diminished the tension one iota, and the best thing she could do for all of them right now was get out of there and let the two of them work out whatever problem they were having.

"Fine," she said, and dug in her bag for some painkillers. Handing them to Lucas, she told him, "When that shot wears off, you're going to need these. Make sure you're close to a bed. They'll probably knock you out of your boots." Waving off their thanks, she slipped out, leaving behind a silence that was thicker than ever.

Neither of them spoke a single word all the way back to the cabin. The tension so volatile it practically set the air sizzling between them, they both stared straight ahead like two strangers caught in a taxi together. Seconds and miles dragged by. Then, before either of them was ready for the confrontation that was sure to come, they entered the canyon. Within minutes, Kat pulled up in front of the cabin and they both silently surveyed the scene before them. Gable's truck—what was left of it—was still in the same spot where she'd originally parked it, but now it was a black, burned-out shell that looked like something out of a war movie. And parked six feet away, untouched by the fire, was Lucas's pickup with his horse trailer hooked on behind. There was no sign of Thunder, but he couldn't have wandered too far among the rocks of the canyon. As soon as Lucas found him and loaded him into the trailer, he could leave.

Blinking back the stupid tears that stung her eyes, she deliberately broke the silence. "You were leaving, weren't you?"

Her tone was matter-of-fact, almost cool, but Lucas didn't miss the hurt that she couldn't quite hide. It reached out of the dark and twisted his heart, and there wasn't a damn thing he could say in his own defense. "I thought it was for the best."

"Why?"

"Because there's no future in my staying, dammit! If you need any proof of that, take a look around you—none of this would have ever happened if I hadn't shown up on your doorstep like a bad penny."

"How can you say that? You didn't do anything."

"The hell I didn't—"

"It was Aaron," she cut in softly, angling on the seat to face him, her eyes dark with entreaty as they met his. "The ugly rumors about you, the vandalism, the shooting—Aaron did it all. And he would have done the same thing if I'd hired the preacher's son or any other upstanding man in the community and gotten involved with him. It had nothing to do with you personally."

His eyes searching hers, he wanted to believe her...so badly he could taste it. But fairy-tale endings didn't happen to men like him. "Dammit, Kat, don't try to whitewash this—you know what I am."

Oh, yes, she thought with a smile. She knew exactly what he was...a good, hardworking man who had fought his way up from the depths of despair and sworn never to drop his guard again. Giving in to the need to touch him, she reached out before he could stop her and laid her palm against his granite-hard jaw.

"You're the man my brothers and some of our best cowboys came running to help when they heard you were in trouble," she whispered huskily as tears spilled over her lashes and trailed down her cheeks. "You're the man I love."

"Don't say that," he groaned, grabbing her hand. But instead of pushing it away as he'd planned, he found himself clutching her fingers as if she was the lifeline that could pull him out of the fires of hell.

She loved him. She'd said it twice now with an ease that slayed him, and if he never heard it again until his dying day, he would never forget the sound of it on her tongue. But she didn't know what she was saying, didn't know what she was inviting.

Trying to convince her, as well as himself, he began, "We're too different—"

"Do you love me?"

"What do you mean, *do I love you?* Haven't you heard a word I said?"

Kat blinked at the sudden fury with which he glared at her, a smile she couldn't hold back curling up the corners of her mouth. "Evidently I haven't. Why don't you try telling me again."

Lucas swore, but it was too late to hide what he'd already thought was patently obvious. "Of course I love you," he growled roughly. "Why else do you think I was leaving? You've had nothing but hell since you hired me."

He loved her. Honest-to-God, head-over-heels loved her. Oh, he hadn't gone so far as to describe his feelings quite that expansively, but he didn't have to. If he hadn't cared that much, he wouldn't have given a damn about the "hell" he'd caused her.

Wanting to throw herself in his arms, afraid of hurting him, she blinked back tears. "I would have come after you," she said with fierce tenderness, so much in love she couldn't stop smiling. "I told you once before I always get what I want, and I want you. Forever."

Her honesty struck him right in the heart and sent his common sense spinning. He tried to tell himself not to listen, not to let himself start to believe that maybe, just maybe, he'd finally met the one woman who could make him forget the past and believe in happy endings. But the words had already been spoken and there was no way he was letting her take them back.

He felt something in him crack, barriers that had been in place so long he'd forgotten what life was like without them. "Come here," he murmured, and reached for her.

She started to launch herself at him, only to stop. "Your arm—"

"Is just fine, thanks to your sister-in-law." Snatching her to him, he ignored the slight throbbing of his wound as he wrapped her close and gave her a kiss that said all the things he couldn't find the words to say...how special she was to him, how he'd longed for her for years and never known it till that first day when she'd stepped out on the porch and told him she didn't have a husband. Chanting her name again and again, he kissed her until they were both breathless, until the need firing their blood burned like a beacon in the night.

"I tried to leave you once," he whispered hoarsely against her sweet, hungry mouth. "I won't ever do it again. We're getting married."

"Oh, yes," she agreed, her blue eyes sparkling as she hugged him tight. "Anywhere, anytime, any way you want. Just make it soon."

Weeks ago, that would have been enough to send him running in the opposite direction. Now it sounded like heaven. He'd always thought he was a man who didn't pray, but without quite realizing how it happened, he found himself sending up a silent prayer of thanks to the man upstairs for sending him to New Mexico the same week the lady in his arms put an ad for a cowboy in the paper.

"We'll talk about it later," he promised thickly, fumbling for the door handle on the passenger side. "Much later. Right now, all I can think about is taking you inside and loving you the way I've been dying to for hours."

Finally managing to get the door open, he stepped out of the truck and held his hand out to her, the heat in his eyes warming her all the way to her soul. "Well?"

"I thought you'd never ask," she said softly. Giving him her hand, she smiled and, without another word, followed him inside.

*   *   *   *   *

JINGLE BELLS, WEDDING BELLS:
Silhouette's Christmas Collection for 1994

Christmas Wish List

*To beat the crowds at the malls and get the perfect present for *everyone,* even that snoopy Mrs. Smith next door!

*To get through the holiday parties without running my panty hose.

*To bake cookies, decorate the house and serve the perfect Christmas dinner—just like the women in all those magazines.

*To sit down, curl up and read my Silhouette Christmas stories!

Join *New York Times* bestselling author Nora Roberts, along with popular writers Barbara Boswell, Myrna Temte and Elizabeth August, as we celebrate the joys of Christmas—and the magic of marriage—with

Jingle Bells, Wedding Bells

Silhouette's Christmas Collection for 1994.

MIRA™

The brightest star in women's fiction!

This October, reach for the stars and watch all your dreams come true with **MIRA BOOKS**.

HEATHER GRAHAM POZZESSERE
Slow Burn in October
An enthralling tale of murder and passion set against the dark and glittering world of Miami.

SANDRA BROWN
The Devil's Own in November
She made a deal with the devil...but she didn't bargain on losing her heart.

BARBARA BRETTON
Tomorrow & Always in November
Unlikely lovers from very different worlds... They had to cross time to find one another.

PENNY JORDAN
For Better For Worse in December
Three couples, three dreams—can they rekindle the love and passion that first brought them together?

The sky has no limit with **MIRA BOOKS**.

Dark secrets, dangerous desire...

Lovers
DARK AND DANGEROUS

Three spine-tingling tales from the dark side of love.

This October, enter the world of shadowy romance as Silhouette presents the third in their annual tradition of thrilling love stories and chilling story lines. Written by three of Silhouette's top names:

LINDSAY McKENNA
LEE KARR
RACHEL LEE

Haunting a store near you this October.

MORE GREAT READING FROM
BARBARA FAITH

If you enjoyed Barbara Faith's DESERT MAN, you'll
want to join her in November as she visits the dark
side of love with DARK, DARK MY LOVER'S EYES,
Silhouette Shadows #43.

When tutor Juliana Fleming accepted an assignment in
Mexico, she had no idea the turn her life would take.
Kico Vega—her solemn, needy student—immediately
warmed to her presence, but Kico's father, Rafael,
showed her nothing but contempt. Until he took Julie
as his bride, ravishing her with his all-consuming
desire—yet setting in motion Julie's worst nightmare.

Take a walk on the dark side of love with Barbara
Faith—only in **SILHOUETTE SHADOWS**

And now Silhouette offers you
something completely different....

SPELLBOUND
R O M A N C E

In September, look for
SOMEWHERE IN TIME (IM #593)
by Merline Lovelace

Commander Lucius Antonius was intrigued
by his newest prisoner. Although spirited
Aurora Durant didn't behave like any woman
he knew, he found her captivating. But why did
she wear such strange clothing, speak Rome's
language so haltingly and claim to fly in a silver
chariot? Lucius needed to uncover *all* Aurora's
secrets—including what "an air force pilot lost
in time" meant—before he succumbed to her
tempting lures and lost his head, as well as
his heart....

The stars are out in October at Silhouette! Read
captivating love stories by talented *new* authors—
in their very first Silhouette appearance.

Sizzle with Susan Crosby's
THE MATING GAME—Desire #888
...when Iain Mackenzie and Kani Warner are forced
to spend their days—and *nights*—together in *very* close
tropical quarters!

Explore the passion in Sandra Moore's
HIGH COUNTRY COWBOY—Special Edition #918
...where Jake Valiteros tries to control the demons that
haunt him—along with a stubborn woman as wild as the
Wyoming wind.

Cherish the emotion in Kia Cochrane's
MARRIED BY A THREAD—Intimate Moments #600
...as Dusty McKay tries to recapture the love he once
shared with his wife, Tori.

Exhilarate in the power of Christie Clark's
TWO HEARTS TOO LATE—Romance #1041
...as Kirby Anne Gordon and Carl Tannon fight for custody
of a small child...and battle their growing attraction!

Shiver with Val Daniels'
BETWEEN DUSK AND DAWN—Shadows #42
...when a mysterious stranger claims to want to save
Jonna Sanders from a serial killer.

Catch the classics of tomorrow—*premiering* today—
Only from ▼ *Silhouette*®

PREM94

SILHOUETTE... Where Passion Lives

Don't miss these Silhouette favorites by some of our most
distinguished authors! And now you can receive a discount by
ordering two or more titles!